IN THE PALACE

OF REPOSE

IN THE PALACE

OF REPOSE

HOLLY PHILLIPS

PRIME BOOKS

Prime Books
www.prime-books.com

CONTENTS

INTRODUCTION

When I was seven years old, I got a copy of *The Hobbit* for my birthday. I read it, loved it, demanded more and got it. I puzzled my way through *The Lord of the Rings* that summer, lying hour after hour on the couch in my grandparents' tract house in Duncanville, Texas. Outside was oven heat, doodle bugs, and a dried up creek that once we found a crawdad in. In the house it was Cowboys pre-season football, my uncles' baseball trophies on the mantelpiece, back issues of *Reader's Digest* (I liked the jokes) and the Bible.

. . . And balanced against all that, swords and hoofbeats and the war-chants of the Rohirrim; Galadriel's mirror; Pippin and Merry bantering amidst the drowned ruins of Isengard. Truths and beauties, as CS Lewis wrote, that pierced like cold iron.

I wanted to go there. Are you kidding? Duncanville vs. Middle Earth?

But some pragmatic part of me—the part that already had caught the Tooth Fairy, and was too wise to buy into the whole Santa Claus thing—was pretty sure there would be no ship to take me to Middle Earth, however much I longed for it, so I decided I would do the next best thing: I would be a fantasy writer.

I rather suspect Holly Phillips has a similar story. Different books, maybe, at a different age; but most fantasy authors are born out of a desire to escape into Middle Earth, or Narnia, or Earthsea; the next generation of fantasists is lying in bed tonight trying to force them-selves to dream about Hogwarts. What makes the connection between me and Holly Phillips a little closer, I think, is that some-where along the way we both got scared; we both began to realize that when we say magic, what we really mean is *life*; and life, it turns out, is dangerous.

The essential Holly Phillips story begins like this: *In a world that felt too little, there lived a girl who saw too much.*

Look, you: magic, it turns out, is not an ability you control, like the super-powers of a comic-book character; it is the apprehension of wildness. To see it is to give it power, to invite it into your life. Bored and safe, you may, like Bilbo, feel a mild itch for adventure; but when bored goes, safe can follow in a hurry. The two halves of the fantasy writer, the one that wishes for magic, and the one smart enough to think that's probably a pretty bad idea, meet in a little conversation in the midst of "The New Ecology."

> "Don't you realize how desperate the world is for a little magic, how badly it needs a miracle? You're keeping it all to yourself, and it isn't fair!"
>
> "Fair. Jesus. How old are you? . . . It isn't magic, and my life is not a goddam fairy tale. . . . It's not an invasion from Fairyland or the Eighth Dimension or whatever you pretend for your little game. This thing that's been happening around me since I was a kid—and don't ask me why they picked me, 'cause I don't fucking know—it belongs to this world. Maybe it *is* the world, even."

Phillips' characters are stalked by wonder. They've been caught wishing for something *more* in life, and are still reeling with the shock of having gotten it. This changeling sense, of having a banal life stolen and replaced with something altogether riskier, runs through many of the stories, most nakedly in "The Other Grace," in which a girl wakes suddenly and inexplicably into her own life, with no memory of the house she has always lived in, no connection to the family she has known from the day she was born.

There is an undercurrent of guilt throughout; these women are pretty sure, at some level, that they brought this on themselves—and they are right. What they have—what Phillips has—is a quickening vision; eyes that see the red blood of the world under its bland skin.

Unsurprisingly, many of her protagonists are artists. Art is a discipline against fear: I conjure life, I control it; and lo! I am not destroyed. (At least, that's the theory; and yet the best work comes, we know, when the djinn escapes us, and so art is a curious dance, almost self-destructive, where we try to let just a little more wildness into the world than is safe . . .)

I am forced to take a moment here to talk, reluctantly, about Phillips' prose. Forced, because her writing is studded with such extraordinary, luminous moments; reluctant, because writers of pretty sentences learn pretty fast that for many people, a phrase like "lyrical prose" is instantly translated as "not enough action." For the record, these are cool stories, and you don't have to give a damn about poetry to enjoy them. But if you are open to the simple pleasures of a ravishing metaphor, Phillips carpets the stories with them, so they release their fragrance as you walk by. For instance, *Thick yellow sunlight filters through and is caught and stirred by dust.*

That's from my favorite story in this collection, "Summer Ice." Manon, the young artist in the story, feels alone and unsure of herself. She has that quickening eye and a generous heart and she tries to do the right thing, even though she feels like she's way out of her depth. At the story's end, Manon is startled to find that it's *enough*: that her quirky gifts are treasured by those around her; that she is loved.

We aren't surprised at all.

The girls who see too much in Phillips' stories are scared, but brave. They swallow hard and they risk it; they dare to live. There's a lot of Manon in Holly Phillips, I suspect. She has worked very hard, often alone, to let some magic into the world, with no assurance that the rest of us will care, or even notice. She has *risked*.

We are the richer for it.

—Sean Stewart

1: IN THE PALACE OF REPOSE

The Ministry car pulled up before the Palace gate and the driver was out and holding the passenger door open before Edmund Stonehouse could get his papers shuffled into order. The top page of the rough draft for his annual finance report escaped and drifted to the cobblestones. The driver bent and picked it up, and Stonehouse gruffly thanked the man. He wished the motor pool people would stop changing drivers on him. Lazy Hawkins had let him open his own door in his own time.

Listen to him. Carping like an old man. He had only turned forty-eight two weeks ago, but a vision of Chesterford confronted him, his aging predecessor bitterly unsympathetic in his cottage on the fell. Stonehouse, younger then, and resisting the temptation to warm his hands in his armpits, had thought that the spot the old man had chosen for his retirement exile suited him admirably.

That fell wind hadn't been any colder than this deepening winter, though. Stonehouse buckled the flap of his briefcase and climbed out of the car.

"Keep the motor running," he told the driver. "I shan't be long."

The driver touched his cap and climbed back behind the wheel, happy, no doubt, to be out of the cold. Stonehouse pulled his collar up around his ears and retrieved the key from his pocket. It was a clumsily ornate bit of ironwork, and the lock on the oak-timbered gate was massive, ugly, and uncooperative in the cold. He wrestled it open, stepped through, relocked it, and set about tracing the cardinal symbols on the forecourt's frost-white cobbles. He was just as pleased to perform the Ritual of Abrogation out of the driver's view. His contemptuous colleagues at the Ministry gave him a sufficiency of grief.

*

Last month he opened the Palace door onto a summer of honey and roses. Today, it is autumn, and bare blackberry canes claw at the foyer walls.

*

He is the Seeker. He presses ahead through thicket and curtain. The canes all have thorns, but they do not draw blood. The curtains, cobwebs, caress him and trail from his coat sleeves. Palace halls have become forest paths, but somehow the farther view is always white with marble, and the floor, though mossy, is polished stone. The Palace Is, always, whatever its sleeping King happens to dream. At least this quest is only a gentle tease, not the ordeal other visits have been. Stonehouse follows a thread of pale sunlight through the half familiar maze, and the rustle in the dead and dying leaves is only mice. The King is willing to grant him an audience.

He sleeps, this Prisoner-King, but even sleeping he is vast enough to be aware. (Though sometimes, it is true, Stonehouse suspects that the King he speaks with is only a figment of the sleeping King's mind. But then, when he has been inside the Palace for too long, Stonehouse sometimes begins to suspect that he is, himself, only a figment.) It had taken the might and sacrifice of a nation to bind a King of such power within this Palace of repose, and the fear and hope of a generation to press him into sleep. When Stonehouse was new in the post, he had believed he felt the weight of the nation's need on his own shoulders, the chains of the future binding his own limbs, keeping him awake many nights, foundering in exhausted sleep the rest. He still feels the weight, but now it is more the weight of history, of a forgotten archive, dusty and crawling with silverfish, to which he has inherited the key, but not the fortune to keep it in repair.

Such thoughts are ill-advised in this place. Even as he chases them from his mind, the brown leaves that drift the floor become scrawled pages, yellowing and torn. Stonehouse's department may have fallen into neglect, but the power it was meant to contain for the sake of progress is undiminished, and immense.

The trail leads him at last into a high gallery. He has been here before. One side of the room forms a balcony with a low railing that overlooks, or has overlooked in past visits, a garden, a pit, a ball-room, and a cistern brimming with dark water. The King's appetite for invention is tireless. Today, the gallery is a high nest or tree house, with the branches of huge trees reaching over the rail. The polished wood of the balustrades is almost hidden behind the tangle of lichens and vines. Two chairs have been set near the overlook, so Stonehouse knows this is where the audience is to take place. He walks over to the chair not hung with a mantle of yellow chrysanthemums, sheds his overcoat, and folds it neatly over the back. The gallery is warmed by the slips of sunlight falling between gnarled branches. It is very quiet. Stonehouse leans over the rail and can just make out the forest floor, green moss rumpled by roots and littered with golden leaves between the columnar trunks of the trees. There is movement down below. Is that—can it be?—a human figure?

Edmund, says the King.

He is in the chrysanthemum chair as if he has always been there. A hard figure to see (some failing of Stonehouse's eyes or brain, not of the air, or the King) he seems to wear a cloak of woven grass and a crown of feathers. Stonehouse bows.

"Your Grace."

The King gestures and Stonehouse finds himself seated in the other chair. His heart races, as it always does, but this time it is more than just the King's presence that shocks his blood. In all the dreams he has walked through, all the dreams his predecessors have recounted in the visit log, there has never been a vision of a human being. The department head of a century ago had written, *Our monarch refuses company even within his prisoner's fantasies. Is he so stubborn in his anger against the humanity that bound him in his Palace? Or has he always been so alone?*

Ask, says the King.

But Stonehouse is too unsure of what he might have seen. He tries to remember what questions he had meant to ask, even though he knows that any paper he might write about the Palace and its denizen will inevitably go unread.

I have had a visitor, says the King.

For an instant the feather crown comes clear: a ragged sunburst of blue and black, kingfisher and crow.

A visitor, says the King again.

"Have you?" Stonehouse carefully replies.

Yes, says the King. Unless I dreamed her.

The King's smile is like the movement of clouds.

Stonehouse clears his throat. "You have never dreamed a visitor before. Have you, your Grace?"

The King says nothing.

"Where did she come from, then, your Grace?"

Unless I dream you, Edmund, says the King.

"Did your visitor come from outside, your Grace?"

Only I am within, says the King. And you, when you have come. "And she?"

Perhaps she is a dreamer, says the King, dreaming me and you.

Stonehouse frowns down at the tips of his polished shoes. The King is patient with such pauses. Stonehouse has never recognized in the King any grasp of time. Yet today the King interrupts Stonehouse's thinking.

A dreamer, a dream, says the King. Edmund, it will be a hard winter. I will think of you.

Stonehouse stares, astonished, but the King is gone. The chrysanthemums cloaking his chair have turned into butterflies, somnolent monarchs breathing with their wings. The audience is done.

I have had a visitor. A glimpse of movement on the forest floor. Stonehouse begins to sweat.

It is impossible, he wants to cry. But he cannot summon a reason why it should be. He has not examined the architecture of the Palace bindings since he was a graduate student, but the purpose of the place has always been absolutely clear: to keep the King inside. Whether there are also wards to keep intruders out, Stonehouse frankly does not know. No one has ever wanted in. Not even the troubled, the suicidal, the mad. No one. Until now?

Well, his duty is clear. He must find the King's visitor, or else establish there is no such person. The first part is only barely possible. The second—

He could spend a lifetime wandering the King's dreams and never find the end, he thinks with genuine despair.

Genuine despair. Yet he is not surprised when the King's visitor finds him at the foot of the gallery stairs.

*

When he led her out of mild autumn and into bitter winter, she clutched his overcoat around herself and spoke for the first time.

"It is *cold*."

*

The Ministry driver got out of the car to open the door for Stonehouse, but when he saw the King's visitor at Stonehouse's side he just stood and gawked, his gloved hands swinging at his sides.

Stonehouse stepped forward until they were almost nose to nose and the other man had no choice but to meet his eyes. "This is a classified governmental matter," he said softly. "It is absolutely top secret. If you breathe a word to anyone you will be committing treason, and I will know. You will never see your loved ones again. Do you understand?"

The driver was younger than he was, with a round chin and full cheeks, a stubby nose gone red in the cold. He blinked pale, watery eyes and choked out, "Sir. But sir."

"Treason," Stonehouse repeated. "Death penalty without the benefit of a trial."

"Yes, sir. I understand, sir."

15

"Not a word," what was the man's name? "Creely."

"Not a word, sir." Creely stiffened until he was militarily straight. His right hand twitched as if he contemplated a salute.

Stonehouse, feeling like an impostor, gave him a sharp nod and then shepherded the King's visitor into the back of the car.

She sat in the corner against the door and rubbed her bare feet with her hands.

Stonehouse could hardly blame Creely for staring. The fact of her was enough to astonish him, but he began to realize, as he cast her glances from his side of the seat, that she was possibly beautiful as well. Possibly. She wore a veil of dreams, or perhaps it was his eyes that were veiled. Every time he looked away from her he felt he had forgotten her face and had to look again. It was a long, finely-drawn oval framed in a tangle of autumn-grass hair. Her eyes were the tip-tilted round of a cat's, but their color escaped him. The shape of her nose, of her mouth— He pinched the bridge of his nose. Oddly, it was her feet and her hands that stayed in his mind, long and slender, with delicate, prominent bones. The pale skin bore a good many scratches, and there was a smudge on her jaw that was either dirt or a bruise.

She tucked her feet up on the seat and covered them with the hem of his coat.

"How long," Stonehouse had to clear his throat, "how long were you in the Palace?"

She drew her eyes from the window. They were the pale green of the inner flesh of limes. She said, "Is this winter?"

Iron-gray clouds over steel-gray river. They were already at the bridge.

"Yes. Winter. What was the season when you went in?"

"It's cold."

Stonehouse opened his mouth, then slowly closed it again. The driver was listening, and for his own sake the less he knew the better. More to the point, it was hard to tell how capable the girl was of answering. Was she simple, or mad? If she had been so to begin with, how did she get inside the Palace when his department held the only key? On the other hand, if she had been sane to begin with, *why* had she wanted to go inside?

Oh, there were a hundred questions. The worst of it was, Stonehouse knew very well that once the Minister learned about the girl he, Stonehouse, would be fortunate to get even a glimpse of some interrogator's carefully edited report. The thought of the Ministry's Special Branch putting their hands on her made his guts freeze; his own powerlessness made him burn.

The girl pointed out the window at pedestrians on the pavement and said happily, "Look! Children! And a dog!"

*

He sat in his office for five days, useless and fuming. Even Brookland, his amiable assistant and only the other member of the department, had not been able to glean any but the vaguest of rumors, and the telephone on his desk was unremittingly silent. He pulled out his notes on his latest visit to the Palace and stared at them, sorted them, shuffled them and dealt them like a fortune teller's cards, but they gave him insight into nothing but the depth of his own ignorance. On the third day he started in on Chesterford's notes, wondering if the department's last head had seen any clues to explain the girl's presence in the Palace. On the fifth day, he shoved them aside and in despair thumbed through the slender booklet that contained the complete list of Ministry staff, from the Minister himself down to the humblest tea lady who served the boiler men in the basement.

Brookland came in a little later. He had been relegated to an unheated anteroom and was always wandering into Stonehouse's office. "I say, sir," he said.

Stonehouse grunted. "Did you know they've got us listed between the Department for the Maintenance of Railway Stations and the Department for the Maintenance of National Museums?"

"Oh, well," said the cheerful Brookland, "everyone involved *has* been waiting around forever. But listen, sir—"

"Museums, railway stations, and the Palace of the King."

"Yes, sir. But about your girl—"

"What the hell is the matter with these people?"

"It's only that they seem to have lost her."

Stonehouse blinked, then closed the booklet and set it on his blotter so that the bottom edge was parallel with the front of his desk. "I'm sorry, Brookland. Could you repeat that?"

Brookland grinned. "Special Branch. Your girl. Lost her."

"Lost her."

"Bloody incompetent so-and-so's."

"The Ministry's Special Branch lost the King's visitor."

Brookland eased himself over to the steam register under the window. "The tale being told 'round the tea trolley has it that they put her in a room here in the Ministry building to wait until they moved her somewhere else out of the city, only they went and forgot which room she was in and by the time they figured it out the door was open and she was gone."

Stonehouse frowned. "I don't believe it."

"Well, you know how tea time can get the old imagination flowing. Speaking of which, I told the tea lady to bring some proper cakes with her this time, so if we're lucky we might end up with a dusty biscuit or two."

"Right," Stonehouse said. He put his hands on his blotter and pushed himself to his feet. "Right!"

He strode for the door.

*

But it wasn't so much that they lost her, the deputy under-minister rather thought, as it was that she wasn't quite worth all the trouble of keeping her around.

Stonehouse sat across from the deputy under-minister's polished walnut desk and wondered if he was going mad. After more than two decades of visits with the King, it was not outside the realm of possibility.

The realm of possibility!

"I beg your pardon," he said politely. "Not worth all the trouble?"

"Listen, old man." The deputy under-minister leaned benignly over his clasped hands. "Of course this girl represents a significant event to you lot—er, to you. But a vagrant wandering into an histor-

18

ical site is hardly worth Special Branch's time, now is it? When you compare it with all the other matters they have to keep abreast of. I mean, it's only been two weeks since the miners were rioting in the south. Three policemen killed. Consider their priorities."

"I beg your pardon. Did you say, historical site?"

The deputy under-minister blinked. "Well, obviously, an extremely significant one. Obviously. It'd have to be to have it's very own department to manage its affairs!" He chuckled.

Stonehouse cleared his throat. Something rather odd was happening in the region of his heart. He felt strangely like laughing. "You are aware." He stopped to clear his throat again. "You are aware, aren't you, that the King still resides in his Palace?"

"Oh, well," the deputy under-minister said uneasily.

"Currently resides," Stonehouse said. "Presently, as it were, rather than historically?"

"Heh, heh, heh," said the deputy under-minister.

Stonehouse blinked into space. *One* of them must be mad. He forced himself to lean back in his chair and return the man's smile. "Heh, heh, heh," he said. "But in any event, the girl has been, er, released?"

"Shuffled off on Housekeeping," the deputy under-minister said with brisk relief. "If I were you, I'd go and have a chat with Albert Snow on the fifth floor."

*

Her eyes were still pale green. Like the ghost of jade, he thought. They were heavenly when she smiled.

"Edmund!" she said, standing in the door to her room.

He was flummoxed. When Snow had given him the scrap of paper with the address of this boarding house by the river, he'd been convinced it was a mistake. Either that, or some bizarre joke of the Special Branch people. Perhaps they had spirited her away and concocted the story of her "release" as a cover. But no. When the land-lady had opened the front door and he'd stammered something barely coherent, she had said blandly, "Oh, yes, they said someone from the

Ministry would be along. Third floor, second door on the left, and go quietly on the stairs, there's a dear, we've had the carpet up for the termite man and Mrs. Heather has the headache from the fumes."

And the girl was here, and her eyes were green, and she knew his name.

"How," he said. "How."

She laughed and took his hand.

*

She wanted to go out, regardless of the bitter cold. The Ministry had provided her with a good wool coat and sturdy boots, which would have astonished Stonehouse if he hadn't had all the surprise knocked out of him already. They walked along the Esplanade in the terrible still air and listened to the sounds the river made as it froze. He felt calm, attentive, and mysteriously at ease.

"Tell me how you got into the Palace," he said.

"I don't know," she said.

They both spoke quietly, every word freezing to an ice cloud in the dusk.

"I don't remember anything from before the Palace. It's a mad place. Oh, well, you know." She smiled at him. "Not mad, but—"

"Bewildering."

"Bewildering. Wildering." She nodded. "Yes."

There was a skinny strip of park between the pavement where they walked and the trafficked road. The trees planted there were sad, puny things in the summer, but now, with the streetlamps coming on, they cast a webwork of shadow across the way. Below, the congealing river steamed.

"Do you know how long you were there?"

"No. I'm sorry. The other men asked me all these questions, you know, but I couldn't tell them either."

"I'm the one who should apologize, plaguing you again. It's only that those men you talked to don't, er, communicate much to other departments."

"Oh, I don't mind talking to you, Edmund. I'm happy to talk to you."

"Now look," he said. "How do you know my name?"

"That's what He calls you. Haven't I got it right?"

There was no question who He was.

"Yes, quite right. But you see, I don't know what to call you. Have you got a name?"

"He calls me Ivy." She paused. "Is that a proper name?"

"It's a very nice name." Stonehouse thought this sounded absurd, like an unaccustomed uncle speaking to his niece. He hurried on, stumbling a little over his words. "Did you, did you speak with him often? The King?"

"No. Not often. No. But he—don't you find?—he speaks to you in his dreams."

Stonehouse recalled the leaves turned to pages and nodded.

"Sometimes I felt as if he were showing me stories, or even explaining things to me, explaining his dreams with his dreams, or trying to teach me some of what he knows. I think he must know everything, don't you?"

He nodded again, but more slowly. "What sort of things did he tell you?"

"Oh, I never understood them." She laughed. "How could I comprehend the dreams of a god who has slept for a thousand years?"

"Not quite a god," Stonehouse murmured, "and rather closer to four hundred."

"I remember the bees, and the room that has a window on the sun. I remember the blue ghosts of mist and birds, and the spiral staircase that echoes the sea, and the sound of a spider creeping over bone." She shivered. "I might be able to show you what they mean, but I could never tell you. I don't think his sense is the kind that can be made to fit into words."

She shivered again and Stonehouse realized she must be cold. He put his arm awkwardly around her shoulders, and as he turned her back toward the boarding house and her room he found he understood why Special Branch had let her go. To anyone who had never been inside the Palace she must sound entirely, though harmlessly, insane.

*

But the following morning Stonehouse began to suspect there was rather more to it than that. When he went upstairs to present his annual report to the Finance Committee, he found the deputy under-minister who had called the King's Palace an "historical site" chatting with the accountants over tea.

*

Autumn has been invaded by the relics of an imagined history. Ivy, brown and sullen green, twines through huge blocks of (perhaps) machinery. The objects, some of them big as railway cars, are complex and have a sense of purpose, of movement stilled, but rust and dying vegetation obscure what details age might have spared. The light is flat and gray, the air hangs heavy with silence, there is a stale smell of fungus and bracken dust. Clinging remnants of vines give the appearance of cracks and incipient collapse to the distant walls. Stonehouse nearly bows under the apparent weight of time.

On his last visit, he was the Seeker. Today, he is the Wanderer. There is no path, only the shifting geography of the Palace and the dream. He becomes uneasy. It is too quiet, too still. How is it possible for the King—font of chaos, spinner of dreams—to encompass this entropy, this end of ends? Death, Stonehouse knows, is within the King's province. He has been the Quarry. He has lived the hunt. The King's death is a fury, a rendering, a celebration, even. Not this pitiless waning. It is neither cold nor warm, but Stonehouse is prickling with sweat and he sheds his overcoat and carries it over his arm. He feels as if he has been here for many dry hours, but there is still no sign that the King cares, or even knows, that he is here. He comes to a wide staircase strewn with ivy trash and bits of bone and wearily climbs.

Everywhere are the huge blunt remnants of this arcane machine. As he paces out the corridors, he begins to realize a kind of pattern to the objects' placement. It is almost as if, within the matrix of the Palace's architecture, they define the lines of another structure altogether. An interlocking marriage of the Palace with this broken, tumbled, purposeless thing. He does not understand, but he is stifled. He begins to forget what it is he hoped to discover here. How could it be possible that the King who dreams this dream should have an answer to any question that touches upon the futures of the living? Even this question falls flat in Stonehouse's mind. The King has never spoken of things outside his dreams. Why has Stonehouse come? He is sure he had a reason—

Footsore and miserable with thirst, he finds the well. It is in the center of a courtyard or room, difficult to tell which. Hulking upright pieces crowd the walls and weave dead vines into a canopy that obscures the blank ceiling or sky. Stonehouse steps cautiously toward the wide mouth of blackness in the floor. The place is profoundly oppressive. The air is so dry it seems to spark as he moves, as he breathes. He shuffles through dead leaves to the edge and looks down.

He cannot judge the well's depth. The mouth is wide enough to swallow his office entire, so the figure at the bottom is either huge or a long way down, as it spans the circular floor. Perspective, perception provide no clues.

Stonehouse does not understand the dread, the terror, the despair that come upon him now. His flesh has gone to morbid dust.

The figure is supine, stiff-limbed, and draped in a coverlet of pale cobwebs that seem to draw light into the well. Stonehouse's vision falls, a strange ocular vertigo that plunges him into intimacy. Webs cling to hair and skin that can only be glimpsed between strand and dusty strand. The details paralyze with their clarity—brittle curve of eyelash, crease of knuckle, arch of rib—yet they cannot be bound together into a whole. Presence without identity. Stonehouse quivers, on the verge, on the brink. The King does not dream men, so this must be he—and yet Ivy was here—and yet, she is not a dream, so this must be the King, and yet, and yet, the King cannot be dead. The King cannot be dead. Whose dream could this be if it were not the King's? And yet, the King does not dream of men.

Stonehouse shakes, he shudders, he gasps for air. The weight of time has become a pressure as of oceans and seas. Dry oceans, dry seas. The broken machine has resurrected its power, and its purpose is to drive Stonehouse down. Down his vision plummets and he sees the grain of the spider's silk, he sees the infinitesimal mote of dust caught on the end of a hair, and choking on panic he runs, runs, leather soles sliding on polished marble, runs for the stairs.

*

The slam of the door broke a flat echo across the forecourt's cobblestones, a shock of sound, of life, of cold that burned Stonehouse's lungs and froze the chill sweat on his skin. He shivered convulsively, his body clenching around the last of his heat. He had lost his overcoat in his flight. The terrible winter air enveloped him as if it meant to consume him, but he did not move from the Palace doorstep. Not yet. He had to draw his mind back from the edge of that well of dust. He had to find his balance. He had to wake into the real world again.

The marks of the Ritual of Abrogation on the courtyard's floor were vague beneath a crystalline dusting of hoarfrost. Beyond the timbered gate a car's engine rumbled. He shuddered, coughing on the cold, and realized that if he waited until he was ready, he would be dead.

*

He was too preoccupied to take much notice of the stares and whispers that trailed him through the Ministry's corridors, but when he arrived at his department Brookland, at the desk in his icebox of an anteroom, frankly gaped.

"Well?" Stonehouse gave his assistant a look that all but dared him to mention the state he was in.

"Yes, sir. That is to say, there's a message from the Minister's office." Brookland glanced at Stonehouse's hair and unconsciously smoothed a hand over his own. "The, er, the Minister requested your presence in his office at a quarter past two. That was," he checked his wrist, "nearly two hours ago. His secretary keeps ringing to ask where you are."

The Minister. Stonehouse was blank. To give himself a moment to think he pulled his watch out of his waistcoat pocket. A large gray wolf spider scampered across his thumb and dropped on a thread to the floor. After a moment, Stonehouse put the watch away without looking at the time and brushed off the silk.

"I see," he said. "Any notion as to what the Minister wants?"

"No, sir. Only—" Brookland shifted his weight in his chair. "Only I ate lunch with Nobby Finch from personnel and he was asking me if I'd given any thought to what other departments I might," he cleared his throat, "be interested in giving a go."

Stonehouse met Brookland's eyes. "I see," he eventually said.

"Probably just idle curiosity, on Finch's part, I mean, sir."

"I should have said it sounds rather more like a warning from a friend."

Brookland cleared his throat again.

"Well," said Stonehouse. It was all dangerously unreal. "You might consider Customs and Excise. At least there you could see a bit of travel."

"Actually, sir, my cousin says the force can always use another man with a degree. Even," Brookland added with an attempt at a grin, "a second in history."

"Oh, yes. I'd forgotten you had a policeman in the family."

"Yes, sir."

"A detective, isn't he?"

"Detective Inspector, yes, sir."

There was an awkward pause.

"Well," said Stonehouse again. "I suppose I've made the Minister wait long enough, don't you think?"

"Look, sir—"

"Not to worry." Stonehouse belatedly began combing his fingers through his hair and brushing down his suit. It was covered in dust and bits of leaf. "I've had a sort of a warning myself, truth to tell."

"But they're mad to do it, sir."

"Oh, yes, quite mad." said Stonehouse. "I'm sure there'll be no end of trouble."

"No end, sir."

Stonehouse started out and then paused in the doorway. "As long as we're still a department, Brookland, you might get on to Transport and wring an expenses chit out of them for a train ticket to Marblepool."

Brookland reached for a memo pad and pen. "First class return?"

"Yes. And come to think of it, you might as well make it for two fares while you're about it."

"Yes, sir."

Stonehouse stepped into the corridor, but then stopped again. "And listen, Brookland. How's your credit with your cousin the inspector? Is he likely to do you any favors?"

"If plied with a pint or two of stout, sir, yes, I should think he would."

"Then get a description of the King's visitor over to him and ask if it matches anyone listed as missing over the last several months."

Brookland's eyebrows crept up his forehead, but he just nodded and jotted another note. "Is it urgent, do you reckon, sir?"

"If you bought your cousin a pint tonight, it wouldn't be too soon for me."

"Right you are, sir."

"Here." Stonehouse reached into his pocket and fished out a coin. "Buy him one on me."

He flipped the coin to his assistant, who was too startled by the small white moth that staggered in its wake to make a decent catch. The coin bounced off Brookland's thumb and fell ringing to the floor.

*

The department had until the end of the year. Three days shy of a month. He and Brookland had that long until their office was turned over to the overcrowded Department of Interdepartmental Relations. The Minister went on with some hearty nonsense about fellowships and endowed chairs and sabbaticals, but Stonehouse managed to cut him short.

"What about the Palace?"

26

"Eh?" The Minister forced his frown to become a reassuring smile. "You needn't trouble yourself on that score, Stonehouse. The entire maintenance budget will be folded into Historical Monuments. I assure you, their personnel and resources are more than up to the job."

"Yes, but—" The knowledge that it was hopeless weakened Stonehouse's voice. "What about the King?"

"Eh?" The frown reemerged.

"What about the King? Are the people at Monuments prepared to keep him contained?"

The Minister harrumphed. "You lot have been fussing over that hoary old legend for five hundred years—"

"Rather closer to four, actually."

"—and what have we got to show for it? Eh? The cost of a monthly motorcar ride across the river and a damn library full of the florid accounts of sinecured historians playing at magic and giving themselves hallucinations! Utter rot! I've heard my grandsons play more rational games, and for a more rational purpose. Why the devil should the honest, hardworking taxpayers of this great nation pay you good money to pretend to be saving the modern world from a threat that has not so much as frightened a maidservant or lit the fire on the end of a match in five hundred years?"

"I see." Stonehouse almost let it go at that, but in all conscience he could not. "I'm sorry, sir, but I would be remiss in my duty—"

The Minister snorted loudly.

"I would be remiss in my duty if I did not point out that the reason the King has not threatened the security of his containment is that my department has worked for a very long time to prevent just that from happening."

"Nonsense. There's been no threat because the only danger there ever was came from our own ancestors' ignorance and superstition, which is now, thank you very much, entirely vanquished." The Minister sat comfortably back in his chair. "Close the door on your way out, there's a good chap."

*

When the train dove into a tunnel, Ivy gasped and clutched his wrist. When it rushed back into the day, a roaring demon-machine streaming banners of sparks and cinders, boiling smoke and billowing steam, its whistle wailing and its wheels shrieking on the rails—she laughed.

*

Chesterford's cottage on the fell was a longer walk from the town than Stonehouse remembered. The lane that crawled up out of the valley was steep, rutted, and patched with frozen mud, but it was the wind that nearly did him in. It poured down from the north like a river of ice and steel, cutting through layers of wool as if they were cobwebs. Stonehouse had dug out his army greatcoat from a trunk in the spare room of his flat, and a knitted hat and gloves smelling of mothballs, and a scarf with the colors of a college team he'd nearly forgotten playing for, and all of it was scarcely enough to keep his blood liquid on the way.

Horrified at the cold, he tried to send Ivy back to the station inn, but she refused to turn back without him.

"I like it," she said. "It's *cold*."

He was not equipped to argue with that. So they walked together out of the town and up onto the fell.

The patches of white on the hillside which he had taken for snow turned out to be sheep frozen dead where they stood.

Madness, he thought. Even if Chesterford had still been alive in the fall (for the former department head couldn't be any younger than eighty) he was certain to have expired in that drafty stone cottage of his. Stonehouse was leading Ivy to Chesterford's tomb, and likely theirs as well. He just wished she weren't so damn cheerful about it.

"But I'm so happy you asked me to come, Edmund. It's a marvel to be outside after being shut in for so long."

Stonehouse knew she meant the boarding house, but he could not keep his mind from returning to his last visit to the Palace. Perhaps, compared to that stifling, deathly silence, this wind might indeed be

28

called invigorating. He certainly preferred to blame his shivering on it, rather than on the memory of fear.

Chesterford's cottage leaned away from the wind, as if its field-stone walls were preparing to surrender to a superior force, but a ragged stream of smoke spun out from its chimney as Stonehouse and Ivy approached the door. He began to shake in anticipation of warmth.

The man who answered his clumsy knock surprised him, not with his age, but with his lack of it: Chesterford had hardly changed in the twenty years since they'd last spoken. He was still tall, stooped, beaky, and disinclined to entertain visitors.

"Yes?" he said without moving out of the door. "What do you want?"

"Chesterford," Stonehouse said, pulling at the scarf around his lower face. "It's muh-me. Stuh-Stonehouse. From the Muh-Ministry."

"I know perfectly well who you are, young Ned. No one else among my acquaintance is stupid enough to be walking on the fell in this sort of weather, for a start. Very well, come in, come in, before you freeze to death on my doorstep." He moved back to make room, and then, apparently for the first time, noticed Stonehouse's companion. Stonehouse, stepping aside for Ivy to precede him, had a good view of Chesterford's face and was intrigued by the expression that passed across it, creasing the old man's frown lines in new and surprising ways. Enlightenment? Surprise? Delight? Stonehouse wasn't sure.

"I beg your pardon for the rustic surroundings," Chesterford said as he pried the door shut against the wind. "I so seldom receive visitors in the winter."

Stonehouse could only suppose he was speaking to Ivy, who looked around with interest and said nothing. In fact, the cottage was somewhat more welcoming than Stonehouse expected. The drafty walls were almost hidden behind glass-fronted bookcases, the floor was deep in rugs, and the cast iron range against the far wall of the main room radiated heat. Or perhaps it was simply that the last time he'd been here he hadn't been cold enough to appreciate Chesterford's meager comforts.

"Come in and warm yourself, miss. The kettle's hot, it won't take more than a moment to brew a pot of tea."

Stonehouse unwound the team scarf from his face and said, "Chesterford, this is Ivy. Ivy, allow me to introduce Doctor Wallace Chesterford, the department's last head. Or rather," he added as he tugged at his gloves, "as it seems I am to be the department's last head, the last-but-one."

Chesterford set the box of tea he'd just taken from a cupboard back on the shelf and turned around. "I see. So it's finally come to that, is it?"

"You were expecting it?"

"Oblivious as ever to the ways of power. Really, Ned, I had hoped for better from you."

"Had you really?" Stonehouse took Ivy's coat and his own and folded them over the back of a threadbare settee. Now that he was no longer in danger of freezing on his feet like the poor sheep, he was feeling remarkably fit and cheerful. Ivy smiled at him.

"You weren't entirely without promise," Chesterford snapped. "I would never have recommended you as my replacement if you had been." He returned to making tea.

"I had always supposed you did that because there was no one else applying for the position."

"There was that blatherskite from Starling College." Chesterford poured steaming water into a fat brown pot. "And I begin to think he couldn't have done any worse than you have." He clunked a pair of pottery mugs on the table and turned his scowl on Stonehouse, but it faded somewhat as his eye lit on Ivy, who was examining his books. He cleared his throat. "But I hope you didn't bring the young lady all the way up here in this weather simply so that she could listen to us reminisce."

"No. No. I'm afraid I've come to ask you for advice."

"Too late to do any good," Chesterford said, "if I'm any judge." And his frown settled back into its familiar grooves.

*

Stonehouse cupped his warm mug between his hands and sighed. "I've always known most people consider us relics. I suspect even historians from the mainstream are dismissed as ivory tower eccentrics. It's this modern obsession with progress, science, money, machines. And there is no escaping it, our specialty is somewhat arcane."

Chesterford snorted. "'Somewhat arcane.' Ned, I despair, I really do. We aren't fusty scholars fiddling about in the backwaters of an outdated field. We're the last, the very last practitioners of the ancient art. We are the last bearers of the key to humanity's truest connection to the fires of creation. We are the final link of the chain that binds our world to the divine. When you and I and that boy of yours are gone, the human race will be adrift, at the mercy of our desires, and our fears."

Stonehouse bowed his head.

Ivy said, "You sound as if you believe that you have been protecting the King from the world, not the world from the King."

"Ah, well," Chesterford said sarcastically.

Stonehouse looked at her. "There was a time, you see, when the power the King embodies promised nothing but chaos. Our ancestors yearned so intensely for order, for peace, for understanding—"

"For the lie of the absolute and the illusion that the ground beneath their feet was certain, eternal, and theirs to do with as they pleased," Chesterford muttered.

Stonehouse shook his head, though not entirely in disagreement.

Ivy tipped her head back and closed her eyes. "I liked the train," she said. "But I don't understand how you can bring yourselves to use magic to keep Magic imprisoned and out of your world."

Chesterford was scowling at his tea, so the answer was left to Stonehouse.

"The problem is, you see." He sighed. "The problem is, there is nowhere else in our world where one can use magic for any purpose at all."

"Yes." She gave him a sweet smile. "I thought you loved him, too."

*

31

It was far too cold to walk back to Marblepool in the dark. Chesterford gave up his tiny bedroom to Ivy, and after a plain supper of barley soup and bread she retired, leaving the two men alone. To Stonehouse's surprise, Chesterford produced a bottle of good brandy and poured them both a generous dollop.

"Go on, then," the old man said. "Ask your question."

"I think you have already guessed what it is."

"How do you keep the bureaucrats and politicians from being absolute bloody fools. Answer: you can't. You never can. You can merely keep to your corner and resign yourself to tidying up once the party is over."

Stonehouse smiled. "Actually, you'll be pleased to know I have learned at least that much from my tenure as department head. No, I wanted to talk to you about something quite different."

"Ah." Chesterford's eyes gleamed within their web of wrinkles. "Go on, then. Ask your question."

*

When Stonehouse and Ivy returned to the city on the train, Chesterford went with them.

"I admit that even a dedicated ascetic can experience a longing for a hot bath in an indecently heated bathroom," he said. "Not to mention something to eat besides mutton and barley."

The cold was deeper than ever, despite the fact that the sky was clear and the sun shining for the first time in days. Particles of ice scintillated in the air.

*

That evening, with Chesterford wallowing in his bathroom and Ivy back at her boarding house, Stonehouse was surprised to hear the doorbell ring. He found Brookland shivering on the doorstep, muffled to the eyes in wool.

"Come in, man, come in," he said.

Brookland entered and began the process of unwrapping himself.

"Sorry to bother you at home, sir. But I thought you might want to know what my cousin had to say."

Stonehouse had thought he'd detected a certain pub-like odor emerging from his junior's clothes. "That was quick work. Come and have a seat."

"No, thank you, sir, I won't stay. It's not a long story to tell. My cousin says he went through the files on missing persons they compile at headquarters and there was no one answering to the description of our visitor."

"He's certain?" Stonehouse said, though he wasn't really surprised.

"Young women with pale green eyes are a pretty rare phenomenon," Brookland pointed out, rather wistfully. "My cousin said he looked back three years and there was no one who even came close."

Stonehouse lifted his eyebrows. "That was uncommonly thorough of him."

"He was raised on stories about the old days and the King, same as me. He said it was fun being connected to it all, even at third hand."

"Fun."

"Yes, sir." Brookland smiled, but quickly sobered. "But listen, sir, if she isn't a missing person—"

"Just so." Stonehouse hesitated. He could hear the gurgle of the draining tub. "Listen, Brookland, if you can stay for a moment, there's something I'd like to talk to you about."

Brookland looked at him, and the blood slowly kindled in his face. "Yes, sir," he said. "If you put it like that, I dare say I can spare you an hour or two." And he grinned.

*

Stonehouse didn't want to risk alerting the Ministry, so instead of calling for a vehicle from the motor pool he and Chesterford took a taxicab as far as Ivy's boarding house, and the three of them traveled the rest of the way by foot. It was another brilliant, bitter-cold day. The river was completely frozen over, but looking down from the bridge Stonehouse thought the water must still be flowing underneath, because the sunlight caused the ice to glow a pale, watery green.

There was no one else on the streets. Even automobile traffic was negligible. The cabdriver had told them he was only able to start his motor that morning because he had had the foresight to keep a paraffin heater burning in his garage all night. Clearly, few people were willing to risk conflagration for the sake of mobility. Most of the businesses they passed were closed as well.

Brookland had arrived at the Palace gate ahead of them and was jogging on the spot to keep his feet from freezing solid. His head was surrounded by a cloud of steam, but it couldn't obscure the worry on his face. He came a little way down the street to meet them.

"I was starting to wonder if you'd changed your mind, sir."

"Sorry to keep you waiting," Stonehouse said. "It took us longer than we'd anticipated to find a cab. I don't think you've met Doctor Chesterford, have you?"

"Sir." Brookland gave a nod that was half a shudder.

"Save the amenities for a more salubrious atmosphere," Chesterford growled. "We'd best be getting on with it before we're frozen in place."

Stonehouse nodded and groped in his greatcoat pocket for the gate key. He had to take his glove off to fit the key into the lock, and for a moment he thought his skin would freeze to the iron. Despite having been carried in his pocket, it was ice-cold. He was very careful not to brush the touchplate with his bare hand. The mechanism revolved with a stiff, grating clunk, releasing the gate, but when Stonehouse tried to remove the key it wouldn't budge. He jiggled it and the haft broke off in his hand.

"Well," he said blankly.

Chesterford snorted. "What did you expect?"

Brookland said nothing, but his eyes were wide with excitement. Ivy watched them curiously.

"Come on, come on," Chesterford said. "I'm too old for all this standing around."

Stonehouse gave him an amused look and pushed at the gate. It resisted. He leaned his weight against it, and then Brookland did as well.

"Hinges are frozen," he puffed whitely.

34

"Shall I help?" Ivy said. She set her shoulder next to Stonehouse's and the gate groaned grudgingly open.

In the shadow of the outer wall, the forecourt was blue-white with frost. The pattern that thousands of repetitions of the Ritual of Abrogation had left on the worn cobblestones had been buried by the cold. It was like a smooth marble floor leading to the Palace's door, with the sunlight streaming through the gate a carpet of gold.

"I wish," Ivy said, "that someone would tell me why we're here."

The three men looked at her. Her eyes were bright, her cheeks pink, her autumn-grass hair burnished by the sun. She was the only one of them who wasn't shivering.

Finally Stonehouse said gently, "You really don't know?"

Eyes wide, she shook her head.

Chesterford nodded. "He would have had to forget himself utterly for the transformation to be complete."

"Who?" she asked.

"The King." Stonehouse's voice was kind. "He must not have known, you see, that his last warden was about to be relieved of duty. His only contact with the outer world was me, and I worked very hard indeed at being oblivious to the bureaucratic reality. If I'd been paying attention, I'm sure he would have taken from my mind the knowledge that his prison was soon to be left unguarded. I doubt it would have taken him long to undo the wards once we were no longer reinforcing them."

"A few decades at the most," Chesterford agreed.

"But," Ivy began.

"I'm suh-suh-sorry to interrupt, suh-suh-sirs," Brookland stuttered. "Can we talk about this inside?"

They started across the white courtyard.

"The last time I was here," Stonehouse continued, "I thought that what I was seeing was a dream of death. But eventually I realized it was actually a dream of abandonment. You see, just as I could not figure out how Ivy might have gotten inside the Palace, I could not understand how the King could dream his own death. I could not believe he could be gone with the dream still alive and the wards in place, yet I saw his corpse. Eventually I realized there was only one solution to all these questions: Ivy was the King, and the corpse I saw was really the empty husk of a cocoon. He had transformed himself—rebirthed himself, really—and I had, myself, escorted him out of the prison I was supposed to be guarding."

Ivy clutched his arm. "But I don't remember any of that! It can't be true. How could I not remember being the King?"

Stonehouse said, "The King is, to all intents and purposes, dead. You aren't him, really, so much as you're his latest avatar."

"But how could I not know?"

Chesterford patted her shoulder. "It might be easier if you thought of yourself as his daughter, with a great deal yet to learn." He nudged Stonehouse's arm. "Open the door, why don't you, before your boy turns into an icicle."

Stonehouse gave him a quelling look, then said to Ivy, "I wouldn't worry if I were you. I'm fairly certain he left everything you need to know inside."

*

He turns the handle and pushes open the door, and like a conjuring trick a flock of doves bursts out to circle against the blue sky.

Ivy looks at him warily. "You aren't going to lock me up in here, are you?"

The three of them smile. Stonehouse says, "Didn't you notice? I broke the key. The Palace can't be locked up again. It isn't a prison any longer." He steps aside and bows. "Welcome home, your Grace."

She looks at him, at the others shaking with cold. A delicious scent as of peaches and cloves drifts against their faces. "Thank you, Edmund," says the Queen, and she steps inside.

Eyes shining with delight, her three ministers follow, leaving the door ajar. Warm perfumed air from the Palace spills out and, with the help of the sunlight, melts a path across the frozen cobbles to the street. With a flash of brown and a whistle of wings, a hawk darts out to scatter the doves still wheeling across the sky.

2: THE OTHER GRACE

i.

As if she dreamed she were walking, and wakes, and is still walking. Hot feet in heavy shoes. Dust and gravel. The side of a road. A car goes by. There is a ditch, a playing field, a mower. A car goes by. Exhaust and the fresh sap of cut grass. Blue sky. A car goes by. Mosaic without pattern. Dream, except she has awakened and the dream surrounds her. Walking. Her arms are full of books. She stops.

The boy beside her says, "What?"

She hadn't realized. She looks. A face, bristle-cut hair. He makes no more sense than the rest. Sensation without sense. Suspended in the fragmentary world.

The boy beside her says, "Are you all right?"

She gasps. She has forgotten to breathe. She is not all right, but she does not know the word to say— She does not know.

"Grace?" The boy takes her arm. "You look like you're going to faint."

His hand is hot.

"Grace?" he says again.

Is that her name?

"Grace?"

She does not know.

A car pulls up beside them. An open car full of boys. The driver calls out, "Hey, Will! We're going to Georgie's for a malted before practice. Did you want to come with?"

The boy with his hand on her arm says, "Ted, can you give us a lift? I don't think Grace's feeling so good."

"Sure, we can make room."

A boy climbs from the back to the front. A car drives around the convertible and honks its horn. The mower in the field chatters and grumbles, close. The boy with his hand on her arm steers her. The boys in the car watch.

"Come on, Grace. Get in."

There is no sense. She doesn't know. The world has come apart and she is being pushed—pushed—

"Grace! What the hell's the matter with you?"

She twists free. Books scatter in the dirt. A bright blue cover slides into the ditch. The boy reaches. She runs.

Running, it is as if she dreams, and, dreaming, cannot wake.

*

ii.

The heat broke with a rainstorm near dawn. The gully where she hid grew slick with mud. It stank. The rain was cold. Her hair, stiff and sticky with something, became tangled when she tried to push it off her face. The rain ran through it into her mouth and tasted of chemicals. The fear that shackled her loosened with the discomfort. She got to her feet and climbed through garbage-strewn bushes to the street. There was a streetlight, some houses across the way. She didn't know what to do, but she was tired enough to be calm and calm enough to know she should do something. She asked herself where she lived but received no answer. How is memory supposed to work? As if some muscle in her head had gone to sleep. How does the body know how to move?

She said aloud, "I don't know who I am." Just to prove she knew the words. Just to prove the words made sense. They did, but there was no sense behind the sense. Behind the facade of reason, only nothing.

The rain matted her hair to her shoulders.

The police found her before the day was fully light, a black and white patrol car that slid past her and stopped. Fear broke through again, but the two men wrapped her up in a blanket and drove her away. Her skin felt strange inside the wet clothes inside the dry blanket. She wondered if it was strange because she had never felt it before, or strange because she couldn't remember feeling it before. But she hadn't noticed feeling dry before, so that was probably normal. People didn't normally get wet and then wrap themselves in blankets.

Did they?

A delicate structure of logic that collapsed when the driver stopped the car at the hospital. She knew what that was, the same way she had known what the police car was, but there was no reassurance in the knowledge. She didn't know what was supposed to happen. A policeman pried her out of the back seat and handed her like a package to a man and a woman in white clothes. They were strong and they barricaded her with their arms. The woman said soothing things, but they gave her no ground to stand on. She heard herself gasp for air.

They levered her up onto a high bed and a doctor came. He was a tired-looking man with neat dark hair and smudges under his brown eyes. He shone a pen light into her eyes and pushed his fingers through the sticky mess of her hair to probe her scalp. It stung when he pulled on a tangle.

He said, "So what's your name, sweetheart?"

She had to reach for her breath. In. Out. In. Out.

"Sweetheart?" He touched her chin so she would look at his eyes. "Do you understand what I'm asking you?"

In. Out. Her body made two false starts before the nod came.

"What's your name?"

The tension in her body spat out in jerks and twitches whenever she moved. She shook her head and the fear seemed to expand, stretching her skin. Other people were watching, a couple of women, a younger man. Nurses, her mind said. Intern.

"I'm not crazy," she said. Gasped. On a breath.

"Okay, sweetheart," the doctor said. He turned his head and spoke to one of the nurses, who parted the curtain around the bed and left. He turned back. "Do you remember what your name is?"

"No." Gasp.

"That's all right. Take it easy. You're doing fine." He peeled the blanket away from her and pulled at her arms. She had them locked tight against her chest. He moved slowly and carefully, but he was strong. "Let me take a look here, sweetheart. We have to make sure you aren't hurt anywhere."

"Not. I'm not."

"Okay. Let's just make sure." He smoothed his hand up the inside of her left arm, and then her right. His skin was dry and warm. The other nurse came over to unlace her shoes. She pulled her knees close and tucked in her arms. The fear was huge and threatened to escape. The nurse who had left came back and said something about a family, with a little steel dish in her hand. There was a needle in the dish. The doctor and the other nurse were pulling at her limbs. If they untied her the fear would get loose. She tried to tell them that, but they didn't listen. Maybe she couldn't get the words out. There were three of them pulling now. She pulled back. The needle was out of the dish. Someone screamed.

A face at the curtain stared in.

The needle was in her arm and a huge relief was drowning her. She had seen that face before. The boy beside her on the road. She remembered. She remembered.

She was gone.

*

iii.

It was a slow awakening, nothing like the walking dream at all. She was so warm and limp in the bed she could hardly feel her legs and arms. In her easy breathing she could feel the soreness of—of the fear— It felt very distant. A fold of sheet lay against her throat, and after a while it began to feel heavy, a pressure instead of a touch.

Somewhere rubber wheels squeaked, voices talked. There was light beyond her eyelids. She lifted her hand to push the sheet away and her wrist was caught short.

Fear took a step closer.

She opened her eyes and rolled her head and saw thick brown leather padded with sheepskin. Buckles, a strap, a metal rail. Both her wrists were bound. She turned her head to look at the other one—fear a little closer still—but there was a boy beside the bed, on a chair looking worried. The boy who'd been by her on the road.

"I remember you," she said. Sleep was thick in her throat. She coughed it clear.

Relief washed over the boy's face like a wave. He would be handsome when he was older, with his knobby nose and big jaw. His blue eyes were innocent under the harsh buzz of brown hair.

She said, "You're the boy by the road."

Relief crashed and died. "Don't you—you don't—remember. Before that."

The sheet on her throat bothered her. She went to push it away and her wrist was caught. "Why am I— What are these for?"

His face pinched, discomfort added to worry. Embarrassment. Shame? "You fought. Before. The doctors."

"I was scared." Her breath left her on a sigh. She looked at the ceiling a while, then the boy. "I'm supposed to know you, aren't I?"

Pain now. She was awed at how clear his face was. He said, muffling the words, "I'm your brother. Willis. Will."

"And I'm, you called me, Grace."

"Grandma's name." He put his elbows on his knees and looked at the floor. His brow was wrinkled, his skin red on pale. When he leaned over like that his face was cut in half by the metal rail on her bed. She tried to sit up but the wrist cuffs grabbed her again.

"Could you undo these for me, please?"

He looked anguished. She felt sorry for him. It was a struggle but with a shove from her legs she sat up after all. The cotton hospital gown she wore slipped off one shoulder. The air was cool. Blushing, the boy—Willis—got up and pulled the gown decent again. He even tied it behind her neck, his touch cool and tentative on her skin.

"Thanks," she said.

He sat and tugged at his fingers.

"I don't think I'm crazy," she told him. "I just can't remember."

"But how— What happened?" He peered at her from under his wrinkled brow, then looked down. "They kept asking, the doctors, about drugs. Did you ever do any drugs, or did you ever drink at school. They said there wasn't anything on the X-ray. They even called the school."

The straps were long enough that she could stretch her fingers within half an inch of the other cuff. That, she decided, was an unnecessary tease. "Did I?"

"What?"

"Take drugs."

"No. I don't know." Then he gave an angry shrug. "No. It's stupid. You didn't even— You don't even like beer."

She bent over to scratch her nose. When she straightened her matted hair fell over her face, and throwing it back made her dizzy. She squeezed her eyes shut, then open, and watched the black spots fade.

He said, "What was it like?"

"It was like waking up."

He thought about that. "I've never seen anyone look so scared."

"Well," she said, "it was scary."

He reached through the metal rails and unbuckled the cuff on her wrist.

"Thanks," she said, and unbuckled the other one. The leather was supple and dark from use.

"I should go tell them you're awake." He got up and headed for the door, then paused to tap his fingers on the foot rail. "You going to be okay, do you think?"

She shrugged and scratched her wrist. The left one had a plastic strip around it, and the cuff had pressed it into her skin.

"I'll go tell them," the boy said, and he left. Willis. Her brother Will.

She wasn't sure she believed it.

The parents looked like real people. Neither beautiful nor ugly, neither young nor old, they were tired and sad and holding themselves up inside. The mother had a graceful form and a rumpled dress with coffee-cream butterflies, black hair in a pony tail and lines and folds around her pretty blue eyes. The father looked a lot like Willis, older and craggier, with a nose crooked as well as knobbed at the bridge, and gray-brown hair cut nearly as short. He wore a blue striped shirt with short sleeves, buttons, and a collar. She could feel their need.

The mother said in a small voice, "How are you feeling, sweetheart?"

The father eyed the unbuckled restraints, then looked at her face and tried to pretend he hadn't noticed.

She said, "All right."

They stood by her bed looking at her and away. They took turns in a fashion that made them seem like a couple, a pair. She tried to use that recognition to open a door onto more, but it didn't come.

"We were awfully worried about you, Grace," the mother said. The father gave her a look that suggested that was something they weren't supposed to say. The mother's blue eyes filled with tears that didn't fall.

The father's eyes were gray. Willis' eyes were blue.

She wondered what color her eyes were.

Fear was inside her again, and a sudden loneliness, her heart locked inside her throat. Her hands pulled blanket and sheet over her lap and burrowed beneath them.

"You don't remember us at all, do you?" the mother whispered.

"I'm sorry," she whispered back.

The father put his arm around the mother's shoulders. Someone outside knocked on the door. The father said, "The doctors need to take a look at you, Grace. We told them we wouldn't be long."

The mother wiped at her eyes and said, "We just had to say hello. So you'd know we were here. So you'd know you're not alone."

"Okay," she said.

Then the doctor came in.

He wasn't the one from before. So far, Willis was the only person who had reappeared. This doctor was older, with a stiff brush of gray hair and eyebrows as black as his glasses frames. He noticed the undone restraints, but then he noticed everything, her eyes, her hands, the way she sat with her knees pulled up tight.

"Don't be nervous." He sat in the chair Willis had used. "I'm just going to ask you a few questions." He lifted the clipboard in his hand. It was thick with papers. "Do you know what a neurologist is?"

"A brain," she cleared her throat, "a brain doctor."

"Right." His eyes noticed her again. "Well, these questions I'm going to ask you are going to help me find out what's happening inside your skull. Okay?"

*

There were tests first. Follow the light with your eyes, stand on one foot, squeeze my fingers. A stick that scraped the soles of her feet. Standing she felt sick and sluggish from the drugs, and cold, but she didn't fall over or try to run. The doctor nodded to himself as he wrote on his clipboard. Then he flipped the page over and the questions began. Where was she, who was the prime minister, what was the year, what was the thing she would look at to know what the date was, what grade was she in, what town was she in, what time did his watch say and was it a.m. or p.m. and how did she know? And a dozen more, a hundred more, and a hundred more after that. Mapping out the limits of what she didn't know. The size of the blank space was terrifying. She knew she was in a hospital, she knew what a calendar was, and she knew it was two in the afternoon because of the light coming through the window, but beyond that was formlessness. Groping in fog, except that again she had the sensation that the part of her brain that was supposed to do the groping was asleep, or missing, or dead. How do you find a memory when you don't know what it is you are looking for, or even how to look?

When the questions finally stopped and he was writing again, she sat in her bed and hugged the fear inside her.

He finished a note and looked at her again. "You can relax, Grace, you're doing just fine."

This was so obviously untrue she smiled.

He leaned toward her. "Tell me the first thing you remember."

"Walking. I was walking, by the road. I had books. Willis, my brother, was there."

"Did you know who he was?"

"No."

"Did you know who you were?"

She shook her head.

"How did you know you didn't know who you were?" He gave a little smile to show he knew how absurd that question sounded.

"He called me Grace. And I didn't know. If that was my name." She was holding the fear in so hard the words escaped in jerks.

"What happened next?"

"I ran. Away."

"Why did you run?"

"I was scared." Almost whispering now.

"Let's go back for a minute, Grace. Tell me about when you were walking by the road. When did you notice something was wrong?"

"I didn't notice. I woke up."

"It felt like you were asleep?"

"Like I was dreaming. Like I dreamed. That I was walking. And then I woke up. And I was walking. And nothing made sense."

"What didn't make sense?"

"Everything. The world. Me."

"You're doing fine, Grace. How didn't it make sense?"

"It was all—pictures and sounds and—smells and—it was all in pieces—everything—was around—me—crowding—in pieces—"

"All right, Grace."

"—it didn't make sense—"

"That's good, Grace, you don't have to—"

"—nothing made sense—"

"—say any more." The doctor stood and put his hand on her

shoulder. "Try to breathe, Grace. Take some deep breaths. That's a good girl."

The fear was tying knots in her body. He went to the door and she was glad because she wanted him to leave her alone. If she could just be alone she could wrestle the fear back again. But then he returned, and a nurse was behind him, and she had a needle in her hand.

"No!" She lunged for the end of the bed. Hands grabbed. She threw herself against them. "I'm not crazy!" And free. She put her hands out, her back to the wall. "Please, I'm not crazy, I'm just scared, please, please, I'm just scared—"

"Grace. We know you're scared. This will help." The doctor stopped and put his hands in the air.

But the nurse stepped forward, and she had the needle.

"No! It makes it like before it's like drowning and I can't wake up I want to wake up pleasepleaseplease—"

The nurse took her arm. She pulled free. The doctor was there too. She fought. The door was open. She couldn't get through.

"I'm just scared I'm just scared please—"

The needle like a bee punch in the arm.

Outside, the mother and the father. Willis. Staring.

Looking as scared as she was.

Before she was gone.

*

iv.

It was June and the air was balmy. Grace couldn't believe how sweet and warm it was. Maddy had brought a summer dress for her to wear, and the light cotton felt so much like a hospital gown she had to check what she was wearing a couple of times. Before they'd left the room, Maddy had taken a pair of tiny nail scissors out of her purse and used them ceremoniously to cut the plastic identification strip off of Grace's wrist. She put the scissors and hospital bracelet in her purse, then pushed Grace's hair back from her face, a self-conscious caress.

"Well, don't you look fine," she had said.

Grace had offered a smile, but she couldn't help looking at the door. Maddy had taken the hint. They'd run the gauntlet of cheerful nurses and candy-stripers, Maddy profuse in her thanks, and now they were outside and the air was warm, like milk and honey against Grace's skin.

The sun was bright, too, glaring off the chrome wings of Nat's new blue Ford. Nat was behind the wheel and he started the engine when he saw Grace and Maddy come out of the hospital door. Willis opened the rear door and held it for them like an overanxious doorman.

"Why, thank you, sir," Maddy said. She climbed in after Grace and told Willis, "Ride up front with your father, Will. Us ladies are going to travel in style."

Willis grinned and slammed the door, and in a minute he was in his seat and they were off. Everything felt strange to Grace. Too big, too bright, too fast. Of course it wasn't the first time she'd ridden in a car, but it might as well have been. She looked at Maddy, at the unaccustomed smile lightening the older woman's face, and thought that Maddy and Nat were bringing their newborn daughter home and they didn't even know.

Of course they knew Grace's memory was still gone. The doctors had confirmed it, as if Grace's word wasn't good enough on its own, but they could not explain how a girl could walk down the street and lose her memory as casually as she might have lost a button off her shirt. Grace didn't need their explanations. She looked in her parents' eyes and saw them see a stranger, and knew that one girl had died walking down the street that day, and another had been born to take her place. But it would have been cruel to say it. She had swallowed the pills and endured the tests, and when the doctors finally decided to release her she had smiled and tried to be glad.

And she was glad. In the back seat of the big new car, with soft air rushing in the windows and the view outside growing greener and greener as they left the town center behind, she was glad.

If only Maddy and Nat and Willis would stop waiting for her to wake up and remember who she was supposed to be.

Nat pulled into a driveway and she got out and looked up at the house. It was a handsome frame building with a wraparound porch, new but with an old-fashioned look. It was finished with white siding, and the upper windows had diamond panes. Everyone was looking at her.

"It's very nice," she said.

In the hall Maddy said bravely, "Will, why don't you show Grace to her room? And I'll start getting lunch."

Willis started up the stairs without looking at Grace. She followed him, her hand careful on the banister. Drugs still washed around in her system and she'd been a long time in bed. Also, Maddy and Nat were watching. They would take her back to the hospital at the first sign of trouble, she knew. She kept her eyes on the risers. The banister was smooth with polish under her hand.

Willis stood in the upper hall flanked by doors. She stopped at the top of the stairs. Willis watched her as if waiting for her to perform. The doors were all closed.

"Which one is mine?"

Willis shifted his weight. "I thought maybe—"

"I think you're supposed to make the miraculous recovery *before* you leave the hospital."

His face grew red. "I thought maybe you'd have, like, an instinct. Even if you didn't. You know. Remember."

"What am I? Your science fair project?" Grace went to the nearest door and opened it. Bathroom. Blue and yellow. Pretty. She closed the door. "Too bad I'm not a white mouse." She moved across the hall and reached for the doorknob.

"That's my room." A blurt, almost hostile. "Yours is at the end, across from Mom and Dad."

"I don't even know if you do science fair projects." She opened the door he pointed at. A room with two windows overlooking the back yard. The floor was wood like the rest of the house so far, but there was a large pink and white rug covering most of it. The walls were busy with posters and snapshots of people. The bed had a pink coverlet and a great many pillows. The poster on the wall at its head was of a sulky young man with blue jeans and hair elaborately combed.

"I did this year. It looks good on college applications."

"Mice and mazes?" Grace went to a window and looked out. The yard was fenced, green grass and a pair of big willows drooping leaves to the ground.

"A suspension bridge. I made it with coat hangers and electrical wire. You thought it was dumb."

"Did it work?"

"Yes."

"So you're an engineer."

"I'm going to be." He said it as if he expected her to challenge his ambitions.

She perched on the windowsill. "Is that what Nat is? An engineer?"

Willis went from defensive to stricken. "Dad's an architect. He designed this house."

"Oh."

He took a breath. He had never quite entered the room. "Did you want me to show you where the kitchen is?"

"I'll give you a yell if I get lost."

"Okay." He hesitated. "You know Mom's making lunch."

"I was there when she said it."

"Right. I just— Right." He was going.

She was abruptly sorry for her coldness. "Wait. Willis, who is that?" She nodded at the sulky young man over the bed.

Willis looked suddenly tired. "James Dean. The actor. You cried when he died."

"Did I?" She made a face.

"I'll see you downstairs."

"Okay."

He went.

It was a nice enough room, she thought. An improvement over the hospital room. There was a desk under the other window and a dressing table with a mirror by the closet door. The mirror was half obscured by photographs taped around the frame. She bent over to look at them and saw her face, thin and pale, framed in loose brown hair. Tired blue eyes. The same eyes looked out at her from a dozen snapshots. The same face, rounder and dimpled with smiles. The same hair elaborately waved. She remembered the feel of wet hair matted with rain and chemicals and grimaced. So did the face in the mirror. She sat on the stool. The other Grace watched her, frozen in smiles, frozen in the past. Grace felt a wash of cold sweep over her, raising goosebumps and a shudder, and she pulled down all the pictures off the mirror. She stuck them together with their tape and shoved them in a drawer.

*

v.

She was sitting on the back porch trying to decide if she should feel guilty for being bored. She had been "home" for a week. That was how she thought of it, self-consciously: "home." She supposed it really was the only home she had, but the other people who called it that had expectations so much higher than her own. Compared to what they thought she should be, she was a transient. A guest. Is a guest with a crippled brain who is usurping the place of the lost beloved child allowed to feel bored? This was what she was pondering when the screen door opened and the girl came hesitantly outside.

"Hi, Grace," she said. She was a small rounded girl with brown hair curled stiffly out above her shoulders. Her eyes had expectations too.

Grace said, "I guess I'm supposed to know you. I'm sorry."

"It's Felicia?" The girl tried not to look hurt. She smiled gamely. "We were best friends? I mean, I *am* your best friend." She came and sat on the top step by Grace's side. "How are you feeling?"

"Fine."

"I'm sorry I didn't come see you in the hospital. I wanted to? But your mom said probably I'd better not."

"That's all right."

"So." Felicia had a charm bracelet that she spun around her wrist. It made a pretty sound. "I'm glad you're feeling better?"

"I feel fine. They just let me out when they decided they couldn't fix me."

Felicia tried to smile without meeting Grace's eyes, then let the smile die. It was clear she didn't know how to respond. Grace was sorry for being unkind, but she couldn't think of anything else to say. She didn't feel up to the responsibility of kindness. The screen door slapped open and Maddy came out with two glasses on a tray.

"I thought you girls might like some iced tea," she said.

As if she'd been on the other side of the screen waiting for her cue, Grace thought. Probably she had been.

"Thanks, Mrs. Elliot," Felicia said, her voice a gush of relief.

Grace took her glass off the tray. "Thank you."

"You're welcome." Maddy paused at the door. "Felicia, did you tell Grace yet about the junior prom? I'm sure she'd like to hear how it went."

"Oh! Sure!" Having been fed her lines the girl was buoyant. Maddy went in, but Grace thought she could sense her hovering by the door, listening to Felicia prattle on about who had danced with whom, who hadn't danced at all. Who had broken up and who was going steady. "And Ted Branner didn't even go, and Lucy told me that he had told her brother Mick that he was going to ask you to go steady!" She turned her face to Grace, and there was such a look on it—of laughter, of pleasurable envy, of pride at bearing News—that Grace had to turn away to hide the hurt. Felicia was talking about the other Grace. She was talking *to* the other Grace.

Felicia fell silent, turning her iced tea in her hands. The charms on her bracelet tinkled against the glass. She said, "Well. I don't want to tire you out."

"It was nice of you to come."

"Well sure! I mean, of course. I'm just sorry I couldn't, you know, come before?"

Grace stood up and put on a smile. Felicia got up as well.

"Okay. Well. I'll see you later. Okay?"

"Good-bye."

Felicia turned at the screen door to give an absurd little wave. Her bracelet chimed. Then she was gone.

Grace wandered onto the lawn to finish her tea in the sunshine. It was good. Nothing in the hospital had been hot and bright, or cold, or sweet. The grass was prickly springy soft to her naked feet. She stood in the sun until she was nearly sweating, and then she went inside.

Maddy was in the kitchen making another pot of iced tea. She said, "That was nice of Felicia to stop by."

Grace took her glass to the sink and filled it with cold water. "Didn't you ask her to come?"

Maddy cut a round slice off a lemon. "She had asked me to let her know when a good time to visit would be." She cut another slice. "She wanted to come see you in the hospital."

"I know. She said." Grace used the dish cloth to wash around the glass rim.

Maddy dropped slices of lemon into the pitcher. "I thought the prom sounded nice, didn't you?"

Grace rinsed the glass again and set it in the drainer. Then she stood at Maddy's side. "You know I'm not going to remember, don't you?"

Maddy was picking mint leaves off a supple red stem. The kitchen smelled of mint and lemon and tea steam.

"You know it doesn't matter who I talk to or where I go. Those memories are gone."

"You don't know that." Maddy went on plucking leaves. "The doctors said you might still—"

"The doctors don't know. They don't know anything."

"I am not giving up on my daughter." Maddy dropped the mint and grasped Grace's hands. Her fingers were cool and damp, her eyes bright with tears. "I am not giving up on you, Grace, and don't you give up either."

"You already have given up." Grace twisted free. "You gave up before you even started. Why can't you let me be who I am now? I don't want to try to be her. I can't be her! I don't know who she was!"

Maddy's face suffused with pity.

*

She took down everything in the room. Posters, snapshots, everything. There was no room in the closet crowded with clothes, so she shoved it all under the bed. Then she rolled up the rug and shoved that under too. Then the coverlet. The stuffed bear on the dresser. The china clown on the desk. Everything. Out of sight. Gone.

*

vi.

The pills for sleeping stood on the table by her bed. The other pills, the heavy tranquilizers in case she panicked, were in the medicine cabinet in Nat and Maddy's en suite. As far as Grace was concerned, they could stay there. She didn't want the sleeping pills either, but Maddy was already upset at what Grace had done to her room. So the pill bottle sat by the lamp, and Grace sat on the windowsill looking out. It was late. A moth drifted in the open casement and wheeled about the light, throwing shadows across the pinholed walls. The willows in the back yard netted the light of streetlamps, reduced it to the spark of deepwater fish even as the leaves breathed a watery sigh. A cricket chirped.

After a while Grace got up and opened the drawer of the night stand, dropped the pills in, and slid it closed. She switched off the light. In the dark she could hear the moth whispering its wings against the lampshade, pat-patter hush. She curled up on the cotton blanket, her arm folded beneath her head, and listened. Patter-pat flick. Poor little moth, lured into nothing. Flut, flut, sigh. The windows became two rectangles of lessened darkness, and gradually, gradually, the first swell of presence began to make itself felt. As if the paper beings exiled under the bed breathed awareness into the room. Grace's body lay as if asleep, but her eyes were fixed open. And against the slowly developing gray of the nearer window a shape revealed itself. A figure, a shadow, the shadow of a girl.

The other Grace.

They stared at each other through the darkness, the dead girl and the live, until Grace on the bed could hardly stand it. She wanted to speak, to move, even just to blink, but she could not. Her body was a stolen thing, unwilling to stir at her command. She felt she could not even breathe. As the other Grace watched, dark shadow against the stars. Timeless moment, small piece of forever. And then the body breathed.

In a convulsive uncoiling, she lunged for the bedside lamp. Numb stupid hands clutched, pressed the switch, knocked over the base. Light flared, glaring off the bare walls, throwing her shadow huge up to the ceiling as it fell. Then the lamp hit the floor, the light bulb burst, and for a frozen moment she was blind.

The door to the hallway swung open.

"Grace?" Nat's hand swept the wall, found the switch to the ceiling fixture. Light sprang out again. "Honey, are you all right?"

She could only stare at him. His hair was too short to be tousled, but his eyes were bleary in the late-night brightness. He wore a white T-shirt and blue pajama bottoms. He sat by her on the bed and put his arm around her shoulders.

"What's up, sleepy head? Did you have a bad dream?"

He was a hot and solid comfort, but he wasn't hers. She propped her head against her knees a moment, then nodded.

"You want to tell me about it?"

She shook her head. He shifted, and she guessed he was looking at the fallen lamp. Then he gave her a squeeze.

"I'll tell you what. I'm going to get you a glass of water. And then I'm going to clean up that glass so's you don't cut your feet when you get up in the morning."

He seemed to want a response so she nodded.

"You'll be all right if I leave you for a minute?"

She nodded again. He gave her another squeeze.

"Hang in there, kiddo." He got up and went into the hall, and through the open door she heard him say, "Okay, Will. Just a nightmare. You go on back to bed."

Then Maddy murmured something from their room, and Grace realized they had all been sleeping with their doors open.

Listening for her.

*

vii.

She felt like an experiment turned inside out. If the mouse escapes, how do the scientists react? She buckled her sandals sitting on the front step.

There was a hopscotch chalked on the sidewalk. She had gone from 9 to 3 when she heard Willis' big feet pounding the pavement behind her. It was Saturday and he had been studying for his final exams while Nat mowed the back lawn. She could hear the mower growl from here.

Willis caught up. "Hey. Where you going?"

"For a walk."

"Anywhere in particular?"

"How should I know?"

"Mind if I come along?"

She shrugged. They crossed the street in silence. Then Willis said, "You know, if it makes you feel any better, you're still as much of a jerk as you used to be."

She looked up at him through narrowed eyes, then laughed. "Thanks."

But that only disconcerted him. He shoved his hands in the pockets of his jeans and slouched along at her side. If he stood up straight he was almost as tall as Nat.

"You know, I wasn't planning on running away."

"Sure, I know." He shrugged. "I just thought you could use some company."

"I guess I know what you thought."

He tucked his shoulders up around his ears.

They crossed another side street. The road they were on began to curve.

"Do you want to go to the park?" Willis said.

"Okay." She followed him around a corner. A bulwark of trees ended that street two blocks away. "You aren't going to fail your exams because of this, are you?"

"Because of walking to the park?" His voice went incredulous. "I'm not that dumb."

"You know what I mean."

"I'm not that dumb."

It was almost stuffy under the big trees, the vegetation green and moist from a morning's sprinkling. Willis seemed to have a destination in mind. She trailed him through the trees and across a stretch of grass and daisies to the park's farther side. There was a baseball diamond there with a little league game in progress. The yells of small boys tagged after them down the grassy bank of a ravine, where a stream crooked its way around big gray boulders. Willis scrambled on top of one of these and sat. Grace followed suit. The stone was rough and warm under her hands and bare legs. The air musical with water. The sunlight dappled. Grace propped her arms on her knees and watched the stream curl around their rock. It curled, and curled, and curled.

"Thanks," she said eventually. "This is good."

"You used to come here a lot."

She didn't know what to say to that.

After another long pause, Willis said, "You know, Mom doesn't mean to upset you. She's just trying to help."

"Is anything secret in your family?"

Your family hung in the air between them. Willis plowed bravely through. "She just wants you—"

"—the way I was. Not the way I am."

"And how is that, Grace?" He was tense. Intense. "You don't say anything to anyone. You don't do anything. How are we supposed to want you like that? It's like you're just, you're locked inside your head and you won't, you don't want to let anyone else—" He broke off. There were some people coming up the beaten path above the stream.

Young men, boys Willis' age. Six of them. They saw Willis and Grace and bumped one another to a stop.

"Hey you guys," one of them said, a tall skinny blond boy.

"Hi," Willis shortly said.

Grace said nothing.

"Hi, Grace," the same boy said.

"Hi," she said.

She doesn't know who you are, one of the other boys whispered too loud.

She doesn't even know who she is, someone else whispered back.

"Shut. Up." The blond boy glared at his gang, then shrugged and tried a grin. "They're just morons. Ignore them."

One of the whisperers shoved him in the back. The other one said, "Come on you guys. We're gonna be late." There was a general movement up the path.

The blond boy watched the rest of them go, then turned to Willis. "We were getting together a game after the kids are done. Did you want to come up? We could use another infielder."

For the first time Grace noticed the glove he carried. Baseball, she thought. Why remember what that was, and not that Willis played? It made her sick sometimes. She turned back to the stream.

"No, thanks," Willis said. "I still have to study for physics."

"Yeah, I was at it all morning. But you go cra— I mean, you can't study, you know. All day long."

"You go," Grace said under her breath.

"I guess I won't," Willis said to the blond boy.

"Okay," said the blond boy. "Well, I'll see you around, Will."

"Sure," Willis said.

"Hey, it was nice seeing you, Grace. I'm glad you're feeling better."

She turned her head and waved, squinting as if against the sun so she wouldn't have to see his eyes. He gave a half-finished wave in return and started up the path.

"That was Ted," Willis said.

"You should have gone."

"Don't have my glove. Anyway, I should get back to the books." He stood. "Are you coming?"

She got to her feet.

"He used to have kind of a crush on—"

"Willis." She closed her eyes. Swallowed. "Please?"

He ducked his head and started up the trail.

*

viii.

She had gotten into the habit of clearing the table after supper. While the other three talked amongst themselves, she could come and go, separate, silent, permitted. Maddy used good china, and the plates weighed satisfactorily in the hand. That night Willis excused himself early to get back to his books. While Grace scraped green beans into the bin she heard Nat say to Maddy, "You have to admit, that makes a nice change at least."

"What do you mean?" Maddy asked.

"Housework and homework with no arguments."

There was a strange pause. Grace stood with the clean plate in one hand, a silver fork in the other, listening. Maddy spoke so low she had to strain to hear her:

"How can you joke? Nathan, how can you possibly joke about this?"

"Maddy."

"After everything—"

"You know I didn't mean—"

"—she's been through—"

"Maddy. Now come on."

"Everything *we've* been through!"

"Maddy, she'll hear you."

A chair scraped. Grace looked at the door to the dining room. The kitchen was lit only by the small bulb above the stove, and the figure in the doorway was silhouetted by the brighter light beyond. She thought it was Maddy at first. But as her sight darkened about the edges and bees began to sing inside her ears, she heard Maddy's feet running on the stairs, and she knew who it was.

The other Grace.

The other Grace wanted to come home.

The plate broke in three upon the floor, and then she

*

ix.

woke in the pink bed. Yellow sunlight slipped through green willow leaves to swim across the emptied walls. She remembered taking the posters down, remembered the hospital, the roadside, the kitchen. The other Grace was gone. She was herself still. Or was it again? She got up, the floor smooth and distinct beneath her bare feet, and found yesterday's clothes atop the vanity table. They were folded neatly but still wrinkled, still with the tiny grass ends clinging to the cotton shirt from when she had lain on the lawn while Maddy fixed dinner, pork chops, new potatoes, green beans that had scattered as significant as a constellation behind the moon of the broken plate—

So. Herself, still. But for how long?

How long?

*

x.

The neurologist ordered more X-rays. Willis graduated with college acceptances already in hand. Summer ripened into something hot, fragrant, and slow. And eventually, after too many careful weeks, Nat and Maddy and Willis all went back to sleeping with their bedroom doors closed.

Grace realized, as she eased the front door shut behind her, that she had not been outside at night since the night she'd spent in the rain, the first night she could remember. It was more frightening than she had anticipated—she was closer than she had thought to that wet and nameless girl—but it was liberating, too. She was free of the expectations she could not live up to, the needs she could not fulfill. Free to be herself, a girl who was no longer haunted by the lost, no longer—she shivered, rubbed her bare arms in the warm, streetlighted midnight air—no longer haunting the family who could not admit they had lost the girl whose ghost she was. So: freedom, she thought. Life.

Willis had taken her on tours of the town and countryside since school had ended. Cruising in Nat's new blue Ford with the radio to fill the silence, or even better, to give them something to squabble over like any brother and any sister— Grace felt a pang of disloyalty as she walked the route Willis had often taken, skirting the park and turning onto the broad avenue that led to the highway. But of course they were not brother and sister, not really, and those July rides had been for Willis what they had been for Grace: an opportunity and an excuse to escape Maddy's watchfulness, Nat's wistful concern. They were waiting, all of them, even Willis, waiting for the other Grace to return. Waiting for the false Grace, *herself*, to disappear.

So she was disappearing. Let them stop waiting, let them get on with their lives. Let her get on with hers. The other Grace could come tomorrow, next week, next year. She could come right now, in the next step, as Grace crossed under the blinking red lights of the deserted downtown street, but Grace would not hold herself in readiness. She was not an empty vessel waiting to be filled. She was going to invent the new Grace so completely, fill herself so full with *herself* that she would never be crowded into non-existence like the other Grace had been.

The way was much longer on foot. There were whole blocks she had forgotten, or never noticed; the neighborhoods that had breezed by under the Ford's wheels, bright, busy, prosperous in the sunlight, were empty and grim, steel grilles over windows and doors, the sidewalk cracked and seeming too wide. She was frightened in the dark, exposed under the streetlamps, rabbit-like before the headlights of the few passing cars. She remembered the black-and-white that had picked her up that night, the first night, and walked warily, watching for the shadows of recessed doors. Her calves ached by the time she reached the on-ramp, and the light-headedness of fatigue gave her something new to worry about.

The aging night grew cool. The highway folded itself into a wood of tall, leafy trees. The smell was delicious, of sap and earth and hidden water, familiar as a dream. Grace shared the verge with bold raccoons and other creatures she only glimpsed in their retreat. Traffic was rare.

At the first gray hint of dawn, she came upon a roadside rest stop. There was a gravel lot, cinderblock toilets, a caged light over a payphone on the wall. A hundred moths swooned into the electric light and clung, exhausted, to the wall all around. Grace went into the toilet to drink cold water from the tap. And there she was in the mirror above the sink, her tan faded to yellow by the ugly light, her blue eyes shaded by fatigue.

Maddy's blue eyes. She turned away from the mirror, and the thought.

A picnic table had been crowded between trees at the edge of the lot. Grace groped her way onto the table top, and although she had only meant to rest until her legs stopped hurting and the sun was up, she lay down and fell instantly asleep.

*

xi.

Sunlight on her face. Birdsong. A car went by. She sat up, stiff, catching herself on her elbow when her arm sagged. Eyes hot, legs stiff, throat dry. A car went by. Her first thought, as always, was not *what happens now*, but *what happened last*. The dark highway, the animals, the fear.

Maddy's wet hands gripping her own.

She rubbed her palms over her face, then sat sleepily, her forearms folded on her knees. There was not much to look at: the highway behind her, the cinderblock building before her and the green trees beyond. A car went by. She thought vaguely about where she was going—somewhere, anywhere, she had thought in Nat and Maddy's house—but her future was blanker even than her past. She tried to imagine adventure, tried to imagine herself competent and brave, but other images kept intruding, her memory so sparse that they leapt out complete and shining. Nat in his pajamas sweeping up broken glass. Maddy slicing lemons. Willis driving Nat's car, working neat's-foot oil into a new glove, walking beside her on the way home from the park—

A car went by.

And suddenly, the fear that had been plaguing her for so long, the terror of losing herself to the self that had been lost, or to a whole other self different from either, reversed itself: a mirror-reflected fear no less grievous than the other.

For she imagined walking down some street somewhere,

anywhere, walking, dreaming of walking, waking to find herself still walking—and no one there beside her to ask her if she was all right.

No one there to call her by her name.

A car went by.

Eventually, after a long, long pause balanced between one fear and the other, Grace levered herself to her feet and walked, limping with a cramp in one calf, to the payphone on the cinderblock wall.

3: THE NEW ECOLOGY

It was almost quitting time when Millennium saw the Nerd again, lurking outside the donut shop in his car. She went straight home to the boarding house and packed her bags.

Sonia from down the hall leaned in the doorway, a newspaper in her hands. "So, what is it? Cops? Debt collectors? Ex-boyfriend?"

Jeans, underwear, T-shirts. "More like Lectroids from Planet Ten." Bike shorts and helmet.

"Huh?"

"Forget it." She tossed the duffel to land with a thump by Sonia's bare feet.

"Hey, watch it."

"Sorry." She zipped up the sleeping bag on the bed, folded it in half and started to roll.

"Well, I don't blame you for leaving, whatever it is," Sonia said, rattling the newspaper. "It's getting pretty weird around here. Did you hear about this thing at the park by the aquatic center? Seems some crazy welder or someone turned the jungle gym into kind of a real jungle—or anyway, a plant, like one of those fly-eating plants, what are they called, Venus flytraps? They say some kid went to play on it and almost got trapped inside. Serves her right if you ask me, you got to be pretty dumb to play around on a thing like that, but can you imagine the amount of work—"

Millennium stopped listening. The sleeping bag's frayed strings were too short, and anyway, she already knew more than the paper did about the kid-eating jungle gym. It wasn't until she heard Sonia say something about their landlord that she tuned back in.

"What?"

"I said, does Mr. Chang know you're leaving?"

Shit. She tossed the bed roll by her duffel bag and looked around the room to see if she'd forgotten anything. "Not yet," she said. "I'll call him from the bus station."

*

Once she'd bought her ticket she used a pay phone to make two calls. The first one was to Mr. Chang.

"Moving out? You mean October first, right?"

"No, I mean five minutes ago." He started to sputter. "Hey, be glad I'm paid up to the end of September."

"One month's notice, or one month's rent!"

"Kiss my ass."

The second one was to her folks, collect.

Press one to accept the charges.

Beep.

"Millie?" Half worry, half hope. "Where are you?"

"Kelowna, mom." A beat to let the relief/disappointment set in. Then, "But I'm moving to Vancouver."

"Oh, Millie."

"It's Em, mom, remember?"

"I thought you liked it there."

"Yeah, well, not really."

"You said you didn't want to go back to the coast after what happened in Victoria."

"I'm kinda running out of places to go, mom." She knew it was a mistake even as she said it.

"You could always come home, Em."

She winced. "You don't want that, mom. Trust me. You really don't want me home."

"Oh, honey, of course—"

"It's getting worse, mom." She hadn't meant to say that either. Her throat started to close. "They're getting stronger. And there's some guy following me around."

Hiss of a long distance line. Finally, "Millie. Come home. We can always find a way to manage."

"You know I can't." She pressed her knuckles hard against her mouth, pain to kill the betraying quaver. "It's better if I keep moving, mom. I'll be fine. I'll call you when I have a place to stay." Before she hung up, she added, "Give my love to dad."

*

What with the Ones getting themselves into the paper again, she'd already been thinking about leaving, even before she saw the Nerd. She had picked Kelowna to begin with because it was a new city with a fast urban sprawl gulping up the farms and sage brush that had once filled the Okanagan Valley. A city too new to have awoken to its power of creation yet—that's what she'd hoped for. Instead it seemed to be working the other way around. The city Ones were far livelier than she'd anticipated, adapting with an ingenuity that was half thrilling, half terrifying: witness the jungle gym. Still, she might have stuck it out at least until winter, when things usually quieted down, if He hadn't found her again.

The Nerd.

A bulky shape behind the wheel of a rusted-out Civic, a face red and shiny in the heat, a plump hand pushing heavy glasses up his nose as he sat reading a book and waiting for her to show.

Nemesis in coke-bottle lenses.

She had to laugh, even as the fear tightened its coil in her gut.

*

Vancouver.

September was a good time for finding work. She moved into a cheap room in a house off Commercial Drive, and by the end of her second day she had a job riding for a courier service downtown. It was Indian

Summer time, warm sunshine with a cool wind off the harbor. Even with the smog trapped by the mountains east of the city the riding was a pleasure, especially after the baked heat of August in Kelowna, and the Vancouver traffic was a thrill, pure distraction from 9 to 5. The rest of the time she waited for the city Ones to know she was there.

She didn't have to wait for long.

The Small Ones found her first, as they usually did. Her fourth night in the attic room that smelled of curry and mold, she heard the scritching of metal claws on the walls outside. Lying on the sagging bed, sleeping bag open to her waist, she turned her head toward the small window across the room. Her skin tightened, trying to lift the hairs on her arms. Her breath came short. She'd never get used to it. Scritch, scrabble scratch. Never. A moving gleam showed in the window, a leggy shadow against the streetlight. There was no curtain or blind. Scritch—tap tap tap.

Bold fucker. She sat up.

Flash, swirl of legs and out of sight. Scrabble scritch and the patter of stucco on the rhododendron two stories below. Not that bold.

Yet.

*

By her second weekend in town she knew it was a mistake to live so near Commercial Drive. Though it was showing signs of the money creeping east through the city, the Drive was still a funky blend of radicals and free spirits, granola and grunge: city life growing wild outside the sober structure of the business center. Too lively in every sense of the word.

By Saturday night, she was unable to sit quietly waiting at home. The air was warm and dry, the smell of summer pavements still strong under the smells of coffee and garbage. Trolley buses whirred by, their cables snapping sparks like the city's neural network there for anyone to read if they could. It was more than Millennium could do—more than she wanted to. But she had other senses and she knew the city was aware of her, watching her as surely as the shaved boy on the corner with steel piercing his lip.

"Spare a quarter? Spare a loon?"

Millennium shook her head and walked on. At least out here with the people and the streetlights all around her the Small Ones could only watch from hiding. But she had to go home eventually, and when she did, they were waiting.

The house was dark, the other inhabitants either asleep or still out. Oversized rhododendrons made black heaps at the edges of the shaggy lawn. A windless night, but leaves and dry grass rustled as she walked to the front door. More than that, there was the sense of eyes, many eyes, down low and watching.

She meant to go in, daring them to risk the inhabited house, but they came out before she could even get the key in the lock. Rustle and the patter of tiny feet. She spun, put her back to the door. A streetlight lit the lawn like a three-in-the-morning stage.

First came a creature the size of a pug dog, a thing of segmented legs that threw themselves over as much as they scuttled forward, like a spider caught in surf. A junkyard spider: the dim light gleamed off the twisted tin of its limbs, the tarry rags of its joints. It scuttle-tumbled to the edge of the walk between the street and the house and stopped with its legs bunched under, ready to pounce. A pause, in which Millennium heard her heart beating loud. Then another came, and then a handful more.

Scrapyard, trash heap, back alley beings. There was, despite the aggravation, something touching in their shyness. They were like children left too soon alone, torn between vengeful pranks and the desire to please, wanting attention and fearing it. A cautious slither of wire and springs to the left, a hesitant leap-frog bound of old shock absorbers and bicycle tires to the right, the eerie two-legged stalk of stick figures made from rebar and broken cement: the detritus of the city, gathered on Millennium's lawn. After a pause, they began to dance.

One of the harmless times. Relieved, resigned, she sat on the step to watch.

Young, half-formed and awkward, the Small Ones danced like marionettes with half their strings cut—and resented their own clumsiness, or so it seemed. One of the rebar stickmen fell over the tumble spider, and when it climbed to its feet it sent the spider rolling with a stiff-legged kick. The shock absorber frog didn't understand the figure at all and bounced about at random until the others shoved it to the periphery. In fact, the whole mood of the dance was more determined than celebratory, as if they were fulfilling an order to dance even though they weren't very good at it, and knew they weren't, and would rather be doing something else. Of course, they had no music beyond the throb of car speakers and the whine of buses on the Drive.

Millennium put her chin in her hands and asked them wearily, pointlessly, "What do you want from me?"

She had never known why they chose her, nor what they needed her for. Maybe for an idol, if it was a kind of worship to drive her half mad with irritation and fear, or maybe a model of how to live in the world—but sometimes she thought she was no more, and no less, than their audience, the observer that proved their existence was real.

And sometimes—more and more often in recent years—she just plain didn't care.

Her question was ignored, of course. Two of the rebar stickmen collided and began to fight, stiff arms and legs beating against each other with a racket of steel bars banging. The tumble spider tried to intervene and was kicked into the wire snake, which tangled its legs. The shock absorber frog bounced excitedly in place. A voice from the sidewalk said, "Wha' the fuck?"

Like cockroaches surprised by light, the Small Ones leapt up and were gone.

The owner of the voice, one of Millennium's housemates, said, "*What* the *fuck*—"

Caught out and thinking fast, Millennium cleared her throat and said, "Raccoons. Baby raccoons. Playing. You scared them away."

Her housemate shambled hesitantly up the walk. He was tall, thin, named Dave, and, luckily, drunk. "Raccoons? They didn' look— Is that Paula?"

"No, Em."

"Oh, hi, Em. I don' think those were raccoons."

"Sure," she said flatly. "I've been sitting here half an hour watching them. What else would they be?"

"Hum," he said, thoughtful. He stood swaying there a moment, then yawned. "Shit am I bagged."

Millennium got up and pulled out her key.

*

Tired, she nevertheless stayed awake staring at the lines of streetlight on her ceiling. The Small Ones would be angry at the interruption. If they were angry enough, they might wake one of the Larger Ones. She lay in a cold sweat, waiting, but the rest of the night was as quiet as it ever was that near the Drive. When she went down at noon, she found the rest of the household speculating about the vandals that had taken all the doors and the front hood off of Paula's car and left them lying neatly on the lawn. The neighbors to either side had suffered similarly. Someone called the cops. On Monday, an opinion piece about imaginative hooliganism on the Drive appeared in the Province.

Two days later, Millennium, riding home from the supermarket on Broadway, saw the Nerd sitting in a cafe window, scribbling in a book.

*

She spent the night in a seething tangle of fury and fear. Bad enough to be stalked by a geek, but at a level she couldn't articulate, she knew that what he wanted from her was not her body, not *her* being, but the beings that gathered to her wherever she went. When she went to get her bike from the back porch in the morning, she found they had garlanded it with a tangle of unspooled audio tape. Gift, prank, or commentary on her situation—who knew? She stripped the shiny black stuff away and said between her teeth, "Enough." She knew of no way to get the Small Ones to leave her alone.

But the Nerd—the Nerd was something else.

*

Of course, when she wanted to see him, he was nowhere to be found. Three times over the course of the week she thought she glimpsed his soft pear shape waddling down the Drive or overflowing a coffee shop chair, but every time it turned out to be a stranger. His absence began to seem as irritating as his presence had been. And the Small Ones were active as well, almost as active as the Ones in Kelowna. Maybe, she was starting to think, maybe that activity hadn't been so much the place as the time. Maybe the Ones everywhere were coming more alive, creating more of their own. How long, she thought one night, before her secret was no longer hers alone to keep, or even a secret at all?

When she saw him at last the next evening, staring myopically at the posters on the Chinese theater's door, she jumped her bike onto the sidewalk and braked at his back.

"Hey, asshole."

He spun, off balance, and gaped. Blue eyes made huge by the glasses, a little nose, a rosebud of a mouth. Thinning hair, though he couldn't have been that much older than she.

"You have something to say to me?" Millennium asked him, voice hard.

"Do I know you?" he said. His voice was right, but he spoiled it by shoving at his glasses while his magnified eyes blinked.

"No, you don't," Millennium replied, showing her teeth. "Which is why I wonder how come I keep seeing you. First Edmonton, then Kelowna, now here. So what's up?"

"I don't know what you're talking about," he said, and squeezed past her onto the sidewalk.

She spun her bike and pushed off at his side. "Oh, come on. You've got my attention, isn't that what you wanted? Or did you really think I hadn't noticed?"

He ducked his head, clutched his notebook, and scurried, jiggling. "I think you think I'm someone else. I've never seen you before. Leave me alone!"

Other pedestrians were glaring at her for having her bike on the sidewalk.

"Aw, come on. Aren't you even going to ask me out?"

The Broadway skytrain station was in sight. He gulped, shoved at his glasses and broke into a run. The sight of his fat bum bobbing down the sidewalk made her laugh. A knot of people waiting for a bus cut her off. She deked out into the street, pissed off a bus driver, jumped the curb again at his side.

"Hey, asshole," she said.

He stared at her, blinking. For a split second she thought she had it wrong, that he was the wrong guy, or it was all some weird coincidence. But past thick lenses and flickering eyelids, the blue eyes watched. Watched. Yeah, he knew who she was, all right.

"Well, if you're not gonna give me a date," she said softly, grinning with rage, "how about a present?"

Before he could react, she snatched the notebook from under his arm and dove into the traffic. Rush hour on Broadway. He didn't have a chance.

*

Guilt almost caught up with her as she wound her way home. But once in her room, still sticky with sweat, she opened his notebook and the guilt blew off her like dust. Outside, a blue spiral-bound book, the cover bent, peeling, and stained by coffee cup rings. Inside, Millennium's life.

A yellowing newspaper article was taped to the first page. *Agricultural Vandalism* said the headline. It was a short column from the back page of a small town Ontario paper. She knew the town, and the story, and the events of which it *spoke.*

London, ON. A new kind of vandalism has struck London's farming communities this week, resulting in thousands of dollars in damage.

One sentence, and memory cast her back. It had been a strange, restless night and she had awoken early in her room across the hall from her parents. Her window looked out through the branches of an old pear tree to the green expanse of the canola fields. She glanced out to check the weather and saw the line of humped earth like a mole's burrow magnified a thousand-fold, leading to a huge black mound in the far corner of the field. She heard her father stirring in his room as she slipped out of the house and ran barefoot across the soft young growth.

For the last several nights someone has been turning farmers' agricultural equipment into works of "art", doing irreparable damage in the process. "I'm actually kind of impressed," sad John Goodman, the farmer most affected. "Whoever's doing this is very creative." Goodman's neighbors are not so philosophical.

Millennium could remember how he laughed when he saw the spiky hedgehog-mole creature his harrow had become. He hadn't understood—and she couldn't explain—either her terror or her guilt. The pranksters, the invisible friends who'd been transforming her toys and playing jokes on her since childhood, were getting out of hand. Way, way out of hand.

Written in blue ink underneath the article, in a tiny exacting script: *Millie (Millennium!) Goodman, 16 yrs old. First occurrence on record, but probably not really the first.*

*

It was nearly dark. She put the light on, got a drink of water, paced. All she wanted to do was burn the book and flush the ashes down the john. But eventually she sat down again and turned the page.

Agricultural Vandals Turn Dangerous. Pranksters who have been vandalizing farmers' agricultural equipment are prime suspects in an assault case, police said today. Last night local farmer John Goodman, whose farm has been the main target of the vandals, was seriously injured in a bizarre attack.

The memories came, vivid and confused. Her father's steps, late, on the stairs. Creeping after him in her pajamas; listening at the kitchen door to the snick-snapping and metallic groans from beyond the barn. Hearing her father's shout—then his scream—then running, running—

Mr. Goodman interrupted his assailants and they attacked him with the harvester they were vandalizing, police said. His youngest daughter heard the assault and scared them off.

There was no "them," no one there at all except for Millennium and her father. No one, unless you counted the combine harvester, alive, deranged, tying itself in knots, a being trying to birth itself out of its own inanimate body. It scarcely even knew her father was there, but it knew her. It knew her.

Millie Goodman, 16, was too upset to talk to police, Constable Griffin said. "We hope when she calms down she'll be able to give us a description of the perpetrators. This was a very serious assault."

And on the facing page, with her high school photograph at the side:

Local Girl Missing. Local girl Millie (Millennium) Goodman, 16, has been listed as a missing person. She was last seen three days ago in the London hospital where her father, local farmer John Goodman, is recovering from an assault suffered on his farm outside of London.

When asked whether Ms. Goodman's disappearance could indicate involvement in her father's assault, an Ontario Provincial Police spokesperson said, "That's one possibility that must be considered." Ms. Goodman is a key witness in the case.

*

And it went on from there. Headlines from the back pages of newspapers in Toronto, Montreal and Ottawa, and then progressively west: Winnipeg, Calgary, Victoria. Edmonton, Kelowna, and finally Vancouver. Some of the articles were grainy photocopies, as though the Nerd had found them in libraries; some of them were on glossy fax paper; some had nothing to do with the Ones. But most of their acts were documented in the Nerd's book, the times their play had come to public attention: the car snares on the 401 outside of Toronto, the park bench alligators in the Rideau Canal, and on, and on.

And although Millennium's name never appeared in the news after London, in city after city that tiny blue writing made note of her address, where she worked, how long she stayed. There was a blurry Polaroid taped on the same page as the Winnipeg incident, her on her bike in a yellow slicker. That was when he must have found her, she thought. That was when the addresses started to appear, and other pictures. Her on her bike. Her shopping for groceries. Her drinking coffee by the kitchen window of the apartment in Edmonton.

Her stomach heaved.

She barely made it to the bathroom in time.

*

Midnight, and the Small Ones were dancing on the roof.

She heard them, their hard feet like hail beneath the rain that had finally come, and somewhere in the dark space between that aware- ness and her rage a plan began to form. She showered and dressed, and switched off the light.

And then she opened the dormer window. Heart beating hard enough to shake her bones, she called softly into the night, "Hello? Hey, you guys. Come down here for a second."

Silence fell with the rain.

"Hello? I need—" A breath. "I need to ask a favor."

A deeper silence yet.

Then the scrape of metal claws on the eaves.

*

The misty night rain cleaned the air and cooled Millennium's face as she jogged down the alley on the Small One's trail. She could feel every block of that day's ride burning in her thighs, but she didn't want to lose the tumble spider leading her on this chase. It was hard enough to see already, half a block ahead and looking like so much trash blown by a nonexistent wind. She almost missed it when it scrabbled up a wooden fence and fell into someone's backyard. She hesitated, wondering if this was just another prank. It was crazy to try this, crazy to think the Ones could ever be anything but a nuisance and a terror.

But then, her whole life was crazy. And what if—she couldn't help the lance of excitement in her gut—what if it worked? What if they learned to take her commands?

She put her hands on the top of the fence, jumped with legs strong from riding, and hopped over. The Small One was waiting on the other side.

Through a side yard, across an empty street, through a gap in a plywood fence that tore her jeans but let her through. Around the edge of a construction pit black with shadow where *something* stirred. The Small One skittered lightly by, a tin can tumbleweed in the dark. Millennium followed on her toes, breath locked in her throat. The *something* was big, one of the Largest Ones, but only half awake. She wished it sleep and crept by, silently cursing her guide. Under the fence through a ditch of wet weeds, across the street, another side yard. The Small One disappeared into the shadow of a house, and didn't come out again.

Millennium hunkered down in the damp shelter of a hydrangea. "Hey," she whispered. There was no streetlight near, but a window on the second floor showed a glow behind a thin blue blind. Otherwise the darkness was almost perfect. Rain hushed in the leaves, a car hissed by on the street. Then something moved on the lighted window's sill. The Small One raised a twisted limb and knocked on the glass.

A minute passed. Millennium realized she was clutching handfuls of wet grass in her tension. She let go, wiped her hands on her jeans. The Small One tapped again. This time, a shadow moved behind the blind. A hand appeared, then the blue paper scrolled up to reveal a familiar bulbous bulk. The tumble spider slipped aside to cling to the wall. Millennium wiped her hands again and stepped into the light from the Nerd's window.

Another minute. The tumble spider waved a few legs in the air like a sea anemone groping after a meal. It was eerie even to Millennium, who had sent it. The Nerd pulled up the window's sash and bent to stick his head out into the rain. The Small One reached two legs pincer-like within a few inches of his ear. He stared down at Millennium.

"What do you want?" he whispered like a shrill hiss of steam.

"I want to talk to you," Millennium said. She spoke aloud, calmly, admitting no doubts.

The Small One reached an inch closer. "I don't know you," the Nerd hissed, oblivious. "Leave me alone."

"That's a good one," Millennium replied. "I bet the cops'll get a laugh out of that when I show them your book. What do you think? A guy who stalks somebody across half the country. You think I should go to the Vancouver cops or the RCMP?"

From the Nerd, nothing. The tumble spider deftly twirled to bring another leg into range. Let him turn his head, Millennium thought, and grinned into the dark. Finally he cleared his throat.

"Wait there," he said, muffled but no longer whispering. "I'll come down." He closed the window and pulled down the blind.

Millennium shoved her hands in her pockets and smiled up at the Small One spinning a crazy course down the wall of the house. It was well hidden by the time the Nerd appeared, but as Millennium led him to an all-night coffee place on the Drive she knew the tumble spider was following. For once the knowledge didn't make her skin crawl. Maybe it was too busy crawling at the proximity of the Nerd.

*

"All right," he said, leaning over the small table at her. "So you found me out. So we're even. What are you going to do about it? And don't give me any nonsense about going to the police. We both know that's the last thing you're going do."

If she'd hated him lurking on the edges of her life, she detested him out here in the open, blinking at her with a nervous triumph. She said through clenched teeth, "Really. Why's that?"

"Because," he said, oozing smugness, "of the small matter of a warrant for your arrest back in London."

"You are such an asshole," she said, wonder in her voice. A pause to let his smugness solidify, then: "There is no warrant for my arrest. There never was a warrant for my arrest. I'm not even a missing person, you dumb fuck, I called my parents when I got to Toronto."

Smugness fell away, leaving him blinking and pale. He shoved his glasses back up his little nose. "Yeah? Well— If you were going to you would have called the cops by now."

"Yeah? Well—" she mocked him. "I can always change my mind."

76

"You won't." The smugness wasn't back, but the sneer he put on was just as objectionable. "You tell them I've been following you, you have to tell them why."

She put on a smile every bit as obnoxious as his sneer. "You mean tell them about how you're so hung up on me you've been following me around the country, committing bizarre acts of vandalism to get my attention and then putting the newspaper articles about them in your pathetic little scrapbook?" She put her head on one side and added sweetly, "You know, I think you're right. I guess I should talk to them after all."

He gaped, blue eyes bulging behind their lenses. "You can't tell them that. It wasn't me. You know it wasn't me! It was them!"

"Who? The cops? Man, you're even crazier than I thought." She pushed her chair back as if to go.

"*Them*!" He slapped the table, slopping coffee. "You know goddamn well what I mean. The Little People. The Fair Folk. The Deeny Shee. Don't you try to put it off on me!" He actually shook his finger at her. "Don't you dare!"

What the fuck were the Deeny Shee? Millennium shrugged and stood.

The Nerd gulped. "There are others who know," he said, voice wobbling. It was obviously his last card. "I'm not the only one. If anything happens to me, someone else will carry on with the mission. You won't get away with this." The last few words disappeared into a squeak under her glare.

"Mission! Are you completely insane?"

But she didn't leave, and by the look in his eyes he knew he had her. She dropped angrily back into her chair.

He shoved his glasses into place and said firmly, "We have a right to know."

"Bull *shit*."

"It is not bullshit." The obscenity was odd coming from his prim little mouth. "What is bullshit is people like you using Them for your own secret ends."

"Using—" But she bit it off. Because she had, hadn't she, that very night. Instead she said, "What do you mean, 'people like me?' What am I, a conspiracy of one? Man, you been watching too many reruns of *The X-Files*."

"Oh, please. You think we don't know about Lucy Woo in Los Angeles, or Peter Legrange in Atlanta? I'm telling you, we've been onto you for years."

A thousand questions crowded into Millennium's brain. Los Angeles? Atlanta? But the only one that made it out was, "Why?"

The Nerd blinked at her. "Why?"

"Why are you onto—us?" Us?! "Why have you followed me around all these years? What does any of this have to do with you?"

"It—we—it isn't right."

Looking into his confused, magnified eyes, she felt fatigue sweep over her. "What isn't right, exactly?"

"That you have this, this secret power and—"

"Power?" Millennium gave a short laugh and spread her arms. "Do I look powerful to you?"

Blink, blink, blink. "I just mean— We all know there's more to the world than what most of us can see, but you actually get to live there. Inside the mystery." He looked down at the table, his voice dying to a sad mumble. "That's all we want. We just want to see inside the mystery too."

Millennium said nothing for a moment. The silence filled with the buzz of conversation, the hiss of steam, Dave Matthews singing *Halloween*. Then she said softly, "Your wanting doesn't give you the right to anything in my life. Do you understand that? Take a look at yourself. You're a stalker. Just because you're not after sex doesn't make you any more righteous, or any more sane."

A tide of red swept up under his fair skin. "I'm not—" He gulped for breath. "I just— It isn't fair! Don't you realize how desperate the world is for a little magic, how badly it needs a miracle? You're keeping it all to yourself and it isn't fair!"

"Fair. Jesus. How old are you?" She propped her elbows on the table and leaned forward. "Listen. I don't owe you a damn thing, but I'll tell you this much. It isn't magic, and my life is not a goddamn fairy tale. For Christ's sake, you think I like living on the road, moving on every time the Large Ones start to wake up? They aren't my friends, and they sure as hell aren't anyone else's."

He looked up with a frown that pushed his glasses down his nose. He shoved them up again. "I don't understand. How can you say they aren't magic?"

"Look, it isn't—" She'd never had to put her years of thinking into words before. "It's not an invasion from Fairyland or the Eighth Dimension or whatever you pretend for your little game. This thing that's been happening around me since I was a kid—and don't ask me why they picked me, 'cause I don't fucking know—it belongs to this world. Maybe it *is* the world, even. Maybe it's the life we've been squeezing out that has nowhere else to go. Do you get me?" By his face, definitely not. "Think about it. We've been trashing the environment for centuries, right? Cutting down forests, putting up farms and cities and dumps and all the rest of that human crap. Whole ecologies wrecked, hundreds of species gone, nothing standing in our way. Well—

"In grade ten biology they taught us about evolution, about how species evolve out of other species to fill in the ecological niches, keep the whole thing going. But these days we're running out of species to evolve from. And more to the point, we're running out of *time*. Evolution takes forever, but the new ecology, the urban ecology, has gaps that need to be filled now. You understand what I'm saying? I mean, Christ, it's in every newspaper you read these days, biological diversity, critical density of ecologies, interdependency, blah blah blah. All it means is there has to be enough life on the planet, doing all the different things living things do to keep themselves and each other going, or everything dies. *Everything* dies.

"And the world *knows*. It knows that plain old animals and plants don't stand a chance against us humans. I mean, they tried, right? Rats and pigeons tried invading the cities, coyotes, raccoons—pests, we call them, but it's just the world trying to mix it up, keep us from taking over and burying everything under concrete. But they aren't enough. It's too slow. So—" She shrugged and leaned back in her chair, more tired than before. "So the world's trying something new. Something tough enough to survive the new ecology. Something so tough it'll maybe even be able to slow us down a little, keep us in check." She drank the last of her coffee. Cold.

The Nerd was staring, his eyelids almost still. "Show me," he said at last.

Millennium stared back. "Excuse me?"

"Show me." He leaned toward her, something inside him taking fire. "Show me what you know. Let me inside the mystery. Let me *see*."

The anger that had dissipated while she talked leapt back into her veins. This asshole hadn't heard a thing she'd said. Fine. *Fine*. She'd show the fucker his mystery and see how much he liked it up close and personal. She smiled a thin, hard smile and stood. "All right. I'll show you. And then you leave me the fuck alone. Deal?"

He gulped and shoved up his glasses. "Deal."

*

After the bright cafe, the construction site was a pit of blackness ringed by a plywood fence. Without the Small One to guide her, Millennium had to grope to find the gap that would let them in. Inside the mystery, she thought vindictively, listening to the Nerd squeeze his bulk through the splintery hole. As her eyes adjusted she could make out the pale blur of his face, the hand that pushed at his glasses, but the excavation remained a sinkhole of absolute darkness spined with rusty rebar. And inside, *something* lightly slumbered.

Largest One.

"What—" the Nerd began, but she shushed him.

"Wait," she whispered. "And whatever happens— Don't. Move."

Largest One. In Victoria, it had been One from the harbor that had woken one night, drawn by her presence. A shambling monster of barnacle-crusted planks, bones, and anchor chains bleeding rust, it had created havoc along the harborfront, terrifying sailors and whores and Millennium alike. She hadn't even tried to deal with it. She just ran, like she always did, hoping it would go back to sleep without her around. They always had, up till now. She'd never deliberately tried to wake one—up till now.

"Hello," she said softly into the dark. "Great One, Mighty One, awake!" Putting on a show for the Nerd. "Tonight is your night to rise. Come on. I know you can hear me. Wake up!"

The Largest One stirred. Millennium was peripherally aware of the Nerd's adenoidal breathing, and even of the more delicate presence of the Small Ones creeping over the fence, but the core of her attention was on the great being half awake and half formed at the bottom of its pit.

"Wake up, you beauty, you darling. It's time to come out, now. It's time to walk in the night."

The Nerd's breathing stopped: he'd finally seen the Small Ones edging into the scant light around the rim of the pit. Millennium ignored him, and them. The Largest One was waking. A slow, deep scraping sound came from the pit.

The Nerd gasped. "What—"

"Shhh!" Her heart was pounding, exhilaration and fear.

Scrape, scra-a-ape, rattle boom.

The Nerd whimpered in his throat. The Small Ones stirred, fell still. The rain glowed with the city's ambient light.

The Largest One rose from its nest.

A damp gleaming angularity of leg. Another. A third. The domed, folded bulk of its core. The muffled fall of earth, the scrape and boom of steel. It rose, unfolding its legs. And rose some more.

Deep in the blood-thrumming moment, a tiny door in Millennium's mind opened on a glimpse of her past: eight years old, folding paper on the top of a scarred wooden desk. Origami. If some vast hand could take half a dozen dumpsters and fold them into a nightmare crab—too many legs with scissor-hinged joints and a body of eye-twisting folds—and if it could be incubated at the bottom of a muddy, garbage-strewn pit, and then wakened on a black wet three a.m—. That might begin to hint at what the Largest One was, climbing up into the city night.

The Nerd whimpered again. Millennium didn't have the breath to shush him. The Largest One paused. One long jointed limb stretched toward them with a faint gritty squeak. Dirty water pattered from the knife point at its end. It groped, delicately feeling the air. Wet mud spattered Millennium's face. Frozen with fear, she could not even flinch. But the Nerd—

The Nerd screamed and turned to run.

Rattle snap boom.

He hung soft and small between two pincer legs, squeaking, before Millennium even registered the cold wind of the Largest One's move. That fast. But then it fell still again, as if it didn't know what to do with its prey now it had him. The Small Ones could have been so much trash. Another door opened in Millennium's mind: her father, pinned within the harvester's writhing frame. She gulped for air.

"Easy—"

The Largest One didn't move, but she felt its attention land on her like a blow.

"Easy, now." The words drifted out of her, gentle as the rain. "Soft little one, he hasn't done you any harm. No threat, no harm. Just a sad little squeaker. You can let him go. There's more to the city than him. There's buses and bicycles and cars. Park benches. Bus stops. Traffic lights and street signs and hot dog carts. You don't need him. You can just let him go. Can't you? You beauty, you marvel. You can just let him go."

The Largest One shifted with a slow hollow grating of joints. The Nerd hung silent and limp. God knew what damage those steel pincers had done.

"Please," she breathed, to the One, to God. "I'm sorry. Let him go." The rain on her lips tasted of salt. "Please."

There was a stir among the Small Ones. The tumble spider crept into the Largest One's shadow, tin can limbs like a tiny reflection of the other's steel. Then another moved, and another—the rebar stickmen, the dumb shock absorber frog—in a creeping, supplicating dance, a little eddy of movement that drew away from Millennium to the far side of the site. The Largest One shifted again, still holding the Nerd but its attention following the dance. Millennium loved them for that moment, those crazy lost little beings doing what they could to help.

She wiped her face on her sleeve, still afraid, but suddenly no longer frozen by it. "Okay," she said aloud. "Just let him down and off you go."

The Largest One paused, attention wavering between her and its small cousins. Then, as quickly as it had snapped him up, it let the Nerd drop. His body hit the edge of the excavation and slid to the bottom in a shower of earth. The Largest One, no longer interested, scissor-scrambled up the other side. It stepped delicately over the plywood fence and was gone, Small Ones scurrying around its feet.

In the silence of the city's hum, Millennium could hear them on the street outside, a rapid pitter-patter and an echoing rattle boom. She took a breath, and another one, and then dashed to the edge of the pit and down.

*

After she'd bought her ticket, she used a phone in the bus station to make two calls. The first one to 911, telling them there was a very dazed and somewhat battered fellow sitting in the middle of a construction site just off Commercial Drive.

The other was to her folks.

Press one to accept the charges.

Beep.

"Em? Where are you, sweetheart?"

"Hi, dad. Um, the Vancouver bus station."

Sigh. "What happened this time?"

"Well, you know— Things."

"Are you all right?"

"Yeah. Actually—yeah. I'm okay. Only it's raining like a bitch. So I thought maybe this time I'd go south."

"Like how far south?"

She took a breath, and realized she was grinning.

"Well, I thought maybe I'd give Los Angeles a try. There's somebody down there I want to meet."

4: A WOMAN'S BONES

Our second day in camp I walked out into the grass. I had forgotten the wind. Born with it in my ears, how could I forget? As constant as a mother's love, unnoticed until it was gone. The wind, at least, I could regain. A vast current of cold air, it sang through the stakes of the surveyor's grid laid across the barrows, boomed in the walls of the tents, hissed and thrashed in the grass. Listening to its voice I did not hear Dr. Cahill approach until he spoke my name.

"I'm sorry to disturb you," he said, always courteous, though as the leader of the expedition he did not need to be. "We seem to have some visitors."

The camp was as it had been all morning: the circle of tall white canvas tents, the untidy cluster of smaller tents and blanket shelters, the neat line of lorries in between. Archeologists and workmen gathered around their respective fires for the midday meal. But beyond, to the south, a dozen horsemen sat their ponies on an invisible rise in the steppe, black silhouettes against the shadowless haze of the sky. The Alyakshin, come to protest the disinterment of those they would claim (falsely, by Dr. Cahill's theory) as ancestors.

They were polite about it. Instead of riding into camp they dismounted where they were, a mile or more away, and began setting up a camp of their own.

"Well," said Dr. Cahill, humor disguising his relief, "at least they aren't riding in waving their spears." He was not a tall man by western standards, with sandy hair and a beard trimmed to a point, and round gold-rimmed glasses that flashed and winked in the sun.

"They will wait for you to invite them into your encampment," I told him. "They mean to be polite about this. It gives them the advantage," I added, not sure he would understand.

"Oh, yes," he said. "Just like my Aunt Hilda." He slapped his hands against the pockets of his khaki jacket, as if confirming he was equipped to handle the situation. "Shall we go?"

"Better, perhaps, to give them a little while to get settled."

"A little while," he repeated, a twist to his mouth that I'd seen often enough on the journey out. It is as hard for the English to live outside the efficiency of clocks as it was for me to learn to live within it.

"An hour?"

He nodded, looking at his pocket watch as I looked up at the sun, a brilliance behind the high white haze. "We can finish the preliminary survey today, start digging tomorrow," he said, as if the Alyakshin protest had come to naught before it had even begun.

*

We walked through grass and wind, Dr. Cahill, Dr. Learner and myself, to meet the riders. Dr. Learner had come fresh from a dig in the desert and was heavily bundled against the steppe's spring chill, his sweaters and coat making him seem even bigger than he was. Dr. Cahill might have just stepped out of a lecture hall.

"Good afternoon," he said, stopping just within earshot of the Alyakshin men.

"Greetings of the day that brings us here together in this place," I translated.

The Alyakshin stood to greet us. Lean, even slight, they did not meet the western image of warriors. They wore felt vests colorfully embroidered, and their long black hair was braided with bright yarn. Their sabers and slender wood javelins had been set aside for a peaceful meeting in another's camp. The leader, a man perhaps a little younger than Dr. Cahill, stepped forward.

"You ride with these trespassers, woman of the steppe?" he said in the formal way.

"Yes," I said. "I have come to speak their words in the Alyak tongue."

"You are from the south. Pelyoshin?"

"I was."

He was polite, he let it go. He said to Dr. Cahill, "You have ridden across grass grazed by Alyak herds, yet you are strangers, not a tribe we have met in friendship, nor yet one we have met in anger. How shall we meet, on this grass the Alyak herds graze?"

I translated, then added, "He's being very formal, very polite in the old fashioned way."

Dr. Cahill glanced at me. "And there's a formal response, I suppose?"

"Assuming you don't want outright war." I gave a faint smile. "From his point of view, inviting him into camp is a bit like a burglar inviting in the man whose house he's broken into, but not inviting him would be worse. Of course he knows—they all know—who you are and why you've come, and that you have government permission to be here. He's just trying to make a point."

Dr. Cahill looked the Alyak men over. "He can consider it made," he said dryly. "By all means, invite them in for a cup of tea."

*

The leader of the Alyakshin was named Kehboryavin.

"It is not the trespass on our lands," he said. "Or not only that. We have learned long since what it means to be conquered by a nation that would put walls around the wind." He paused to let me translate and sipped his tea. It would seem insipid to him, I knew, even with a spoonful of condensed milk stirred in, but he drank it, unremittingly polite.

"Is that really what he said?" Dr. Learner said. "'Walls around the wind'?"

"Jack." Dr. Cahill was repressive.

Kehboryavin went on. "But this is not a matter of grazing, or water, or camping rights. This place is a place where the dead wait. You are not of the plains, any more than the hillmen who give you permits to come here, so perhaps you can be forgiven your ignorance. But since I now tell you, you will know: there is a great power buried here that must not be disturbed."

Dr. Cahill spoke with long pauses for thought. "Tell him it is true there is something powerful buried here. Tell him I know this. Tell him the power here is the power of knowledge, the power of the past. There is no evil to be unearthed here, only a link in the chain of history, and of the lives of the people of the steppe. Tell him that the power we recover, the knowledge, will give his own people strength, like the strength a deep taproot gives to an ancient and flourishing tree. Tell him it is for his people that we have come here to dig."

The trees on the steppe are stunted, wind-tormented things. The plainsmen trade hides and furs for wood straight enough to make tent poles and javelins. I didn't mention this to Dr. Cahill. It is difficult enough just to translate the words, never mind the assumptions behind them.

Kehboryavin studied me when I finished, then turned his dark gaze on Dr. Cahill. "We know what is buried here," he said flatly. "It is you who are in ignorance. Will you listen to the words of one who would teach you what you must know?"

"Yes," said Dr. Learner before Dr. Cahill could speak.

"Jack," said Dr. Cahill in exasperation.

"Speaking as an anthropologist, Tom, this is gold he's offering us. The oral history of the place, of the people buried here, to compare with what we actually find? It's a gold mine!"

Dr. Cahill frowned. "You know the modern plains people are the descendants of a different group entirely from the barrows people. They supplanted the barrows people more than a thousand years ago."

"I know that's what you're digging to prove. But this could give us a whole new insight into the way populations meet and replace one another. We don't even know if there was direct contact between the barrows people and their successors. Does the oral tradition about this place actually start with these people's ancestors finding the barrows and inventing a reason for them, or is it a borrowed tradition from the barrows people themselves? Or was there even an intermediary group between the two? It could be a whole new facet to the investigation here!"

Dr. Cahill sighed. "If we tell him we want to hear what he has to say, it will only give him false expectations. I'm certainly not delaying the dig for you to catalog his superstitions."

Leroy Paltz, the expedition photographer, said quietly, "If we say we're interested in his knowledge, give him a role in the dig, some stake in the outcome, he might end up an ally rather than an opponent."

"Yes," said Dr. Learner emphatically, and two of the graduate students murmured their agreement.

"Very well." Dr. Cahill turned to me. "But make it clear that we are going ahead with the dig regardless."

"Tell him we value his knowledge and are eager to make use of it to direct the excavation and to help interpret what we find," Dr. Learner said.

I told Kehboryavin. He looked at me a long time, while the wind slapped the fire down and shook the tents. "I think they said much more than that," he said finally.

"I told you everything they asked me to tell you."

His expression did not change, but I could feel a door close behind his eyes. "Tell them I will take their words to the elders. Tell them it would be better for them to wait to dig until they have heard what they must hear. Tell them they do not know what danger they could raise."

Dr. Cahill listened, politely, and nodded. "Thank you," he said. It was a dismissal. Kehboryavin set his cup aside, stood, and walked away.

When he was out of sight beyond the tents, Dr. Cahill chuckled. "What dig is complete without a superstitious native or two?"

Everyone laughed.

Even me.

*

The Alyak riders left as simply as they had come, returning to the rest of their tribe to report. For the next six days we labored over the barrows, cutting the recalcitrant sod and sifting the fine loess that the wind blew into everything, eyes and tents and food. Dr. Cahill set the workmen and students to excavating alternate squares along the spines of both barrows, reserving for himself and Dr. Learner the shallow dome-like mound where the two long barrows met in a T.

When I wasn't relaying instructions to the workmen I assisted Leroy Paltz, the photographer. The blowing grit was a menace to the fragile mechanism of his camera, and even more so to the treated glass plates of film, so we spent a lot of our time constructing and reconstructing a kind of canvas blind, and Leroy had me back up every exposure with a sketch. It was tedious work at this stage, but Dr. Cahill's enthusiasm kept spirits high—at least, the spirits of the academic contingent. The workmen were growing quickly sullen, but I put that down to the unaccustomed labor (they were all drivers and mechanics, men of status in the city where they'd been hired) and to having to take orders relayed by a woman. But one night, lying awake listening to the wind throb in the walls of my tent, I heard their voices rising in unison from their camp and realized that instead of the songs and boasting stories of earlier nights, those men were singing prayers.

Superstitious natives, Dr. Cahill would say.

My dreams were empty of everything but wind.

*

The Alyakshin returned at noon.

This time only Dr. Learner and I walked out to their camp, Dr. Cahill grudging any time away from his dig. The whole Alyak tribe had not come, I saw, but a fair proportion of it. Women were setting up the felt and lathe ghurdis, while men cut fire pits and kept an eye on the ponies and long-legged sheep grazing south of camp. They were a traditional lot, the Alyakshin, following their herds across this remote reach of the steppe, a long way from the encroachment of civilization. Most of them would never have seen a truck before, or a blond man, or a woman wearing anything but the long tunic and wide felt trousers dictated by tradition. The Alyak women were too busy, the men too polite, but the children stared and stared.

The man Kehboryavin met us on the edge of their camp with three elders, a hearty grandmother almost as broad as she was tall, and two sexless beings withered so dry by age it was a wonder the wind did not snatch them up and scatter them into dust.

Dr. Learner said, "Good afternoon."

I said, "He gives you good greetings this day, honored elders, and wishes of health and fair journeying to you and yours."

The ancients nodded. Kehboryavin studied the work taking place over my shoulder. The grandmother said, "My, such fine manners in a foreigner. And so much said in two little words!"

I blushed. "It was his meaning, grandmother."

"Hmm." She studied Dr. Learner a moment, then turned to me with shrewd black eyes nested in wrinkles. It was a look that took me back to childhood. She said, "Pelyoshin, I think my grandson said?"

In the grip of manners and memory both, I told her my name, my mother's and grandmothers' names. She took in my jodhpurs and plain shirt, and the bobbed hair dictated by both fashion and practicality, then dismissed me to say to Dr. Learner, "You are the one who is willing to hear the truth of this place."

He gave a short, jovial bow. "I am he, madam."

She looked, as her grandson had never ceased to look, at the industry taking place half a mile to the north. "You should have waited. Come tomorrow after dawn and we will begin."

Dr. Learner bowed again, making no effort to hide his amusement, and turned away. Before I could follow, the Alyak grandmother said to me, brooking no argument, "You will stay. I have work for you."

"I should go back, I—"

"I have greater need of you here. Come with me." And when I hesitated, aware that Dr. Learner was watching with interest, she snapped, "Come!"

It was the voice of my childhood, the voice that could not be disobeyed. I went.

When I returned to camp a little before sunset, Dr. Cahill glanced up from the fire he was building to say mildly, "We could have used your help this afternoon."

I flushed, grateful for once that my skin was too dark to show it. "I beg your pardon. It—" I wanted to explain the imperatives of a grandmother's voice. But one thing all my studies have taught me is that some things truly will not translate. I finished lamely, "It won't happen again."

He nodded, his mind already back on his fire, or more likely on the dig.

Dr. Learner clapped then rubbed his hands together. "And tomorrow, the great mystery revealed!"

*

Grandmother Kehboryana sat by the fire, her broad, round-shouldered form dark against the newly risen sun. The cold wind was laden with dew, drenched with the scent of grass. My stomach growled at the smell of fried mutton stew.

"The Story of the Conqueror Yulima," Grandmother Kehboryana said through me, "is the oldest story of the Alyak nation. It carries the names of our ancestors and of the lands they rode to find this place, their home. On this day, for the first time, those not of Alyak blood will hear this truth. Already, the Alyak heart becomes divided." That said, she began the story. "These are the events that occurred in the days before days were numbered—"

There is a thing that happens to me when I translate. Perhaps it is common to all translators, I don't know. But sometimes it seems that the two languages meet and mirror each other, word for word, without any involvement on my part at all, except the rudimentary cooperation of ears, lips and tongue. The rich phrases, soaked in the folkways of the Alyakshin, became straight and stiff and alien when clothed in English, like foreign students at the University clothed in their uncomfortable new tweeds. Dr. Learner fell into a trance of his own, writing, and I, as distantly as if I were reading what he wrote, saw the pageant of the Alyakshin story, their oral history, their truth, roll across the background of the windblown steppe. The people from beyond the known world who swept up the armies of a dozen nations and remade them into their own. The powers that let them conquer, and conquer again, and yet that drove them as unmercifully as they drove the lesser folk under their sway. The lust for the riches of the far west, the only land that resisted their coming and thus, like the winds of frustration, drove their desire into ungovernable need.

"—like the unceasing wind of the east that drives the summer fire until it consumes all the grass under the western sky," Grandmother Kehboryana said. "And in that time a child was born."

The sun had risen above the grandmother's shoulder by this time, sending her shadow streaming across the grass. The clang of shovels and picks rang clear from the dig, counterpoint to the bleating of sheep. Several of the children had settled nearby to listen to the story, sneaking glimpses of Dr. Learner's pale hair, and of his long hands doing incomprehensible work with paper and pen. Grandmother Kehboryana directed one of the girls to pour out the sugared tea that had been steeping to syrup by the fire. We both sipped before she continued speaking through me, trailing her images across my mind.

"A child who was no child, for, though she was as fine to look upon as any babe, with as sweet a voice and a smile more like sunlight than gold, she bore from the dark of her mother's womb the hungry soul of a demon. She was the Conqueror Yulima—"

Dr. Learner would occasionally nod at a phrase or a metaphor. I had taken his class on folklore—in fact, it was he who had recommended me to Dr. Cahill as the expedition's interpreter—so I also recognized what he was hearing. The story contained echoes from a hundred different cultures: the great and terrible leader who nearly transcends his own wickedness by the height to which he brings his people; the challenge to the gods that can not be borne; the humble hero who lays the prideful low. The one moral truth imperative to the primitive society, according to Dr. Learner. The individual with the power to wreak change upon the community must bow to tradition, or be buried by it.

The only new thing here was that the individual, the great leader, the Conqueror who threatened change upon the world, was a woman.

"—That first man of our people, he cried, 'Wind of the north, wind of the east, wind of the south, come to me! The killing in the west has raised such a darkness that heaven itself has turned black. Come to me, and join your brother of the west to end the dying.' And of course the winds came, for all the winds are the breath of the gods' will. And the Conqueror Yulima could not stand before them. Her armies were scattered beyond the earth and she was blown here, where the ancestors of our ancestors, who had been left behind, buried her beneath grass and stone, for of course a woman such as she could not be killed. And here she has lain, for an age and an age, waiting for her tomb to be breached so that she may once again rise to conquer the west."

*

The circle of silence the old woman had created with her storytelling closed in around us, a wall of wind separating us from the bleating sheep and the hard labor at the dig.

After a moment, Grandmother Kehboryana drew in a slow breath and let it out, her hands dark and gnarled in her lap. "So you see what you risk with your digging."

Dr. Learner set his notebook aside and stretched, pressing his hands to his back. "Tell her she has all my thanks. Her knowledge can only add to the knowledge we will gather from the dig. And tell her that if this is the Conqueror Yulima, the stories *she* will tell us will be given in turn to the Alyakshin. It is the greatest gift we could possibly give them: a return to the present of the power of their past."

Grandmother Kehboryana thought about this when I had finished. "Tell him this, granddaughter. Tell him we, who have seen our children seek out the knowledge of his cities and come home dying of that knowledge—tell him we know the price that is always paid. All knowledge, and all power, comes at a cost. He would do well to listen."

When Dr. Learner returned to camp, I went with him, quickly, before the grandmother could call me back.

*

That night, alone in my tent, I dreamed. No great vision of the myth-ical past, no window onto the days of the Conqueror's triumph and fall. The dream I dreamed was an old one, familiar as the sound of loose canvas in the wind. There were the noble buildings and crooked quadrangles of my college. There were the echoing wooden floors, slate blackboards, and diamond-paned windows. There was the mellow chapel bell, the flutter of academic gowns, the pervasive smells of dry rot and tea. And there, where they never had been, never could be, was my family. Mother, brothers, aunts, who'd died so long ago they scarcely had faces, setting up my grandmother's striped ghurdi on the green rolled grass of the Fellow's Lawn.

I woke, as I always did, sweating and sick with shame.

*

The dig was going well, despite the growing reluctance of the native help. The students worked themselves into exhaustion every day, inspired by Dr. Cahill's fireside lectures in the evenings. I don't think you could even say he disregarded the grandmother's warning, so utterly did it fail to impact on his consciousness, but the Conqueror Yulima's story was the wind that blew his ambition, his desire to know, into a conflagration. Every night he spun a new strand of theory from Dr. Learner's account of the tale. Each mention of a people conquered, each stage of the conqueror's journey, was pinned down on the map of the world he carried in his mind. One night, Dr. Learner said, "So what's next after this dig, Tom? When do you start to trace the Conqueror's people back to their origins?"

We all called the barrow's occupant "the Conqueror" now.

Dr. Cahill smiled. "What are your plans for next season?"

Everyone laughed, but I didn't think he was joking. Once a man like Dr. Cahill creates a map of the world in his mind, the next, the only, thing for him to do is recreate the world in the map's image. The people of the steppe travel thousands of miles across the seemingly unlandmarked plains, they have done so for countless generations, but they have never even invented a word for "map." The first time I ever saw one was in the orphanage school far to the south, where I learned a hundred words for things I had never known, and was commanded to forget the names of everything I did.

While Dr. Cahill ordered the past for his students beneath the springtime stars, the diggers told their own stories over on the other side of the camp. The lore they traded was all modern, and mostly to do with the money they were earning and how it would be spent once they were home, but one night, standing in the dark outside of camp, I heard a slow, measured voice explaining the doom that would fall on any man who touched, by accident or design, a bone from under the barrow. "Even the dust," said the senior driver. "Even the dust." And after a silence they all began to pray.

"They are wiser than your learned men."

I jumped. It was Kehboryavin. I had not heard his footsteps under the hush of the wind. The Alyakshin had remained camped a half-mile or so away from the dig.

"Were you at the barrow?" I demanded, shrill with shock.

His face was all gray angles under the quarter moon. He looked at me, then away to the camp, where the two fires burned orange, like beacons, or eyes.

"You always share the westerners' fire, never your own people's. Why is that?"

"The drivers aren't my people. Anyway, they wouldn't want me to."

"I did not mean those *piyevya*." The word meant, literally translated, "weak without walls." "I meant my grandmother's fire. She has been watching for you."

I was silent a moment. "You aren't my people, either."

"And they are?" He gestured towards the other fire, where Dr. Cahill's glasses caught the light, circles of fire in his sunburned Englishman's face.

"—'the gold and amber fields of the west' could be a reference to the ancient Celtic trade—"

Kehboryavin listened to words he could not understand, or to my silence. Then he said, "Pelyoshin was never Alyakshin's enemy," and walked away.

I don't know what moved me to spit at his back, "Pelyoshin is dead!"

But he didn't respond.

I had said it in English.

*

In only two more days, the sod and dirt was cleared from the T-shaped barrow. Leroy Paltz, the photographer, and I worked late into the day, even after the rest had cleaned off their shovels and headed for their tents to rest for the evening's celebration. The sun was a searing orange flame on the horizon when Leroy exposed his last plate. I held the camera's black shroud against the wind, while my eyes took their own picture of the barrow's central dome. It was huge and dark, its rough granite stained by centuries under the earth. It seemed to lean away from the bitter wind, yearning for the golden fire of the west. Covered with sod it had been merely a hump in the plains. Marked with string and cluttered with students, shovels and sieves, it had been—what?—an artifact. Helpless, quiescent. Dead.

Now, though. Now.

The wind blew more fiercely in the wake of the sun. I swayed and Leroy said my name. He was finished, already packing up his things. "Are you all right?"

"Tired."

"It's the wind," he said knowledgeably. "It'll dry you right out. A cup of tea and a glass of beer, in that order. Can you take the tripod?"

It wasn't easy, turning my back on that resentful heap of stone. But it was good to head into camp with the prospect of a sponge bath, clean clothes, and something to drink before me. Leroy was right, the wind could take it right out of you.

I had hardly drawn my ration of bathwater from the drum, however, when Dr. Cahill came to find me.

"There you are," he said. He was impatient; some snag had interrupted him savoring the approaching triumph. "If you wouldn't mind, the drivers seem to want a word."

I was surprised. I had assumed any problem would be the Alyakshin.

The drivers stood in a group on the scholar's side of the line of lorries. Their leader, a man with a broad, dark, furrowed face that always reminded me of a tilled field, barely acknowledged me with a glance. He kept his eyes on Dr. Cahill as he spoke.

"He says they will not dig any more."

"Tell him there isn't any more digging to do. For heaven's sake, they know very well we've uncovered the stone structure! How can they see what we've accomplished and still complain about doing farmers' work?"

Dr. Learner and the others had approached by this time, one or two carrying lanterns against the gathering night, so the two groups confronted each other across the trampled grass, with me between. Some instinct made me glance up and away, and I saw not far off three horsemen silhouetted against the last of the light.

Dr. Learner said to me, "Tell them the work they'll be doing from now on is the most important part of the whole job."

"Tell them," Dr. Cahill interrupted testily, "I'd do all the rest myself if only I could. Tell them they're bloody lucky to have any part in this enterprise at all."

He was missing the point completely, but it wasn't my place to say so. I told the drivers what the two doctors had said. The drivers' elder went into some detail about the threatened doom of any who touched the Conqueror or her minions' bones.

When I'd finished, Dr. Learner said eagerly, "Ask them how they know about the Conqueror."

Dr. Cahill said coldly, "I know bloody well how they know about the Conqueror, and so do you."

He was staring at me, and the blood began to burn under my skin as Dr. Learner and then all the students understood and stared as well, or, embarrassed, looked away.

"I beg your pardon, Dr. Cahill," I said. My voice was low enough, but I couldn't keep it from trembling. "But I didn't tell them anything about her."

Leroy Paltz stepped forward from the group. "It isn't as if the men couldn't talk to the Alyakshin if they wanted to, Tom."

"It's quite a different dialect," Dr. Learner said. "Still, it wouldn't take much more than a word or two, their own imaginations would do the rest."

"It isn't as if this kind of thing hasn't happened before," Leroy added. "Think of Egypt in 'Fourteen."

Dr. Cahill glanced past me at the drivers. "Well, it hardly matters how they got onto it. The point is to get them off. Tell them—"

I told them. I told them repeatedly and at length, but Dr. Cahill might as well have been talking to the grass, or the wind. Eventually he threw up his arms and pretended to laugh. "Superstitious savages! You can give them lorries instead of horses, but you can't bloody civilize them. All right! Come on you lot, if we're going to be shifting stones tomorrow, we'll need a hell of a good dinner tonight. Who's for beer and jerky stew?"

Dr. Learner and the rest trailed after him, quietly, heads down. They knew as well as I that, for all his laughter, he was furious. Yet, at the same time, I knew that he had said nothing less than the truth. If he could have done it all himself, he would have.

The oldest driver knew it too. He said, "What kind of a man is that? He'd rather fuck a pile of bones than a live woman?" He looked me over and spat, just to one side of my feet.

A javelin's point slid out of the darkness to tap his jacket over his heart. "Go back to your sty, city pig," Kehboryavin said. "Speak to a woman of the tribes in such a manner again and I'll see you roasting over a dung fire on a spit."

Dr. Learner was right. Different dialect or no, he got his meaning across. The drivers shuffled off with only an evil look or two, leaving me alone with the tribesman. The light from the two camps only seemed to cast the space between in deeper darkness. I was not unaware of the irony.

I said in English, "The noble savage rescues the beleaguered maiden." It was a scene caption from a moving picture I'd seen just before we sailed.

Kehboryavin said, "Grandmother sent me to ask you to eat at her fire tonight. She'll be in a bad temper if we are late, but I did not wish to interrupt. Perhaps it will sweeten her mood if I can tell her there is a problem with the digging."

"Tell her what you like," I said, and started for my tent.

"You aren't still hoping you belong with them, are you? But then, it seems living between walls makes all the rest of them fools, I don't know why you should be any different."

I stopped. "May I ask you something, young chief? If you are such a bitter enemy of the westerners and those who take up their ways, why do you oppose waking the Conqueror?"

His laugh was indeed bitter, but his answer surprised me. "Why do you think I do oppose it? It is my grandmother who is so afraid of change. For myself, I say some change might not be so terrible a thing, if it should blow these men and their cities and diseases and laws from the grass." He laughed again. "But you know as well as I do, the Conqueror is only bones, and a woman's bones at that."

*

Because the ocean of grass really does swell and move with the tide of wind, the ground level of the barrows was nearly three feet below that of the present. Alyak territory isn't quite far enough north to mean permafrost, but the yellow loess clay stays cold and saturated late into the spring. Good for the grass, but a bad sign for the archeologists. However, as drainage ditches were painfully dug and the base of the long barrows was revealed, hope among the expedition members grew. They had rallied behind Dr. Cahill after the drivers announced their strike, and although their cheerfulness had been somewhat forced to begin with, it took on strength as the intact masonry was gradually revealed.

Dr. Cahill apologized to me: an exercise in good manners, since he no longer required my services as an interpreter. Unlike his colleague, Dr. Learner was actually quite pleased by the turn of events. Now that I was freed from having to relay instructions to native diggers, I was available to act as guide among the Alyakshin, and Dr. Learner could at one stroke advance his own work and avoid the back-breaking labor of the rest. I wasn't sure that I wouldn't rather have joined in with pick and shovel, but the scholars had been uncomfortable with me since the confrontation with the drivers. I decided ruthlessly that if I was going to be unhappy wherever I was, I might as well choose the work that left me free from aching muscles and blistered hands.

That was what I thought before we actually approached the Alyakshin camp. Any suffering of mine wasn't because the ostracism was worse. In fact, the Alyak manners were exquisite, by my grand-mother's reckoning.

And there lay the source of my misery. Not the polite welcomes, but the memory of my aunt snapping my ear when I was rude. Not the buttered tea, but the memory of sipping from my mother's cup, nestled in her lap, listening to her sing. Not the elders' stories, but the stories of my own tribe, so like and so very different, with every name echoing the names of my family. Dead family, dead stories, dead tribe. Dr. Learner asked me about the differences. I pretended not to remember, and then lay awake half the night listening to the wind, afraid it was not pretense but truth. Yet why should I be afraid, when I had done nothing since I was a child but try to forget everything I had ever been? To forget was to attain all the goals that had waited for me at the end of the long road to the west.

My mistake was that I had turned my face back towards the east.

*

The long barrows were sound, but the leaning dome was in danger of collapse. Dr. Cahill had a nightly argument with himself about whether he had been right to strip the sod and earth from the struc-ture. Every night he absolved himself, but he worried endlessly at his structural diagrams, his dusty hair standing in spikes and his glasses flickering in the lantern light. "It's all guesswork, that's the trouble!" he said once in the middle of dinner. "How is it propped up inside? What's the condition of the foundation? The whole thing is more than twelve degrees off true."

"It's a sophisticated structure," said one of the students who'd been with him at other digs. "Surprisingly sophisticated, considering they were a people who never invented the wheel. It's a true dome."

"Eskimos build domes—igloos—and they never came up with the wheel either. It's not sophistication, it's an imitation of nature," someone else said.

"Perhaps that's all wheels are." I spoke to the tin plate on my lap, not intending to be heard, but a silence fell.

"The wheel is one of the fundamental machines of civilization," another student said.

I looked around at sunburned faces hidden and revealed by the wind-tossed fire. "A fallen tree rolling down a hill. A water-rounded boulder tumbling in a stream. Eskimos live surrounded by ocean and ice. The people here—" I gestured at the night. "What would suggest a wheel to you here? Even if you came up with the idea, what would you make one with? Grass? Wind? The ancient Britons who built Stonehenge moved all those stones by sledge and raft, and they must have been surrounded by rolling trees and tumbled boulders. In fact, wasn't it the Romans who introduced the wheel to Britain? Along with plumbing and heating and bricks and—"

Leroy Paltz laughed, and the tension broke.

"In any event," Dr. Cahill said. "There's no sense in speculating about cultural sophistication at this point. The barrows and dome are an impressive show of engineering—though perhaps not quite on the level of Stonehenge—" more laughter "—but it's what's inside that will tell us the most. And to find that out, we have to get in without bringing the top of the dome down on our heads. Now, this is the best plan I can come up with—and if doesn't work, on my own head be it."

The students got up from their camp stools and gathered at his shoulders to peer at his sketch. Around their own fire, the drivers were praying. The Alyakshin camp was nothing but a point of light in a sea of black.

*

I didn't sleep that night.

The wind boomed and sighed and muttered around my tent. Some-

101

times I thought I caught a new note, an eager whining voice wrung from the rough corners of stone. That wind had traveled over a thousand thousand miles of grass, I thought. Surely it would recognize something that did not belong.

*

They used boards taken from the truck beds to prop the leaning side of the dome. The many cracks between stones seemed much blacker than they had, and there was some worry that the wind, or simply the process of drying, had done structural damage. But the foundation was exposed and drainage ditches dug, and still there was no sign of movement. Finally, everyone climbed out of the ditch and watched while Dr. Cahill walked the base of the dome, from the point where it met the long barrow on the east around to the west.

It was at the end of the day. The sun was a blaze of light that seemed to burn through my eyes into my brain. Green-gold grass washed towards it in waves, hiding the slow rise and fall of the steppe that was itself, grain of dust by grain of dust, moving ahead of the wind. The scholars, mud-caked and leaning with exhaustion, were gathered by the north arc of the dome, keeping out of Dr. Cahill's light. The drivers were there, too, a clump of dark, suspicious men farther to the north. And out in the grass, a line of horsemen.

Dr. Cahill spoke. "It looks good."

A sigh of released tension passed over the archeologists, and for a moment they seemed to sway like the grass.

"So." Dr. Learner walked to the ditch, an iron wedge in one hand, a sledgehammer in the other.

Dr. Cahill squinted at him through his dusty glasses, then looked at the watch from his pocket, as if he were blind to the sun. "We've only got an hour or so of light left. It would make a lot more sense to wait for—"

He was drowned by a chorus of groans. Dr. Learner laughed. "Come on, Tom, you know as well as I do, you're not waiting for anything."

"I only said it would make more sense." Dr. Cahill grinned and reached for the hammer.

He meant to pry out only one block of stone in the course above the foundation, close to where the dome met the long barrow, in the assumption that the barrow wall would act as a prop for the weakened dome. He chose a big block, twenty-eight inches square by the tape, big enough to allow him to crawl through the space it left behind. It was hard work, forcing the wedge into a gap and then heaving with the iron pry bar, over and over, but no one offered to help. It was a kind of honor they did him. He grunted, his whole weight on the pry bar, his boots scrabbling for traction in the slick yellow mud of the trench bottom. One of the drivers lit a cigarette. The scent streamed by on the wind. Shadows grew long, and longer still.

When the stone block fell, the wind leapt into the square black hole with a sound like tearing, or fire.

"My God, Jack! Did you hear that?" Dr. Cahill turned his face to look at his colleague, but the setting sun forced his eyes closed even behind his dirt-streaked lenses. He turned back to the tomb. "It was sealed. It was bloody sealed!" He stuck his head in the gap.

"Tom!" Dr. Learner, no doubt like the rest of us, thought he was about to enter blind.

Dr. Cahill looked up from the trench and snapped his fingers at me. "You. Run to the camp and get a lantern. Quickly!"

I ran, anger and excitement and a strange kind of grief at war within my breast. I snatched a lantern from the door of Dr. Cahill's tent and a box of matches from the table inside, then ran back. I lit the lantern with shaking hands and without waiting to be told slithered into the muddy ditch.

Dr. Cahill held out an imperative hand.

I clutched the lantern tight and, ignoring his unspoken command, bent against the stone to reach the light into the ancient darkness.

If the Conqueror truly slept within, I would be the one to wake her.

5: PEN & INK

The flashlight flickered, then steadied into a dimmer radiance that allowed the blacks and grays of the midnight mansion to ease a little closer. The intruder wanted speed, but she forced a careful pace, slippered feet silent on hardwood, whispering over oriental rugs, creaking minutely on the stairs. The yellow circle of light conjured wraiths of porcelain and marble, slumberous fires of silk, glass, gold.

Be ghost, the intruder thought. Be smoke.

There were bedrooms on the second floor, their occupants in sleeping ignorance. Also a study, half office with computers humming on standby, half library with shelves of leather-bound books and cases of jade miniatures so delicate they could have floated on a breath. The intruder was momentarily tempted to set them free, but she lost the thought. The flashlight had moved on to open a window on another world.

Despite long training in disappointment, a seed of hope quickened in the intruder's breast. She stalked down the path of the flashlight's glow, narrowing the circle of illumination until all was darkness except the painting inside its rosewood frame. The Madonna sat by a window, her head weary against the wall, her child sprawled across her lap. The child was plump-cheeked and rosy with sleep, fat-creased limbs escaping the shawl that hid the mother's hands with its fringe. The mother had creamy skin, tawny hair, heavy eyes. Her child was ruddy-brown, coppery in the morning light that streamed over her shoulder. In a courtyard below the window, half-realized in the half-shade of a silvery olive tree, a man stood with his back to the viewer, his right hand holding an axe by his side, his left hand clasping the back of his neck. His lowered head was black with curls, his face hidden. The intruder stepped closer still, until the flashlight illuminated nothing but the man, the mother's arm, the child's face.

"Dad?" Less than a whisper. A breath. Gloved fingers grazed the polished wood of the frame. "Daddy?" Grief bloomed, a loss rehearsed a thousand times.

For while the trembling light shivered the leaves of the olive tree and stirred the fringes of the shawl, the figure in the courtyard did not turn.

*

She went to her mother's house, pretending, until she was nearly there, that she was headed somewhere, anywhere else. Early morning painted the water, the seawall, the low clouds in varying shades of gray; the iron railings that hemmed the sidewalk on the ocean side of the street were black as prison bars against the ebbing tide. Eyes burning dry within heavy lids, she sat on her mother's step, pulled her sketchbook and pen from amongst flashlight, gloves, ballet slippers, lock picks, wire cutters, patch cords, circuit boards. Opened the book on her knees, uncapped the pen with her teeth, and drew.

The sash window above the door shuddered open. "Cézanne?"

Her mother's voice, weary as the Madonna's eyes. Cézanne muttered something around the pen lid. She did not look up, but could not keep her shoulders from stiffening. In a moment the window chattered shut again. Not long after that the door at her back swung open. A wave of warmth and the smell of her mother's sandalwood soap curled around her.

Jule, her mother, said stiffly, "I'll put coffee on. Come in when you're done."

She *was* done. Black lines, white space, ink threaded through the paper's weave. When she was sure her mother had retreated down the hall, she slipped book and pen into her pack and stood, taking care the bag was zippered all the way closed before she went in and shut the door.

Against the warm gleam of the kitchen, the morning outside faded to barely dawn. Polished copper reflected movement, light. Terra cotta floor tiles echoed red granite counters, the cupboards were butter and cream. Jule's whole house was like this, its colors chosen to compliment them both, Jule's paleness, Cézanne's cinnamon brown. Cézanne sat on a stool by the sink and watched her hand, spread for balance on the countertop, curl into a fist.

Jule shook grounds into the filter, found mugs, sugar, cream as the electric kettle began to mutter. Her springy hair lay like a mane across her shoulders, the color of beach sand, tawny-gray. Her robe was cream silk. Her eyes were the Madonna's eyes, greeny brown like a hazelnut's shell, tired with motherhood, their lids creased and smudged with shadow.

Cézanne dropped her gaze before their eyes met, just. "The school called you?"

"Not before coffee," Jule said.

The kettle growled and snapped itself off. Jule poured the water into the filter, searched in a disinterested way for rolls, oranges, left-over quiche. Cézanne ate cold quiche, hungry, with her fingers, before the coffee was even poured. Then she dumped sugar and cream into the mug and stirred, her spoon clinking in counterpoint to Jule's. Jule sipped, and sighed, and sipped again.

Finally, she said, "Three days. Three days, Cézanne." She waited, or at least was quiet a while. Then, "Do I want to know where you were? Should I just be glad you're still in one piece?"

Cézanne chased a loose ground on the surface of her coffee with her fingertip. "Will they take me back?"

"Do you care?"

She caught the ground, flicked it onto the counter. Looked up and met her mother's eyes. "You know I won't live in this house."

"Cézanne, stop. Please, stop. I can't—" Jule thumped her mug on the counter, scrubbed her face with both hands, pushed her fingers through her hair. "Yes! They'll take you back!"

"Good!" Cézanne shouted back, buoyed by the relief of anger.

Jule let her hands fall to her sides. "I'll drive you when I'm dressed. Will you just, please, promise me you'll stay there for longer than a month?"

Cézanne picked up her mug and held it before her mouth. "No," she said, and drank.

*

The curator made it easier for her by coming during the day.

The girl's school had a stone wall around the perimeter, low, but mounted with motion detectors; the administrators operated as if they were under siege. They had made Jule sign a paper, several papers, but had otherwise evinced no great concern over Cézanne's habit of escape. They were too frightened of what might get in to worry about Cézanne getting out. The alarm system had been valuable in her education. She had never had reason to think that it gave the curator any trouble at all.

The lawns were groomed even during the winter, but the band of trees that bordered the wall was half wild, a circle of woodland where leaves were allowed to lie where they fell. Waiting, Cézanne sat on a punky stump and sketched the skeletons of maple leaves while a chill breeze toyed with the edges of the paper and flipped the hem of her uniform skirt above her knees. A shadow fell across the page. She looked up, pen in hand.

The curator was tall and thin, had deep grooves chiseled across his forehead and around his mouth, fine gray hair beneath a tweed cap. From her low vantage Cézanne could see dirt smudged across the knees of his trousers and the hem of his raincoat, but she took nothing for granted. It was easier to imagine him walking through the wall than climbing over. He was as much a mystery to her now as when he had first approached her. She looked down, closed her sketchbook, capped the pen.

"Did you find the Madonna?" he asked in his light, incurious way.

"Yes."

"Was it the one?"

She stood up. "No."

"It is an early work." He looked at her face, but avoided meeting her gaze. "But of course you knew that."

"Yes."

His eyes touched on the trees around them, the stump where she had been sitting, the pen in her hand. The bag at her feet. His gaze flinched from that as from her eyes. She bent and opened the zipper. Only then did he ask, "What did you bring me?"

A small square of canvas, edges frayed where it had been taken off its stretching frame, stiff with oil paint.

"Ah." The curator made his first gesture, reaching with both hands for what she held. "The study for *First Summer, Then Wine.* Yes. Yes."

She held the canvas against her, paint side in. "What did you bring me?"

His hands twitched, closed. If hands could carry expression, these set one aside, picked up another. Prosaically, they opened raincoat and suit jacket, reached into a pocket for a thick envelope. "The Birdwell Foundation bought *The Gate Behind Them.* It's a later work. Very," his eyes flinching again from the canvas she held, "very powerful. It has been lent to a private gallery in Midford. The insurance company demands a security guard as well as the alarm system— But this will tell you everything you need." He held out the envelope.

She took it, passed him the small canvas. He barely looked at it before he slipped it inside his jacket, did up the buttons, tied the raincoat's belt. She dropped the envelope in her bag and tried to pin him with a look.

"You know these aren't the ones I want. They're all too early. I need the last ones, the ones he was working on before he disappeared."

"The ones your mother sold." The grooves around his mouth implied another smile. "I know. It isn't easy. They were all private sales. Some of them may even have been gifts."

"No. She sold them." Cézanne could not catch his gaze. Angrily, she said, "I'm not going to go on giving you everything I have left of him unless you give me what I want!"

"I will find them. I want them, too."

She cooled. "I won't steal them for you. You know I'm not a thief."

"I know." He pressed his hand against his side—against the study for *First Summer, Then Wine*, but it looked as though he were in pain.

*

As he had said, the envelope contained everything she needed: circuit diagrams, floor plans, lock types, personnel schedules. She finished the day's classes, had dinner at the scarred refectory table, isolated from the other girls by her preoccupation. Later, sitting at the desk in her small room, she worked through algebra problems and the rough draft of an essay on Hawthorne and Poe. The curtains were open on the night, so the desk lamp made a mirror of the window. She looked up often to see the blunt bones of her skull shaping her cinnamon skin, the springing black umbra of her hair. After a while she closed her school books, tied the fat curls back with an elastic, opened the envelope and spread the papers across her desk. It was hard to concentrate on the details. She was waiting again. She locked the papers away in her trunk.

The trunk held her tools, also her father's sketches, studies, even brushes and palette knives: everything she had stolen from his studio during that brief time between his disappearance and her mother's treason. She could not have said, now, what had prompted her to steal. She had been so terribly surprised when she came home to find his studio stripped, all his last paintings gone, that she could not believe she had somehow suspected Jule's intentions. The surprise had been like a wound. So it must have been instinct, a faulty instinct that had reached without knowing what for, or that, knowing, had not dared to reach far enough. The paintings themselves were too large, too valuable, too great with power. Even the small things in her trunk burned with it. It pained her that they should spend themselves in the curator's hands.

And even as she thought it, green light seeped through her reflected eyes.

First summer, then wine. An alley of grape vines, perspective bearing the viewer's eye off to the right and away. The foreground filled the frame, light-filled leaves, hidden grapes small as pearls, the twisted feet of vines digging into earth. Breathless with summer heat, sweet with the promise of juice. Somewhere, a thin man with gray hair and hungry, cowardly eyes entered that lustrous summer day and drained its warmth.

Somewhere, a painting died.

When the vision of green was gone, Cézanne, sick with grief, with guilt, with envy, with need, crawled into her dormitory bed and cried herself to sleep.

*

She trailed the security guard softly from room to room, the easiest way to avoid being surprised. No need for the flashlight. The gallery was a series of white-walled, birch-floored rooms, track lights burning low for the guard's sake. In the light, Cézanne was too dark and solid to be ghost or smoke. She thought of cats, and felt small, silky-soft and prowling through the gallery's treasures. The guard's shoes squeaked, always a room ahead.

The Gate Behind Them had a wall to itself. Two tall canvases, a foot of white space between them. On the right, Eve, naked, her tear-streaked face half hidden in her tawny tangle of hair, her left hand curved protectively, sensually over her belly, her right hand, open, reaching. On the left, Adam, dark skin smudged with lighter mud, right hand clenched protective over his heart, left hand, big knuckles swollen and scarred, reaching. Eve looked ahead shyly through her tears. Adam craned to look behind him, his broad shoulders twisted, his face almost hidden but for the line of a scantly bearded jaw. The space between them white as a burning sword, forever separating their reaching hands.

Cézanne stepped close to touch Adam's painted hand. She did not speak, her throat swollen with hope, with awe, with, strangely, sympathy for Adam's plight. But the fingers did not warm, nor turn to clasp hers. The guard's shoes began to squeak their return path through the gallery. She let go and ghosted away, even under the lights her substance gone.

Easter came early that year. The school refused to allow her to stay in residence over the holiday, and Jule was nearly as adamant, so she went to the house by the sea. The first night Jule made a supper of appeasement, spicy goat with rice and aki and peas. It was good after the relentlessly institutional food at school. Cézanne ate steadily, hungrily, and felt Jule across the table from her relax. This, at least, was normal: a hungry daughter home from school. Cézanne kept her gaze on her plate. She could not look at Jule without seeing the Madonna's tired eyes, Eve's rounded belly and breasts. Adam's averted face.

The next morning they walked together to the big park around the community center. The Japanese garden had recently been refurbished, and it was a good day for a walk, a subtle day of fog and sunlight, of sea breezes braided with calm. There were others in the park, but it was quiet among the green paths and damp gray stones. Moss, cool light, running water. Alleys of bamboo. Jule left Cézanne at the teahouse, a tiny structure of bamboo and stone, while she walked the perimeter. Cézanne sat on the bench that overlooked the small lake, its craggy rocks and reeds, the arched bridge. She pulled out her sketchbook and pen.

It was uncanny, the way so much solidity and distance, so much color and depth and light—so much reality—would consent to be bound and anchored by a few lines of black ink on a page. It almost frightened her at times. The hand moved, the pen let down its ink, and the garden was reborn, twinned. A whole new world recreated from the old. A whole timeless age born from a captive moment. The reality of earth and water and growing things snared in all its power and forced to serve—

"You," someone said, "are your father's daughter."

The pen froze. She looked up, disbelieving. The curator, here. Standing at her shoulder. She had felt no presence at all.

His hungry eyes were on her sketch. She closed the book and his gaze flickered away across the lake.

After a moment he said, "I may have found one of the paintings you wanted. One of the last. One of the untitled ones. I thought you would want to know."

Cézanne capped her pen, trying to shield her shaking hands from his gaze. She coughed to unfreeze her throat. "How did you find me?"

"Do you want to know? I could tell you." His voice was cool. "I could probably teach you how."

"It doesn't matter." She hunched her shoulders to disguise a shudder. "Which painting? Where is it?"

"You know I have never seen them."

She could feel him look at her, and belatedly stood, sketchbook and pen in hand. He stepped away, putting almost the whole width of the teahouse between them.

"Where is it?" she said again.

"Quite close. I have the address here." He opened his raincoat, slipped a hand inside his jacket, then paused. "Do you have something for me?"

"At school. It— I didn't think I'd see you. Here." She swallowed. "I can give it to you when I go back."

The curator withdrew his hand from his jacket pocket. He held a slender envelope, white, unaddressed, sealed. "Of course I trust you."

She started to reach for the envelope, but he did not hand it to her.

"I do trust you. So I am willing to accept, shall we say, a down payment?" His eyes flicked to the sketchbook in her hand, to her face, and away.

She looked at the book herself, her throat stiff again, her eyes unaccountably hot.

"Really?" he said, as if it didn't matter to him. "A schoolgirl's sketch more valuable than a Russell Porter?"

"No," she whispered. Her fingers were stiff and cold as she opened the book, tore out the page, traded it for the envelope. She did not watch as he folded the sketch and tucked it carefully away.

He said, "I look forward to hearing about the painting. Perhaps" the grooves deepened around his mouth "perhaps you might make me a sketch." He walked away.

She slipped the envelope with the book into her bag, then looked up to see Jule standing on the arch of the bridge.

*

Jule was up late that night. Cézanne sat on her bed, in the dark, her pack in the cradle of her crossed legs. Cars swished by outside, the sound mixing with the draw of the waves, while the headlights swam between the opened curtains, in and out again, a fluid gesture of light across the empty walls. Jule came upstairs finally, clattered and splashed with the bathroom door open, the habit of a woman who lived most of the time alone. Cézanne clenched her teeth, listening. It was hard to wait until the house was quiet, harder to wait the time it would take for Jule to fall asleep. Did Jule usually sleep well? Would having her daughter in the house make her more likely to lie awake, or less? Cézanne gave her an hour, then slipped out of her room and down the stairs.

She was almost to the front door when Jule's voice came from the darkened living room. "That bloody school might not care. I do. When you're in my house, you'll damn well stay put."

Electric jolt of shock to the heart. Then fury: if she had been so careless in another house, she would be facing a bullet, or jail. Rage, at first self-directed, spilled over.

"Your house. *Your* house." A snarl through the darkness between hall and living room. "Who do you think you are? This is *his* house, bought with *his* work that *you stole!*"

A hint of movement that was Jule standing up. "Those paintings were all he left us—"

"No shit they were all he left us!" Cézanne was breathless, incredulous. "Is that supposed to be a reason?"

"They were all he left me to support you with. What the hell do you think pays for all these fancy schools? These expensive schools that you insist on going to, and that you keep getting yourself kicked out of!"

"Don't give me that. Don't you dare give me that. I don't give a sweet goddamn about what school I go to, and you know it."

"Or where you live? You want food on your table? A roof over your head?"

"You call waterfront property *necessity*? You call no fucking job *necessity*? You sold those paintings out of revenge. At least have the guts to admit it when you know I know!"

"He left us! He walked out the goddamn door without a goddamn *word*!"

"Oh my *god*!" It was a cry. "You *know* he didn't walk out of any *door*!"

Silence from the living room. The darkness flashed in time with Cézanne's heart; traffic and tide boomed through the pulse in her ears. When Jule spoke again, her voice came as almost as great a shock as the first time.

"Cézanne. Oh, my love. Where do you imagine he's gone?"

"You know." A whisper. "You know."

"Sweetheart." Was Jule's voice patient, or careful? "Russ loved you so much. But responsibility was so hard for him—"

"Is this still some kind of revenge? Pretending his paintings are nothing but oil and pigment and cloth? How can you, when you know where he has gone?"

"How can you pretend," Jule flatly replied, "that they are anything else?"

A slow breath in. A long, shaking breath out. "Oh, god, no wonder he left."

When Jule said nothing more, Cézanne moved to the front door, undid the deadbolt and the chain, stepped out into the sea- and gasoline-smelling air. Paused a moment on the step.

Shut the door on the dark and the silence behind her.

*

A small house in an exclusive neighborhood, its walls crowded with treasure, as though the owner made a collage of paintings, drawings, etchings, prints. Priceless things guarded by a simple alarm and a dog who whined with pleasure at being let out into the night for a leashless run. The flashlight shone bright with new batteries, dazzling Cézanne's dark-adapted eye with color and line. Russ's painting had pride of place on the dining room wall; the glass doors

114

that opened on the living room framed it beautifully, cleverly: the painting itself was a view through an open door.

A rain-washed courtyard of tilted stones—a kitchen yard, old, with a crooked, gap-planked gate onto a garden, rakes and hoes propped leaning on the vine-clad wall. There was a shed stacked with flowerpots, a rusted wheelbarrow tipped up on its wheel. Such details hardly mattered. The real subject was the rain; the painting, a portrait of a rainy day. Luminous with cloud light, the courtyard was a reservoir brimming with color and damp air, the gate that sagged on its broken hinges like an immanent breach of the dam. The whole painting was as urgent as a flood.

Cézanne followed the flashlight beam around the long table to stand at the visual threshold where the true image threatened to dissolve into the equally true mechanism of brush strokes and paint. Through the gaps in the gate she could see the green of the rain-fed garden, and the figure of the gardener stooping among the rows.

"Daddy." She put her hand on the painted doorjamb, stared through the circle of light until the figure almost seemed to move. "Please." This time. *This* time . . .

She pressed her face against the canvas, her tears dampening the painted rain, until the happy dog came and barked to be let back in, and she had to run.

*

Jule had put the chain bolt back on the door. Cézanne sat wearily on the stoop without trying the bell. Dawn hovered in the misty air, just beginning to dim the streetlights ranked along the seawall. She was too tired to think what came next. She hugged her arms around the knapsack in her lap and tilted her head against the door, watching as mist and damp concrete and ocean water swelled with color and light, and iron railings became black ink strokes against the gray. She remembered the sketch she had made two weeks ago; that memory blurred into the sketch of lake and reeds and arching bridge, the sketch the curator had taken. Poor payment for so much pain.

At the thought—as if, this time, the curator had been waiting for her—memory blurred into vision. Still water, reflected arch making a ring of the bridge, reeds threaded by mist, the open wall of the teahouse a frame like a mockery of her father's courtyard door. The picture was vivid against the gray of early morning, stunning in its color, no picture at all, but a window on a perfect moment of time—until color, depth, life drained away, were sucked away, leaving thin black lines across a marginless expanse of white . . . until those lines were sucked away as well, stolen by the curator's hunger as blood might be stolen from her veins—until there was nothing left but white—

*

She woke confused. She should have been on the hard step, but she lay across something soft and warm. She was not on the hard step, but there was the street before her, the railings with their compliment of seagulls, the restless sea beyond. She was outside, but the air smelled of sandalwood and brewing coffee. Confused, she stirred, and Jule's arms tightened around her. She lifted her head, and Jule's tears fell against her cheeks. She blinked and thought of rain.

*

The curator would be coming for the rest of his payment soon. Cézanne could not bring herself to think about this directly. Guilt and fear got in the way. What had she been doing to Russ all this time? What had she been doing to herself? She did not know, but the memory of white haunted the background of everything she saw. So she hid her mind in her schoolwork, hid her indecision in meaningless activity.

Her art teacher had set the senior class to putting together portfolios to send to universities and art schools, and she did that. She leafed through drawing after drawing, pencil, charcoal, pastel, watercolor, ink, and the teacher would peer over her shoulder and say *Those could be a series* or *I'd like to see another figure drawing to balance the still life's*, as if it mattered. Paper, marked and smudged,

116

sifted through her hands like dead leaves. Only one stopped her, a pen and ink portrait she had made from a memory of Jule. There was something of Russ's Madonna in it, something of his Eve. *You are your father's daughter*, said the curator in her mind. But the portrait was, more than anything, a picture of the woman who had held her daughter on the steps at dawn, the woman no one but Cézanne had ever seen. Before she could hide the sketch, or destroy it, the art teacher saw it, exclaimed over it, took it away to be mounted, and Cézanne could not summon the will to retrieve it. She was braced too hard against action, any action.

And then the afternoon for meeting the curator under the greening trees came and went, and she knew, finally, with sickening clarity, that the not-deciding had been transformed by time into a decision, and that the decision had been the wrong one. She should have met him, though she did not know what the consequences of having stayed away would be.

The drawings were fixed to squares of matting and filed into big, false leather cases labeled with prestigious addresses and stickers that said Do Not Bend. The art teacher made a small ceremony of collecting them, and after the last class several students, Cézanne among them, made a parade of bearers carrying the portfolios to the main administration building where the courier would pick them up. Cézanne stacked her load with the others by the reception desk and would have left except the teacher wanted to talk to her, to infect her with some of the appropriate feelings of anxiety and hope. Cézanne stood sullen as a rock in a stream, all but deafened by the stifling approach of doom. Finally, the courier came. The teacher fussed around him as he loaded the cases into the van, but Cézanne did not—could not—take the opportunity to escape, because the courier was the curator. The courier was the curator. She did not understand at first. But when, as he slid the van door shut, he met her eyes and smiled, she remembered the drawing uprooted from her heart and eaten.

And then she remembered the portrait of Jule.

She ran, pointlessly, down the long curving drive to the gates. The van's tires spat gravel at her at first, but then it pulled ahead, stopping only briefly at the gate before turning onto the road and accelerating away and out of sight. Cézanne stood on the blacktop and panted in the exhaust-tainted air. The spring afternoon was cool enough to chill her through her uniform blazer and stockings. She knew the art teacher would be wondering, perhaps following after to question and soothe. She knew the school security system would be recording her image as she stood helpless in the road under the camera mounted on the wall. Without thinking, she started to walk in the direction the curator's van had taken.

*

Jule's house was still lit, though it was very late by the time Cézanne arrived footsore and cold. No van was parked out front, but there was a Mercedes she did not know, its silver paint hazed by the silver fog that shone in the light from the streetlamps. She could not spy on the house, the curtains were all closed, but she felt that she did not need to. She remembered the curator saying, when he came upon her in the park, that he could have taught her the method by which he had found her. She thought now that she did not need to be taught. She could feel his skulking hunger inside her mother's house, as though the meal of her drawing had forged a bond between them. She sat on the cold iron railings above the waves, holding her skirt tightly between her knees against the groping fingers of the fog, and waited for him to feel her waiting and come out.

He made her wait only long enough to make her powerlessness clear.

She stayed perched on the railing as the door opened on warm light and two silhouettes, as it closed on one, as the other became a figure crossing the empty street. She stayed as the figure became the curator, dressed in raincoat and cap, gray and cold as the fog. He came to stand beside her, not too near, and rested his hand on the railing.

"You show real promise," he said.

"I want them back."

His hand moved on the railing, flicking bits of rust into the sea. "You can always make more. Can't you?"

"I want them back." Her voice was almost as soft as his, but brittle as the rusted iron flaking away under his fingers.

"They are hardly of exhibition quality, however. Not yet. You have some growing to do, still."

"They are mine, and I want them back." Her voice cracked against his silence. "Give her picture back!"

"Or you will do what?" Flick, flick. The sea swallowed up the sound. "Or should I say, *and* you will do what? As I recollect it, you still owe me from our last transaction." Flick. "Still. I might be persuaded to consider this little collection of yours as, shall we say, collateral on payment due."

She whispered, "I have more of his things. I have his sketchbooks, I have—"

"No. I have taken a great deal of trouble to aid you in your peculiar quest, and this defaulting in payments angers me. You will pay me the interest you owe before I will consider a return to our earlier arrangement. You will have to work to regain my confidence—and your mother's portrait."

She had forgotten the cold, but she was shivering. He might just as well have said, *To regain your mother.* "What do you want?"

He took his hand from the railing and drew an envelope from the inner pocket of his jacket. She hesitated about accepting it, confused, but he held it out to her, white in the fog-shifting darkness, and finally she took it.

As soon as it was in her hand he said, "Don't test my patience, please. I expect to have the painting by this time next week."

"Have—?" She held the envelope out as if he might take it back. "I'm not a thief!"

He folded his raincoat closed and tied the belt. "Your mother is quite good company—which is to say, you captured her likeness very well. I would rather have your father's painting for my permanent collection, but it is up to you." He turned to cross the street.

"Wait! I'll do it, I— Give me her picture and I'll—"

"This time next week," he said over his shoulder, "or not at all." He crossed the street, climbed into the Mercedes. Started it with a quiet rumble and drove smoothly away.

Cézanne, shivering on the railing above the sea, raised the envelope to her face and breathed in the mingled scents of musk, sandalwood, and rust.

*

She went back to the school to collect her gear. She did not speak to Jule. She could not bear to see the curator looking back at her out of her mother's eyes.

*

Black midnight, a circle of light. Like a wand, the flashlight conjures out of darkness rich colors, shapes and shades, moments out of time, windows on another world. Or are they only scraps of wood and canvas, layers of oil, acrylic, tempura, ink? Too opaque to let in the light, or to give a view on the world as it is, right now, on the moment that moves always into the future, out of the past. What is real? What the flashlight illuminates? Or what lies in the darkness all around?

Russ's picture hangs in the midst of a great white expanse of wall, isolated from the rest of the vast room, the vast house. When she catches it full in the flashlight's beam, it seems to float, a fantastic jewelry ship adrift on a night-time sea. The colors shine so brightly it is as if her light has been answered by another, stronger light within, or behind.

And it is the picture, she knows it is, the picture she has been searching for all along. The knowledge, the certainty, is a bonfire lit beneath her heart. This, *this* is the painting she must steal to ransom her mother's soul.

There is a house, a low, rambling farmhouse with plastered walls and a tile roof, crowded by a weedy, exuberant garden. There are trees beyond, with deep shadows beneath leaves bright with wind, and a blue sky sketched with clouds—oddly sketched, as if the painting were not quite finished—and through a window there is just the hint, the suggestion, of a man, a painter standing at an easel, and Cézanne knows, as surely as she knows that tears taste of salt, that the painter is her father, and that the sky is still undone because he is in there now, right now, painting in the clouds.

She steps closer, one step, and another. She speaks his name. And she waits, waits for him to turn, waits for him to open the door and let her in.

Waits, knowing that she cannot wait for long.

6: ONE OF THE HUNGRY ONES

When Sadie entered the underpass between the Avenue and the park, she found Raz and a couple of his boys hanging out there, at one with the mold-and-urine smell and the insomniac sodium light. Raz, who somehow knew her name.

"Sexy Sadie," the pimp sang, a line from an old song. "Sex-y Sa-die."

She fixed her eyes on the tunnel end, where a flight of stairs led to the dusk of grass and autumn trees, and walked, her face stiff with a mask of no-fear.

"Hey, Sadie, are you hungry yet?" one of Raz's boys whispered at her back. The tunnel magnified his voice, her footsteps, the growl of traffic overhead. "Are you hungry yet?"

"Sex-y Sa-die."

*

As much as she hated the tunnel, she loved emerging into the freedom of the park. A dangerous place after dark, people said, haunted by rapists and crazies who treated insanity with alcohol and crack. Night was the time street kids came together to canvass the restaurant diners and movie crowd, and to share their scores in the cold of an abandoned store. Safety in numbers. But Sadie hated the press of dirty bodies, the mumble of drugged voices, the grope of unwanted hands—hated the pack and hated the fear that dragged them all together—so when the whisper had come her way, Mullein's Park on Friday night, she had determined to come, Raz or no, shadows or no.

Under the trees the air smelled of burning leaves.

It was Rayne who had whispered in her ear. (How did Sadie come to meet them, Rayne and Leo and Tom? They must have spoken to her first, she was too shy, too wary to talk freely to strangers. But she had watched them since her arrival on the Avenue, spent weeks yearning after their cleanliness, their fierce swagger, their mysterious affairs. They were bright as firelit knives, shining as jewels.) Rayne, slip-thin and blond, had sauntered over to Sadie panhandling on the corner and whispered, promise or tease, *Mullein's Park on Friday night*, and it was the smell of her, soap and new leather, that had conjured Sadie's need. Need, not courage. Courage is a flame that requires fuel, and Sadie was too hungry to sustain that kind of fire.

Too hungry for that, not hungry enough for—*Sex-y Sa-die*—

A breeze scattered frost-dried leaves from the trees. The rustle made a screen for footsteps or voices. Sadie doubled her oversized cardigan around her and started down the gravel path. Mullein's Park covered a whole block. There were a lot of tall lamps casting pools of light, a lot of trees shedding black skirts of shade. The three could be anywhere, if they were here at all, if Sadie wasn't too early, or too late, or otherwise entirely wrong. She couldn't think what she had done to earn this invitation.

Someone was running towards her, dashing from shadow to man back to shadow as he passed through a lighted space. Sadie caught a flash of his face—beard and weathered skin, eyes wet with fear—then he was in the dark and past her, and all there was left of him, all there was left of any human thing in the night, was the stink of aged sweat and the phut-phut of newspaper shoes retreating to the tunnel stairs.

Then a woman laughed. The sound was a bright echo to Sadie's fear, a spark to warm her hollow gut: relief as the three of them walked towards her into the round of light. Rayne, tall catling with a tuft of pale hair and a silver ring in the curve of her smile. Tom, like his name, big, soft-walking, ruddy and cool of eye. Leo, with wind-tossed straw for hair and the loose-limbed, big-handed grace of an athlete. The warmth in Sadie's middle grew, tentative, but strong enough to light a smile.

"Sadie!" Rayne cried.

"Sadie," Tom murmured.

"Sadie," Leo said, smiling and reaching out a friendly hand.

And she was among them. Rayne laughed and slipped an arm around her shoulders. "A true name three times spoken," she said. "You're ours, now, Sadie."

Sadie didn't know what she meant, but it sounded like a joke, so she laughed.

*

They took her to a house on the other side of the park. It was a neighborhood she hardly knew. Old houses, some indifferently kept, some fixed up like new, most guarded this month by a candlelit pumpkin scowl: a welcome for children, but not for the homeless or the lost. Even in company she shrank a little in her thrift-store clothes. Be invisible, instinct whispered. Make yourself too small to see. She dragged her feet through harsh leaves when the trio turned off the pavement and onto the front walk of a house.

But Rayne tugged at her sleeve, her silvered grin bright in the streetlight dusk. "Come on, Sadie, don't be shy. We'll get you all dressed up and you won't have a thing to fear."

"But I don't have any clothes?"

Rayne laughed. She had an easy laugh, a tripping chuckle that sounded happy and true. "Trust Sister Rayne," she said. "We'll find everything you need."

"Don't worry," Leo added, more sensibly. "The owner's a friend. He lets us keep our things here."

"And he'll lend you a mask," Tom finished.

"A mask?" This brought Sadie to a stop. "But it isn't Hallowe'en for—" But she wasn't sure what day it was, maybe the month's end was closer than she thought.

"'Tis the season," Leo said, smiling. "Hallowe'en all October, just like when we were kids."

"Only more fun." Rayne hummed it in her ear, and somehow she was moving again, along the walk and up the stairs. There was a glass panel in the door, stained glass that flashed as the door opened, something red, something green, and a creature's snarling or laughing face, white fangs and cat-languid eyes—just a colorful glance as the door swung open and she passed through, and then she was inside.

The hall was dark save for the glow that came through a doorway on the right. The air was warm and smelled of honey, beeswax, maybe, for the banister on the stairs caught a yellow gleam. The place was so alien to her after a summer of living city rough, Sadie felt disoriented, almost dizzy. She looked at smiling Leo, at Tom's watchful eye.

"Come on." Rayne slipped her arm through Sadie's. "We still have to wash and change before everyone else arrives."

Shower? Clean clothes? Sadie let Rayne pull her up the stairs, still dizzy, but now it was luck that spun her head, and warmth, and the sweet welcoming smell of the house. Trick? Or treat? She did not have to ask.

*

Thick candles that slumped under their own heat. Deep tub, hot water, vanilla foam. Oval mirror in a swivel frame. Sadie stroked the wet cloth up and down her skin and watched while Rayne came in to try her costumes in the mirror. Every passage made the candle flames jump and flicker; Rayne's reflection shimmered with mystery. Sadie was fascinated to see the same gamin face and pale shock of hair become twenties flapper wearing a sheath of blue-green beads, renaissance lady in an embroidered bodice, fantastic pirate in tight leather and parrot scarves.

Sadie wrung out the cloth and draped it on the rim of the tub before soberly clapping her hands.

"Yes?" Pirate Rayne cocked her head in the mirror, studying Sadie's face rather than her own form.

Sadie twisted her hair into a knot on her neck and reached for the towel rack. "Yes."

Rayne quit posing long enough to hand her the towel, then turned back to the mirror. For a moment her face was still, almost numb, all the life in her searching eyes. Then, as Sadie stood in the tub, dripping foam, and steam swirled through the candle light, Rayne planted her fists on her hips and threw back her head, arrogant and laughing.

"Yes!"

*

There was a bottle of wine in the next room. Glasses, too, but Rayne-the-pirate drank from the neck of the bottle, and Sadie did the same, when she wasn't burrowing in the deep closet full of clothes. The smell was strangely delicious: rich fabrics, faded perfumes, and the dim hint of strangers' skin.

"Your friend must have a lot of parties," Sadie said as she emerged with an armful.

"He loves them," the pirate said, swigging. "He lives for this time of year."

Sadie spread her choices on the bed. A double bed with a brass frame and wine-dark spread, it was the only furniture in the room. The window, uncurtained, looked out on the back yard. Sadie was wary of the naked glass, suspecting eyes in the night beyond, but Rayne was careless, so she pretended she was as well.

"Here," she said, holding a gown against her toweled body. It was Ginger Rogers elegant, with a fringe of fluffy feathers at hem and shoulders.

Rayne made a face and shook her head. The feathers felt good on Sadie's skin, but she put the dress aside. "How about this?" Another flapper dress, peacock-beaded with a fringe.

"No," Rayne said, reaching over her shoulder. "This."

*

In the mirror she looked surprised. The silk frock coat, blue-white-gold, was a little too long in the sleeves, the matching breeches a little tight in the ass, but the ruffled collar and buckled shoes made her, even with her damp brown hair tangled on her shoulders, a youth from one of the French Louis' courts. Blinking her surprise away, she tossed her head and tweaked the lace of her sleeve. Rayne, just a scarved head at her shoulder, grinned and nudged her elbow with the bottle, now mostly empty of wine.

*

The boys were waiting at the top of the stairs, Tom in a Chinese robe of crimson silk and dragons, Leo a cheerful Hamlet in black doublet and hose. The hall below was still dark, but through the lighted doorway came the murmur of voices and the melancholy dance of a gypsy guitar. Leo clapped as Sadie and Rayne came up. Tom padded round them, nodding his approval. Enjoying their scrutiny, Rayne struck a pose, and Sadie bowed, a little drunk, a little happy, and trying not to wonder—*why me?*

Another pair of hands joined Leo's applause. Sadie, who'd almost forgotten the host she had yet to meet, straightened with a flush. He was tall, taller than Leo, and like Leo dressed in black, but the blackness of his clothes, the straight simple cut of them, made Leo seem like the imitator, himself the original. He wore a tight cap of black hair and, making Sadie stare, a mask, skin-tight black velvet with eye-holes rimmed in black sequins, and mouth outlined in red.

"This is Sadie," Rayne said, nudging her in the back.

"Sadie." The masked man's clapping hands drifted apart, white against the black of his coat. "Sadie." His voice was musing. His teeth were white as he smiled. "Sadie, you are welcome."

"Thank you," she said, remembering the manners of another life. "It's nice of you to have me."

"Any friend of Rayne's." Her host's laugh was dark and velvet as his mask. "Any friend of Rayne's is a friend of mine."

She knew, then, that there was something wrong here. Knew it in the way Rayne went stiff and still at her back, in the way Tom's eyes drifted to a far distance and Leo's smile grew wide and false. Knew it, most of all, in the way her own skin shivered down her spine. Instinct sang a warning. But it's Rayne, Sadie thought, and seeing the slant of the masked man's look, she was sure. Rayne, not her. Relief, a buoyant burst of defensive anger for her friend (Rayne became her friend in that instant), even a dark slink of curiosity, they all crowded out the twinge of fear. The wine probably helped as well.

"Thanks," she said again.

Then their host took them aside to choose their masks.

*

Leo: a black domino, diamond slits for his nervous eyes.

Tom: a snarling dragon, red and gold to cover his own stiff calm.

Rayne (hesitated, started a hand for this one, fiddled another's ribbons, bit her lip over a third): finally: a spangled cat drawn in crazy lines that made her eyes seem not fearful but wild.

And then Sadie. The room was all masks, on tables, on stands, on hooks on the walls. A crowd of eyeless orbits and breathless mouths awaited life. It was strange, so strange, and then the others' faces were hidden, and she was the only one exposed.

"Here," said their host, though he had stood silent in the corner shadows while the rest had made their choices. His white hand offered Sadie a pale mask formed in wicked, laughing lines, an imp's face, a cheerful demon's. It was not quite ugly, but not what she would have chosen. She wanted something to suit her costume, something gilded from the Sun King's court.

But, "Take it," their host said. "I insist." As if she hesitated because she thought the honor too great for her to accept.

So she took it, and she put it on.

*

A mask's eyes are brighter than the eyes in a naked face. They are livelier, more intelligent, more eloquent of meaning: doorways onto being, windows on the soul. Eyes. And mouths, lips taut or smooth, humorous creases, lascivious tongues. And the voices that spill forth. The laugh that, by a twisted lip, is proved a lie. The word that, by the witness of the shining eyes, is proven true.

And the touch of her own mask, at first cool and clammy leather, but quickly like a second skin, and the play it gives her, herself a stage, her every breath a performance, and yet (herein lies the magic) also and entirely true. Every game, every lie flirting and cruel—and the house is full of them, games and lies—is real as knives, for the masquerade has come to define the night. The false face of everyday, that hides reality beneath flesh and skin, is itself hidden beneath the fantasy that, because it is a product and reflection of the mind, is an honest facade. Sadie has lived a wary, defensive life, always urged by that self-preserving instinct to stay small, hidden, safe. She did not know she had an imp inside her until she wore it on her face.

Of course it lived inside her, somewhere deep within. What else drew her to Rayne and Leo and Tom to begin with? What else carried her through risk to their meeting place, and from there, here, to this stranger's house?

The imp, who knew where freedom waited.

And now it's free, indeed. Sadie-imp, frock-coated and masked, has become the perfect androgyne, and therein lies the heart of her game. A broad man with a grizzled braid and the mask of a weary angel feeds her tiny pastries (cheese and herbs, she's greedy for them, and bites the tips of his fingers to catch the crumbs) and then stands confounded while from a bare-breasted Kali she teases sips of wine, importunate youth from her tangled hair to her buckled shoes. And that's only one game, there are a dozen more, until she's bored and so:

she dances to campfire music of guitars and drums, as like to the mechanical rhythm of a rave as the giddy wine is to the chemical sterility of the pills she's swallowed there. No, here, *here* is life, here is the blood leaping wine-bright in her veins. She dances, imp-Sadie, with men, with women, with no one—once in the arms of dragon-Tom, who moves softly on his feet—once (or did she only glimpse his mask in the whirl?) with their host all in black, his red-sequined mouth smiling, white teeth agleam—once with Rayne, whose laughter sounds like wine in the neck of a bottle, like water cascading down a drain—

then, though the music comes tangled behind them, they are not dancing but running through the wild-tree moonlit-lawn park, the park grown to woodland, an autumn forest all in a city block, running, no, hunting (but still dancing, too, perhaps this is a dream?) imp dragon cat and leaping Hamlet chasing after their quarry

poor shambling bear, shaggy and lost in the forever city-block wood, weeping when they bring him down

and then there is wine again, poured from a weeping bottle opened by imp's needle teeth and passed all around

bright wine in all their veins

*

Or perhaps this is a dream?

*

Sadie sat on the park bench in the morning drizzle, elbows on her knees, head in her hands. She sat for what seemed like a long time, watching a dirty trickle of water run between her feet toward the middle of the path, nothing much in her mind. Then someone sat down beside her and said in a half-familiar voice, "Hangover?"

She straightened and turned. Leo, in jean jacket, sweater, jeans. She, also, was in her usual clothes, though she couldn't quite remember changing, or how she came to be sitting here. Too much wine. Leo looked tired, incipient lines running from nose to chin, his eyes a little sunken into shadow. Half-familiar, half a friend.

She remembered his question and said, "Not yet."

He smiled, but she hadn't meant it as a joke. She felt odd, not sick, not hurting, but weirdly, ominously full. Not just in her belly, but under her skin as well, as if she'd been inflated like an inner tube. She glanced at the backs of her hands, but the bones were as prominent as ever, the veins like faint blue worms.

"Have a good time last night?" Leo asked.

She looked at him again, but he was watching a puddle form. The rain was cold in her hair, heavy on her shoulders. She'd been sitting there a while, then. "Yes," she said. "Yes, it was amazing."

He nodded, then swallowed as if he didn't feel too well himself. "Good." He passed his hands over his hair, making it stand out in all directions, then turned with a smile and a nudge to her arm. "C'mon. Let's go find some breakfast."

"I'm not really all that hungry."

He laughed. "Coffee, at least. Yes? Coffee? My treat."

As if the word conjured the reality, she could smell the possibilities, dark roast, hot steam— "Coffee. Yes."

*

When they were sitting in the café, immersed in the Saturday morning crowd, Sadie asked Leo, "Why did you guys ask me to go with you?"

Leo lifted his brows. "Why wouldn't we?"

"You hardly know me."

He carefully tore the corner off a packet of sugar and poured it into his cup.

"We know you better now."

*

Somehow she thought things would change. Maybe she thought she would be included in the trio's mysterious business, maybe she just thought her luck had turned. But after Leo said good-bye that noon, she did not see them for days. Days of *Please can you spare some change?* in the October rain. Days of grocery store alleys at closing time, waiting for the bruised fruit and stale bread to be thrown away. Nights huddled with others as cold as herself, wondering if it would be the cops or the suburban punks who would roust them next. Wondering if she'd been forgotten. Wondering if she shouldn't, herself, forget.

It would be easy to forget such a night, its passages so like a dream's. Yes, she'd gone to the house, had a bath, drunk wine with Rayne. The clothes, all right, she remembered the feel of silk on her skin. But the masks? The black, white-handed figure of the nameless host? Yet she also remembered the feel of cool leather on her face. Indeed, sometimes when the rain touched her cheek she started, surprised even after so long to find her face exposed. But the chase in the park-that-was-a-forest—the bear hunt in the trees—that had to be a dream. So where did the real night end, and the dream night begin? That was what troubled Sadie.

That, and why her new friends had decided she was not one of them after all.

*

One night, cold and hungry and numb, she passed Raz on the street.

"Sex-y Sa-die."

"Leave me alone."

"C'mon, Sadie-girl. Let me buy you a hot meal. A nice hot meal, and then maybe you and me can party, after. You like to party, don't you, Sadie-girl? Sexy Sadie. Aren't you hungry yet?"

"Not enough," she said, and he let her pass.

But, "You will be," the pimp said to her back, and she went on sick with the realization that it might, it just might be true.

*

Then Friday night came around again, the month creeping farther into the hunting season, and because she couldn't help herself, she went to Mullein's Park. No Raz in the underpass this time, just a couple of winos sharing a bottle.

"Nice night," one said as she passed. "Nice night to stay in out of the rain."

His voice reverberated in the tunnel. Like his own echo, he mumbled the phrase over again, as if he couldn't figure out how it worked. *In out of the rain. In out of the rain.* Sadie climbed the stairs

132

to the sharp bonfire smell of the park, the treed darkness run through by the lighted paths, and felt the week's misery cut loose by hope. Maybe— Maybe—

Rayne, with a whoop, grabbed her in a hug, big-handed Leo ruffled her hair, and even cool Tom was grinning. She was home free.

*

Only the second time, and already it had the feeling of a ritual: the bath, the wine, the clothes.

This time Rayne was a spacewoman in white zipper boots and a skin-slick jumpsuit of green. She wet her hands in Sadie's bath water and smoothed back her pale hair, becoming sleek and cold, while Sadie, already feeling the wine, slithered into silk pantaloons and flowing robe and became a Persian prince. Like an older sister, Rayne pulled the tangles out of her hair and wrapped it up in a black fringed scarf. Ready, they stood for a moment at the mirror, Rayne a long cool pillar at Sadie's back.

Sadie, stupid with pleasure, said, "I thought you'd forgotten about me."

Rayne ducked to prop her chin on Sadie's shoulder. Now they were two faces on one body. "Nope."

"I never saw you all week."

"Places to go, people to see." Rayne tipped her head against Sadie's. "You shouldn't have worried, Sadie-girl. Didn't we say you were ours?"

Sadie flinched at the echo of Raz.

"What?"

"Nothing. Just don't call me that. Okay?"

Rayne looked in her eyes, reflection-wise. "Somebody giving you a hard time?"

Sadie shrugged, making Rayne's head nod. Rayne wrapped her arms around her.

"Don't worry. We take good care of our own."

She smiled, and Sadie smiled back, but she was thinking, *Like you did all this week?*

But the hug felt good.

Leo was a medieval alchemist with a skull cap and spangled robe. Tom was a British huntsman, red coat, tall boots, riding crop and all. Spacewoman, magician, huntsman and prince, they stood at the top of the stairs and watched as people came through the glass-paneled door, into the dark hall and the lighted room beyond.

"They all have their own masks," Sadie said.

Tom put a heavy hand on her shoulder. "It's only special guests who are granted access to Mr. Nero's private collection."

A warm buzz of excitement grew in Sadie's belly, fed by the touch, by the pleasure of watching unseen from above, by the anticipation of the revels to come. She was glad, too, to finally know their host's name.

"Nero," she said. "Wasn't he an emperor or something?"

They all laughed.

"Probably," Tom said.

"Or something," Rayne said.

"The question is," Leo murmured, "what is he now?"

Sadie turned to look at him and saw a ghost at his back. She yelped, jumped a little. Tom's hand held her fast. The ghost stepped forward and she saw it was their host, Mr. Nero all in white, his mask of clinging feathers white as swans save for the corners of his mouth that were splashed with macaw scarlet. Only his hair and his eyes were still black.

He bowed. "My friends. Another night, another dance." He looked at Sadie and held out his hands. "And you have come back again."

Guided by the pressure of Tom's grip, she stepped forward and put her hands in Mr. Nero's. Slender and strong, they closed about her fingers. His eyes were bright as a bird's. "Sadie, lovely Sadie. Welcome."

"Thank you," she said, breathless.

He did not let go. "I hope this means you enjoyed yourself a sennight ago?"

"Last week," Tom murmured in her ear.

"Yes, thank you. It was— It was—"

"Yes." Mr. Nero squeezed her hands, his teeth bright in his smile—and her blood seemed to ebb and draw strangely through her veins—and then everyone was laughing, and he let her go. "Yes," he said, "it always is."

*

The mask touched her face damply, like a kiss.

*

Imp-Sadie dances with the red-coated hunter who wears the fox's face, with the magician who has a bat's visage, with the tall all-in-white birdman. The spacewoman with the fractured-glass ice-mask eludes her.

"Have you seen Rayne?" she asks the satyr while his hands burrow like moles beneath her robe.

"I'm looking for Rayne," she tells the Egyptian slave who bows his jackal head against her thigh.

"Do you know Rayne?" she asks the King's Fool, who capers and howls, "Not well enough to come out from in!"

Come out from in. In out of the rain. Rayne? It's raining, it's pouring, the old man is snoring—

There is a game. Everyone is looking, everyone has a clue to give, no one knows the object of the search. There is much hilarity. The imp finds a button lost from someone's costume and yells, she has the prize! Then spins off and away through the crowd leaving a tangle of would-be captors behind her. Hide it again, hide it again! Shivering with silent laughter, the imp slips through a door into a darkened hall and is hunting out a corner when she comes upon the fox-faced hunter and the alchemist-bat conferring beneath the stairs.

The bat says, "It's wrong."

The fox says, "I agree that if she's going to go through with it, she should at least be here."

The bat says, "You know what I mean. The whole thing is wrong."

The fox says, "And losing Rayne would be right? The girl is—"

135

"Right as rain!" the imp cries. "Come on, you guys, shouldn't we dancing?"

So the white-bird man calls for music, and so the musicians play.

*

A princely imp goes dancing, she-prince, Persian djinn, fire-dervish of the Eastern sands. Dancing, dancing, the Eastern night hot as blazes and lit by lampshade stars. Her court is a wild place, rowdy randy and raucous, and a white bird hangs over all, black eyes bright with reflected glory. Greedy white bird with a red beak wet with the juice of the Persian fruits, berries plucked from burning coals. Dancing, dancing, huntsman-fox and squeaking bat and ice-cool spacewoman who melts in the heat of the star-lamps, dancing, dancing, caught in the whirl spun by the dervish-prince and the white bird's fanning wings, dancing, dancing, until the fever races them out of doors into the cold, the dark, the giddy giddy night where the fox blows his horn and the sweet bat sings and the ice-woman runs into rain and the princely imp wins the game, a button, a bottle, a bear!

*

And pours them all a glass of the red, of the red, of the blood-red wine.

*

With the end of the month and the beginning of winter in sight, Sadie was not willing to be ignored.

She waited two days, three days, though not patiently. She was so restless in the daytime she could not settle on any corner but walked and walked, listening for three bright voices and gleaning no money at all. Nighttime, too hungry to sleep, she haunted lit sidewalks, ignored by the roaming police cars (no need to hide from the indifferent) and almost too angry to hide from the scavengers who preyed on the abandoned.

Almost.

Though angry was perhaps the wrong word. Wounded? Yes, but fiercely so. Everything was fierce, her hunger, her hurt, even her fear. Perhaps the imp inside her, twice released, was less content to hide beneath her weekday face. Finally, midweek, she gave up the pretense of survival and on the Wednesday dusk dropped down to the tunnel to Mullein's Park.

There was a crowd in the sodium-lit underpass. A conclave of bums. Like dead leaves washed into the gutter by rain, the homeless littered both of the tunnel's curved walls, leaving a narrow alley down the middle. Some stood, some sprawled, most hunkered down. The stink was of old sweat and older piss, of wood smoke and booze, and the sound was a growl of low voices and ruined lungs.

The weird thing was, it wasn't even raining.

Sadie walked by the bleary, crazed, grieving eyes, startled a little way out of her mission, though not much afraid. These men and women were far more likely to be victims than perpetrators—more likely even than she was. Towards the park end, one man in a burn-scarred army coat raised a bottle to her in a toast and said, "Nice night."

"Nice night to be in out of the rain," she said impishly.

He peered at her, then slowly pulled his bottle close to his chest, eyes widening with—what?—shock, fear—recognition—something that shocked Sadie in her turn.

Taking this exchange for encouragement, the woman crouched beside him held out a cupped palm. "Pardon me, ma'am—"

But the man in the burned coat pulled at her arm and whispered in her ear, and she clasped both hands beneath her chin, staring at Sadie with the same wide look.

"Sorry," she said. "Sorry, sorry, sorry—" echoing down the tunnel as Sadie hurried to the stairs and climbed into the park.

Not her, the crazy man in the burned coat had said, his voice magnified by the steel walls. *She's one of the hungry ones.*

The sun had shone for a while that afternoon, and now the evening sky was deep and blue above the waking streetlights, the air sharp with the coming frost. People lingered, ordinary folks taking advantage of the fine weather and the unusual absence of beggars. Sadie got a few wary looks (street kid, watch your purse), but nothing to match the tunnel people's eyes. *She's one of the hungry ones.* An after-work jogger pounded along the path, his sweatshirt going from gray to blue to gray again as he passed beneath a lamp, and Sadie felt a surge of dizziness.

The runner goes from gray to blue to gray.
from shadow to man back to shadow
Not her. *She's one of the hungry ones.*
beard and weathered skin, eyes wet with fear
a button, a bottle, a bear!
Flicker, flicker, like flames catching a draft, just enough seen to make up a dream. What did it mean?
the blood-red wine
Sadie bent double on the path and retched. Too long since she'd eaten, too long since she'd slept. The park was darker now, and emptier. When she spat out the taste of bile and straightened, no one was watching. There was no one near enough to watch. She wiped her mouth, her sweating face. Ran her tongue over her scummy teeth.
She's one of the—
She shook her head, chasing out the lunatic's words and the dizzy delirium they had conjured. Just a crazy bum. Just a street kid too long without food. Too long without friends. She followed the path to a water fountain and drank, filling her belly with a water ballast to keep her steady. Then paced back to where she'd met them before, under the street lamp, gravel gritting under her feet, thread of breeze pattering through the last of the leaves. The park was hemmed in by traffic, yet somehow the trees' bare limbs invoked a kind of silence, a listening quiet, an expectant hush. No peace, though, no tranquillity. Sadie paced the diameter of the circle of light. Traced the circumference. Measured out the geometry of waiting and found it added up to nothing. Nothing.

The imp was jumping inside her skin.

Brisk and sure, as if she knew what she were doing, she left the park. Not through the underpass. Across the street on the other side.

Heading for Mr. Nero's house.

There were children everywhere. Innocent witches, monsters, heroes, ghosts, small and colorful, with treasure sacks in their hands. Party guests, Sadie thought, and then she shivered with hot and cold: not children, not in Mr. Nero's house. She was confused, she hadn't noticed, or had forgotten, what day it was. What night it was. She tried to remember the taste of chocolate melting on her tongue, and could only conjure the dusky warmth of wine, the scent of honey candles and vanilla foam, sweeter than candy, warmer than the pumpkin lanterns grinning at her from every step. A guardian parent herded his clutch of movie stars and thieves around her, protective as a sheepdog in wolf country, and she realized she was standing in the middle of the side-walk. Before her, the gate, the narrow walk, the door with the stained glass panel faintly lighted from within. She looked away from the father-shepherd's eyes and headed for the stairs.

Knock? Ring the bell? There was no bell that she could see. Her fist hovered over the half-visible face of the creature in the glass, then touched, knuckle to cool, too softly to make a noise. She stepped close and pressed her ear to the panel. The glass seemed to hum, but to traffic or music or voices inside? Children were shouting up and down the street. Sadie couldn't tell. Her hand closed around the doorknob. She let it turn. The door was open, and she was in.

The party, if there was to be a party tonight (but of course there was) had not started yet.

Halfway up the stairs, she heard voices and paused. Her heart was beating hard, and yet the familiar dark, the scent of beeswax and wine, reassured her. She was even strangely elated. This was not survival, she realized. This was an adventure!

Then a door slammed upstairs and feet clattered in the hall—she was frozen, caught—and Leo was running down the stairs.

"Sadie!" He rocked to a stop one step above her.

She craned her neck to look up at him, unsure if she should laugh or run. "The door was open."

"Christ!" He wiped the back of his hand across his mouth, his eyes staring at someone, something, else. "What the hell are you doing here?"

"Looking for you," she said. Then, hearing how that might sound: "Looking for Rayne."

His eyes did see her then. He rubbed his knuckles against his palm, then reached to put his fingers against her cheek. He was so much taller, and she was a step down. She might have been a child next to him. "Listen, Sadie," he began, very sober.

A man was speaking, coming towards them from the back of the house.

"Shit," said Leo. "Come on." He grabbed her arm and pulled her up the stairs. But in the upper hall they heard a door shut, and footsteps, and Leo, quick as reflex, opened the nearest door and shoved Sadie inside.

"Don't move until I come for you. Don't!"

Then he pulled the door shut and she was standing alone in the dark, listening to what happened on the other side.

*

Rayne's voice: "You weren't in there, were you?"

Leo's: "No. Well, yes. I do, sometimes, just to look. Don't you?"

Rayne: "Not anymore."

Brief pause.

Leo: "They're waiting."

Rayne: "Leo—"

Pause.

Rayne: "I know you're angry at me."

Leo: "I'm not."

Rayne: "I don't blame you. I don't like it either. You don't think I wanted this to happen, do you?"

Leo, sighing: "No."

Rayne: "It was Tom that brought us here."

Leo: "Don't blame Tom! We all wanted to be here. We all wanted—"

Rayne: "Yes. We all wanted. And we still do, don't we?"

Long pause.

Rayne: "Don't we?"

Leo: "Yes."

Rayne: "Then Sadie can wear the mask the third time and I—"

Leo, interrupting: "Come on. We're already late."

Footsteps retreating.

*

Sadie put her back against the door and slid to the floor. I can wear the mask the third time and she—what? What?

Light from a street lamp came through the bare window. As her eyes adjusted she began to see the eyes and mouths crowding the room. The mask room. Staring eyes and gaping mouths, mindless, breathless, lifeless. Sadie shuddered, folded her arms around her knees.

They all wanted—what?

The masks seemed to hoard what little light there was. Beak, horn, scale, howl, laugh, scream—the night wore all the faces, watching and waiting for someone, for Sadie, to put it on. Put on the night, dancing prince, courtly youth. Sadie, imp, put on the night and run.

Not her. She's one of the hungry ones.

Hungry. Well, she was, as hungry as anyone, as empty. Empty eyes, empty mouths, empty, empty—except—one? On the table beneath the window, propped on a stand so that it could peer down at Sadie sitting huddled on the floor. Slant-laughing eyes gleamed with lamp-shine, shifted, looked her up and down as a car on the street drove by, headlights shining. Crooked grinning mouth ghost-gleamed with teeth and lapping tongue. A wind tilted through the tree outside and the left eye winked. Sadie, imp, put on the night and run.

Sadie leapt to her feet and slapped at the wall by the door. One mask flew, another, a tick-patter of broken beads. Then her hand found the light switch, and lamps on the walls blinked on.

*

When Leo came back, she was at the window, watching the groups of children that still prowled the street, although it was getting late. The imp mask was on its face beneath the table.

He slipped through the door and said, "You shouldn't have turned the light on."

"It was dark."

"You don't know what kind of trouble you'd be in if he caught you here. Especially in here." His eyes pointed out the faces on the walls, as if she might have missed them.

"You opened the door."

"I didn't want Rayne to see you. You shouldn't be here!"

"You mean, I shouldn't be here *yet*. Or aren't I supposed to be invited tonight?"

Leo said nothing.

"Why shouldn't Rayne see me? Isn't she my friend?"

It was a challenge. He hissed at her to keep her voice down.

"Well, isn't she?"

Leo pressed his hands to his eyes. His mouth twisted as if he were crying. "Shit. Shit. Shit."

"Leo." Sadie waited for a response, then picked up the imp mask by its ribbon ties and held it out between them. "Leo, what happens when I wear this the third time?"

He pulled his hands away from his face and looked bleakly at the mask. It swiveled on its ties, glaring at the populated walls. He said, "The same thing that happened the first two times."

"And what," her voice was husky, she coughed, "what happened? The first two times?"

"You—we—you led the dance. And the hunt."

The mask was still, staring now at Leo's feet.

"The hunt," Sadie said. "The bear. Only the bear isn't a bear. Is it? Leo?"

He looked old and bitter, his shoulders slumped against the door.

"The third time isn't the same, not really, is it?"

"The same." He licked his lips. "Except after—there is no after. You can't take it off. You lead the dance, and the hunt, forever."

"Forever?"

"Until it kills—until something—someone—"

"Until one of you kills me."

"To be free," Leo whispered. "If we ever want to be free again."

They stared at each other. The masks, silent audience, watched. The imp danced, impatient on the end of its ties, as Sadie's hand sank to her side.

"Why?" she said. "Why me?"

"Because Rayne wore it." Leo took a ragged breath, leaned his head against the door and closed his eyes. "Rayne wore it twice. We love it, the dance, the hunt." He sighed. "But you know how it is."

Sadie bit her lips. She knew.

"He loves it too. Mr. Nero. He lives for it. Tom realized he was waiting for Rayne to wear it again, to keep it always hunting season, and we—Christ!—we love it but we love her more."

"So you found someone expendable. Someone you didn't care about, who would wear it for her," her voice shrank, "for all of you."

Leo squeezed his eyes tighter, then opened them to meet her gaze. "Yes." He said it simply. "Yes."

Her hand shook, throwing the imp into a giddy spin. "So that's how it is."

"That's how it is."

Silence spilled from the mouths on the walls, loud enough to fill her ears. She began to wonder if she would ever hear, ever speak again. What was there left to say?

Leo said it, pushing himself away from the door. "We're supposed to be going to meet you, but I'll get them into the kitchen. Give me a couple of minutes, then get down the stairs as quietly as you can and out the door." He reached for the handle. "Two minutes. Got it?"

"But," Sadie said. "But."

"Just do me a favor." He looked at her, and his eyes were narrowed, his teeth showing, it was so hard for him to say. "Take that thing with you. Burn it and wash the ashes down the drain. Can you do that for me, Sadie?"

She took a long, stuttering breath. The imp's ties were tangled in her fingers. Its chin nuzzled against her leg.

"Sadie?"

"Yes."

He nodded and opened the door. "Two minutes."

Then he was gone.

*

Down the stairs, out the door, running light-footed into the street. The night air was sharp and cold. There was a moon cruising white among remnant clouds, only a few children's voices crying the sweet seasonal choice. Trick or treat? Sadie ran, the imp gyrating on the end of its ribbons, ran because she could, because her blood was on fire and she needed to gulp the cooling air. Free again.

Leo! she wanted to shout. Rayne! Tom!

Free!

Across the street and into the park. There were no children here. Folded into darkness, she slowed to a jog, to a walk. To a halt. For a moment she'd forgotten how hungry she was. Her head whirled. The imp mask nudged her leg.

Burn it and wash the ashes down the drain. Fine. All she needed was something to light it with, something to help it burn. And then—

And then?

"Sex-y Sa-die."

That damn stupid bit of song.

"Sex-y Sa-die."

The call of the hunter who stalks his game through the dark. She flinches, deep inside. But the imp, ah, the imp does so love to dance—to hunt. The mask's ribbons still tangled in her fingers, she turns, slow and graceful as a line of music, gravel biting under her heel.

7: BY THE LIGHT OF
TOMORROW'S SUN

I arrived by boat, because End Harbor is an outport and that's the only way to get there. Jacques Devries came to pick me up at Kiet's Inlet in his dad's old diesel-powered troller. He looked so much like his old man, with his black hair tucked under a greasy John Deere cap and deep grooves already around his mouth, it shocked me when his young man's bawl rang out across the wharf. "Daaaaan- yuuuuuuul!" He slapped my shoulder and called me a city slick, and carried my duffel bag down the gangway to the float as if he didn't trust me not to fall in the drink. But the subtle shifting of the boards was intensely familiar to me, like the slap of the oily water under my feet, the creak of boatlines, the stink of fish, diesel exhaust, and the sea. So terribly familiar I didn't know if it was love or panic that filled my chest. I sat in the wheelhouse with Jacques and we talked, of all things, hockey.

When we arrived I could see the End was the same as it always had been. And yet, that's a lie. Though I'd lived there all my life until I ran away, there were things about the place I hadn't known. Or rather, I knew them only at the roots of me, in my cells, not in my mind.

But I had no trouble recognizing the village's unpainted frame houses strung together by floats and boardwalks and stairs. The old cannery still leaned on its pilings across the inlet, its steel roof a sagging tent of rust, and the crescent of beach was still tucked at the far end like the web of flesh between a finger and a thumb. And the trees still hung above it all, giant firs black with shadow, feathers on a raven's wing that reached to snag the fog.

There's always fog on that stretch of coast. Sometimes, like it was that day, it's a thin veil that glitters in the trees when the sun eases through the clouds. Other times it submerges the world under a breathable ocean of gray. Days like that the only clarity is at the still surface of the ocean, where a seal coming up to gasp for air sounds like a message from another world. And that was the surprise I felt, the new recognition of the old, old truth: End Harbor looks like nothing but what it is. The meeting place of worlds.

Jacques slowed the boat, killing our wake before it could rock the floats, and glanced my way. "Hey, Dan. Glad to be back?"

I couldn't say it, but I was. I was.

God, how I loathed myself for that.

*

The house I grew up in was on the ocean side of Tempest Point, a twenty minute walk from the village through the trees. The warm mushroom smell of decaying fir needles filled my lungs, an earthy undertone to the rank green of the wet salal and thimbleberry that lined our way. Black mud oozed under my boots, long stretches of the trail so smooth I could see that only deer had been that way since the last big rain.

It being the coast in springtime, the last big rain could have been that morning, but Harold Peach said apologetically, "It's been a while since anyone's been out there. Your granddad made it plenty clear he didn't need no visitors, and Dick Turnbull took out a box of groceries last Sunday, so—"

"You know the old man," Jacques added. "Grumpy as a sea lion in rut."

Jacques and Harold Peach had volunteered to walk out with me. As much to make sure I actually went, I thought, as to offer me support. They knew I would never have come back if Margaret

Peach, Harold's wife, hadn't tracked me down and told me to. The old man was failing, she had said, and the house was falling into the brine. My mouth was full of cold saliva, a result of the nausea of fear. I wanted to push my way off the path and lie down under the ancient trees, to disappear under the blanket of moss. Why had I come? But even as my mind flailed, my bones knew. Fate gripped the back of my neck and marched me to the end of the trail.

Falling into the brine. It was no exaggeration. The house hung at the edge of a cliff, the stumps of its foundation posts buried in earth that was being eaten by the waves. Like an organic glacier, the thick black forest duff, that was centuries of dead needles, dead animals, dead trees, poured off the mountainside and into the sea. Underneath, frangible basalt cracked and crumbled away, bedrock less certain than water. The house had been twenty feet back from the edge and twenty feet above high tide when it was built. This winter past, according to Harold Peach, storm waves had washed the back porch, warping the wood and worrying the foundations.

"You can see the lean in her," he said, and he was right. I could. Small weathered house, its roof of cedar shakes green with moss and infant trees. I felt a visceral dismay that the whole thing hadn't been washed away. As a blank space at the edge of the world, it would have been beautiful.

"Gotta take a leak," Jacques said, heading around the side of the house to the cliff edge.

Coward, I thought at him, who'd once been my best friend.

Harold Peach climbed the stairs to the front porch and stamped his feet to clean the mud off his boots, better than knocking. "Matwa? It's Harold Peach." From within, silence. "Hey, Matwa! Come see who's home!" He turned to slip me an uneasy wink. The only sound was of the waves beating the shore below. I stood stupidly on the bottom stair. Even the hand of fate couldn't drag me any further. Again, I thought, why am I here?

Then Jacques shouted, a wordless yell of horror.

A cold sheet of sweat washed my skin. A tide of sick relief.

"That's why." The words escaped my mouth. Harold Peach gave me a strange look as he ran past me down the stairs.

*

But of course it wasn't what I hoped. The old man had fallen, yes, but he was still alive.

*

The cliff below the house wasn't a clean knife cut. Nibbled by storms, it fell by stages into the waves, a rough slope of earth and roots above, and then steep crannied stone down to the water. Slow waves sloshed against the shore. It was low tide and the tumbled lumps of black rock at the base of the cliff were clad in white barnacles, purple mussels, green and russet weeds. Spring kelp was visible beneath the surface just beyond the intertidal zone, and then, beyond that, the smooth blue swells of the ocean. The clouds were breaking up, letting sunlight through to dazzle on the water. I squinted, some relic of a habit making me search the horizon for strange ships. Usually they appeared after storms, or on the still gray days when they got lost in the fog, but we always looked when we were kids, wanting to be the first ones to wave them into the harbor. The visitors, the strangers, like Matwa my grandfather once had been.

"Hey. Daniel. We could maybe use your help here."

Harold Peach was crouched at the edge of soft dirt staring up at me. God knows what he thought, me gazing out to sea with the old man stranded down below. One of Matwa's canes was there by the house's corner foundation post, its rubber foot clotted with mud. I picked it up and propped it against the wall. Harold Peach was easing himself down to the ledge where Jacques perched by the old man's side.

"He must of fallen last night," Jacques said looking up at us. "He's good and wet. I can't believe he's alive."

The old man was an ungainly huddle against the dirt. He'd drawn his crippled legs as close as he could for warmth, and he had his right arm hooked around an exposed root. The trees that might have stabilized the cliff edge had been cut down to build the house and expose the view, but their huge root boles had remained under the ground until now. Dead and buried, keeping him alive. Saliva filled my mouth. Jacques was wiping mud off the old man's face, that was dark and heavy with bone, strong even when it was slackly unconscious. There was no sign of the other cane. I turned against the wind and spat.

Harold Peach was digging rough steps in the earth with his boot heel. He said without looking up, "Dan, find a couple blankets and a rope. We'll wrap him tight and pull him up."

"If he busted something when he fell—" Jacques said.

Harold Peach shook his head. "Looks to me more like he climbed down and got himself stuck." He was still kicking at the dirt, and starting to pant. "Come on, Daniel, get to it."

Eels in my gut, my feet clumsy as anchor stones, I climbed through the side rail to the back porch—the steps hung out over pure air—and went inside.

Everything that was End Harbor was in that house. The wholly prosaic: homemade cedar table and chairs, iron stove, kerosene lanterns, braided rugs. And the wholly wonderful: the silk cushion embroidered with four-legged birds, the harpoon of shining golden stuff that wasn't gold, the hide of the sea-beast with the long scaly neck and black flippers like wings. Mementos from the sailors who found themselves in the End, hopelessly lost, but still willing to trade. There were glass net floats on the windowsills, too, frozen bubbles of pale green and blue, but those had mostly washed ashore from Japan. I pushed into the old man's bedroom, trying not to look at anything while I pulled a couple of wool blankets off the sour tangle on the bed, but on my way to the front porch for a length of nylon line my eyes fell on the trunk by the door. Dark wood bound in brass, carved with letters only one man on this earth could read. There was still a gleam of old polish under the dust. When I'd taken the coiled line from the hook in the porch roof I went around the house instead of cutting back through the inside.

Harold Peach had finished his stairway and was teetering at the old man's feet, telling Jacques what to do. I passed down the blankets and line, and then stood there feeling sick and useless while they wrapped the old man in his cocoon. He moaned once, his eyelids flickering to reveal yellowish whites, but he didn't come to. Harold Peach and I hauled on the line from above while Jacques pushed from below. Jacques's footing on the unstable ledge wasn't good, and the strain was visible in his face. Right past his head I could see the water, bright green now in the sun.

We got the old man onto level ground and then Jacques, clumsy probably with relief, slipped. He wasn't in much danger, but he threw himself in a belly flop against the slope, scrabbling with his hands.

"Shit," he gasped. "Shit!"

I left the old man to Harold Peach and ran to grab Jacques's wrist. He grunted, but he didn't look at me, or even try to pull himself up.

"Come on, man." I gave his wrist a yank.

"Hang on." He twisted his wrist out of my grasp. He was still scrabbling at the dirt, but not for purchase. "Jesus," he said. "I don't believe this." His voice was blank, almost mild. Beyond shock.

His searching fingers had uncovered a skull.

*

By seven o'clock that night there were half a dozen people in the house, and a carefully wrapped bundle of bones on the back porch. The old man was in his bed. He'd come to long enough to drink down a cup of sweet coffee, but he was back under now. Margaret Peach had gone in to see him, and came out shaking her head.

"Still out," she reported. "His breathing doesn't sound too good, neither."

This was accepted without much response. The silent consensus was that maybe it'd be easier on everyone if he never woke up at all. The discussion about whether to get on the radio phone and call Kiet's Inlet for the RCMP had been perfunctory. Then there had been a lot of concern about the bones: how to get them out of the mud, and clean, and sorted away. But finally the skeleton was recovered, and now they were all inside, the leaders of End Harbor. The Peaches, Jacques's folks, the Turnbulls that owned the store. They'd found themselves seats in the crowded living room and were all of them looking at me.

"So," Margaret said. "What do you know about all of this, young Daniel?"

The endless waves sounded like they were right under the porch. Thud, rush, sigh, like the blood through my heart. I looked away to a dark corner, the skin around my eyes tight and sore.

"It's obvious, isn't it?" I said. "It has to be Lise."

"It could be a stranger off a boat, or a body what washed ashore." Harold Peach spoke so promptly I could tell he had been thinking it over for a while. I could also tell the alternatives were offered purely as a formality, like the offer to call the police.

"It's Lise," I said with too much certainty.

Lucy Devries looked at me out of hollow eyes. Her husband echoed Margaret: "What do you know, Daniel?"

Jacques, their son, Lisette's brother, didn't look up from the floor.

I said, "Nothing you don't know. My folks took grandma up to Kiet's Inlet to see the doctor, and the fog rose, and they never made it back. The old man went nuts. Lise disappeared. What more do you want? I mean, Jesus!" I couldn't get enough air. Their stares were crowding it all out of the room.

"Is that why you ran away?" Mr. Turnbull asked. He was a short, graying bear of a man, one of those quiet men who are listened to when they speak.

"Listen," I said. "You don't know what he was like after the boat disappeared. He was crazy. He stayed all night on the cliff screaming at the ocean. Half the time he said he should have been with them, half the time—" I caught my breath.

"Half the time?" Margaret said.

I couldn't bear their eyes. I looked at the floor, muddy from all our boots. "He said we should go after them. Him and me."

"You mean looking?" Jacques said. "In a boat?"

"No." My throat was so tight it was a whisper. "Not in a boat."

Margaret sighed and shook her head. "Still, Daniel, crazy with grief is one thing. Killing a little girl is another."

There was a general stir of discomfort. "Now, Margaret," Mrs. Turnbull said in her soft way, "as far as that goes, burying someone isn't to say the someone was killed."

"You don't know what he's like!" It tore out of me, beyond control. "You never knew him, none of you did! You all saw him fall in love with grandma and stay behind when his ship pulled out, so you all thought, how romantic! As if that's all there was. You don't know how hard it was for him to learn the language. You don't know how he kept after my grandmother to live by his people's ways. How he kept after my dad even when dad was grown. Even when I was a kid, he was always— You don't know the stories he used to tell about murder and war and sacrifice. Sacrifice!" I wrestled myself silent. Finally I wiped my face with my sleeve. "You're right, Mrs. Turnbull, I don't know. I don't *know.* I just know what he was like, and I know Lise was supposed to come out to see me the day she disappeared."

The silence was different then. There was compassion in the way people looked away. The surf washed underneath the porch where Lisette's naked bones lay. Boom, hush, sigh.

Finally, Mr. Turnbull let out a huge gust of air. "I remember. We searched all the woods between here and town."

"And the shorelap," Harold Peach agreed. "For two weeks we had our boat out every time the fog lifted, looking for a sign."

"Oh, yes, that was a terrible year for the fog, wasn't it?" Mrs. Turnbull said. "Days at a time socked in, and when it lifted not a ship in the harbor nor a crab in the pot."

"And the old man sitting out here," Margaret said, as if she'd no patience for their attempt to ease the heartbreaking tension. "Sitting out here alone, and young Daniel coming into town for a bite to eat and a civilized word."

"And I remember," Burt Devries said, "how the old man said he was looking for our daughter on the day he fell on the rocks and broke his legs, when none of the rest of us had set eyes on him the whole time we were searching."

*

People who live in the End have a way about them. A sort of philosophy developed over generations living in a place where other worlds come to call. They leave room for the mysteries. They let silences speak. They allow you to find your own way through the fog.

I knew that I was absolved from suspicion by the way Mrs. Turnbull and Margaret Peach washed the coffee cups and heated me a tin of soup. There was no argument when I declined Jacques's offer to stay overnight. Even if the old man was a murderer, he was old and crippled, probably dying, and I was young. But there was a promise in the look Jacques gave me, and in the way his father shook my hand. The question of Matwa's guilt remained.

When they were gone I ate the soup, though I wasn't hungry. I washed the pot and bowl, swept the drying mud from the floor, built up the fire in the stove. Old habits still lived in my hands, doing the work without any direction from my mind. I knelt for a while, the dry heat of the coals stinging my face as I watched the seasoned hemlock start to burn. They had taken the bones from the porch, but the dead still spoke in the spaces between the waves.

I walked out the back door and vomited all the lies over the railing into the sea.

*

Lisette was a year younger than Jacques and me, twelve to our thirteen the year she died. She had stiff black hair and brown eyes that tipped at the corners, a straight nose and a round brown face, and I thought she was beautiful. She had a terrible temper. If she thought she was being teased she'd throw whatever came to hand, a book or a rock or a handful of salt water. She loved End Harbor. She was one of those who lived with the awareness of the magic shining through their skins.

"Look at her," my grandmother used to say. "There's one child who really belongs in this place."

While the old man, who had never belonged, would scowl and look away.

I went in to check on him. The hoarse labor of his breathing filled the room, echoing the drag of the surf on the rocks. I stood over him, watching the lantern light waver across the harsh bones of his face.

He didn't seem to have changed at all. He only had to open his glaring yellow eyes and he would be the same man who had lured Lisette to her death.

Who had made me lure Lisette to her death.

"She's the only one who can help us," the old man had said to me. After days of rage, wild cursing, violent tears, he had fallen into a long, thinking silence. Where this sudden calm came from I did not question, any more than I questioned the subject of his contemplation. I clung to his surety like a starfish clings to a rock in a storm. He said, "Your grandmother is right. The girl is part of the presence of this place. She can help us tap its power. She can help us bring them home. You must tell her to come."

Matwa's people knew about magic, about imposing the will upon the world. I did not have to forget his bloody tales of where their power came from. They were buried as deeply as my parents and grandmother were buried beneath the waves, or beneath the gray fog that swept the End, giving and taking away. I swore Lisette to secrecy and told her to come. She agreed without pause, her dark eyes shining with a child's curiosity and an adult's compassion. The idea of magic was as natural to her as the idea of breathing, and she wanted to help. So did I. I knew when the old man went out into the woods back of the house to make his preparations. And when he returned and said he'd been in the village, when he said he'd seen Lisette and she'd told him she couldn't come after all, I knew it was a lie. He sent me down to the cove on the other side of the point to gather driftwood—an ingredient in the spell, he said. I circled round through the trees until I could see the house, and I waited, as he waited, for Lisette to come.

This I remembered, as the surf beat beneath the house's foundations, and the breath rasped in the old man's throat. I remembered everything.

*

The fog crept in before dawn and drowned the world. As the dim underwater light grew, I sat by the open front door with my face to the trees, but they never came into view. I might have been on a raft,

154

surrounded by the rhythm of the waves and the groans of the house as it leaned over the brink. On a raft, drifting into the unknown, with the fog a cool touch on my skin. I held my hands out before me, as if the damp air alone could wash them clean. It carried strange scents into the house, a powerful ocean smell one moment, a delicate spice like birch bark and cinnamon the next. I knew all the signs. It was a stranger's fog, the fog of change.

Jacques came out early, as he'd said he would. I heard his boots on the muddy trail long before he appeared out of the gray. I wiped my wet hands on the tail of my shirt and carried the coffee pot out onto the porch, along with a couple of cups.

"Hey," he said as he climbed the steps.

I handed him a steaming mug. "The old man's dead."

He looked up from his coffee, dark eyes searching my face through the steam. "How'd he go?"

"I was asleep." I turned my shoulder to Jacques to pour coffee into my mug. "He wasn't breathing so good when I went to bed, but it wasn't any worse than before you left." I shrugged. "I could have stayed up with him, I guess, but I don't know what I would have done."

"Not a lot you can do if somebody stops breathing." Jacques settled himself against the railing and looked out into the fog, but he might as well have been staring at me still, the effect of his attention was the same. "You really think he killed Lisette."

I swallowed bitter coffee. "I guess I have, subconsciously, for years." I drew a slow, careful breath. "I'm sorry, Jacques."

"You said it yourself. The old man was nuts." His voice was brusque with an old grief. He gentled it some when he said after a while, "We're going to bury her today."

I nodded. "He can wait till tomorrow, then."

Jacques turned and looked at me strangely. "Why should he? Put them down together. That way it'll all be finally over."

Without warning, tears spilled out of my eyes. I could not seem to control anything anymore. I raised my arm to wipe my face on my sleeve, but when I took it away I could see Jacques was crying too. So we stood there together and silently wept, while the trees dripped, invisible in the fog.

The murdered and the murderer went in the ground together, side by side. There's no preacher in End Harbor, and no undertaker, so funerals are a community affair. The women lay out the bodies and sew the shrouds, while the men dig the graves. It's hard work, digging a deep hole in the heavy, root-clogged earth. Jacques and his father dug Lisette's grave together. I dug Matwa's alone.

Sweat soaked my shirt and stung my eyes, while blisters burned on my hands and fog moisture gathered in my hair. Every spadeful hurt, the sodden dirt as heavy as the old man had been when we carried him wrapped in blankets from the house to the Peaches' boat shed. He lay there now, washed and bound in linen and cedar bark, ready for the end. Old Mrs. Reedy, Margaret Peach's mother, lined the graves with damp hemlock boughs, and then they were ready as well. Tired as I was, I could imagine lying down there on that fragrant furry green to sleep. Sleep as black and heavy as the earth.

The dead were carried up from the water's edge to the graveyard above the village. Men in clean sweaters bore the biers, while women walked behind, singing. Not hymns, but children's songs for Lise's sake, eerie in the fog. For Matwa there would be nothing.

He had spoken so gently to Lise, there at the foot of the cliffside cedar near the house. I think that must have been why I in my hiding place felt no fear for her, although it was utterly contrary to his usual manner. I could hardly recall an instance of kindness from the old man, yet Lise even laughed once at something he said as he cut symbols into the tree's bark. The sun was golden in the vapor that slid high among the branches of the trees, and seagulls were dancing on the wind. How many times had we stood on the back porch, Lise and Jacques and I, throwing scraps for the big white birds to catch in their yellow bills? Laughing ourselves sick when two gulls fought over the same tidbit, tumbling fearlessly toward the waves. As fearless as Lise, trusting Lise, who wanted to help. Who stood while Matwa dug his symbols in the flesh of the tree. Who fell when that same blade released her blood to flash like a scarlet banner across the air.

The violated earth of the graveyard smelled just the same as the ground where I had pressed my face. Hiding from the sight, burying my screams.

*

There was food at the Turnbulls' after the funeral. I stood alone in the crowd, sick with a decade of silence, while End Harbor ate and talked, talked and ate. I was lost in time. I was the same boy who'd stood quietly at Margaret Peach's side while the village mourned the loss of my family. The same boy who'd trailed after the searchers, suffocating with the need to speak, choking on the words I could not say.

Choking, because—deep in my heart, in a place neither words nor conscience could reach—I was waiting for Matwa's magic to work. I was waiting for the sacrifice to bring my family home.

*

The fog was only just beginning to thin as we filed out of the Turnbulls' onto the boardwalk below their store. The evening sun was a white ball balanced at the mouth of the inlet, weaving its cold light through the skeins of mist above the water. The tall ship riding the tide into harbor was a ghost, a wraith, a mockery of all my sins.

"Eh, there, wouldn't you know," Margaret sighed. There were sighs like hers all through the crowd, an acceptance that was half humor, half exasperation. "Trust the fog to bring 'em now," her husband said, and someone answered, "Death and change, Harold Peach. Death and change."

I stood at the boardwalk railing with the rest of them to watch the ship drop her anchor and lower her boat. She was a three-master, her square sails hanging lank and white as shrouds in the dimming air. The water of the inlet was a still dark perfection, a mirror, the inter-face of worlds. Men rowing the boat called out even before they had reached Turnbull's dock, asking in a harsh alien tongue where they were. Mr. Turnbull and his tomboy daughters went down the gangway to take their line. The Turnbulls were long accustomed to offering reassurance without words. They would take the strange ship's officers in, give them a good meal and warm beds, and tomorrow there'd be trading. Used to this schedule, the adults of End Harbor were saying their goodnights and gathering up their reluctant children.

Margaret touched my arm. "Come on to our place, Dan. No need to risk your neck in that ill-omened wreck of a house tonight."

I shook my head, then cleared my throat and managed, "Thanks, Margaret. I'll come by in a bit, if it's all the same to you."

She patted my arm, then took her hand away. "Take your time, lad. Take your time. Dinner'll be waiting when you get there."

"Thanks, Margaret. I appreciate all you've done, the both of you."

"Well, I knew when I told you to come home it'd be hard on you, but I never thought it'd be so bad as this. I'm sorry I ever called, so I am."

"You were right, though. I had to come."

She gave my arm a final pat, then collected her husband and headed for home. The lost sailors were climbing out onto Turnbull's dock, talking amongst themselves as they interpreted Mr. Turnbull's pantomime. Listening to the voices ringing in the quiet evening, I felt myself tumble through another layer of shock, as my grandfather must have tumbled down the cliff when he'd gone to see if Lisette's first grave was still hidden. Shock, because I could understand some of what the sailors said. They were men from my grandfather's world, from the island he called home. And hearing them swear in their confusion, I heard again his fury as he cursed me from the rocks beneath the cliff, the rocks where he'd fallen, shattering both his legs, after I'd pushed him off the porch.

*

"You said they'd come back!" I screamed at him the day Lisette had been given up for lost. "You said you'd bring them home!"

And he'd shouted back at me, in the language he so rarely spoke, "They are dead, you stupid boy! Dead and gone! It is I who should be going home!"

That was how I knew. He had not killed Lise to bring my family back to me. He'd killed her to bring a ship to take him back to his blood-soaked world.

His magic had failed us both.

I shoved at him with all my strength, and he fell off the porch steps, off the clifftop where he'd killed and buried my friend's sister, my first love. I pushed him onto the rocks where he should have died, and ran.

*

That night at the Turnbulls' I acted as interpreter, to the relief of the ship's captain and the bemusement of everyone else. There was a good morning's trading, while the last of the fog cleared and the wind rose up to tip the blue waves with white out beyond the harbor's mouth. And when it was done, and there were handshakes and hearty thanks all around, I asked the captain if he'd give me passage. He gave me a long, wary look, as if he thought I was insane, but he took me on with the understanding I would work for my passage. The Turnbulls would have tried to dissuade me, I think, but I gave them no time. I climbed into the dory and took up an oar as if I'd been doing it all my life, and we rowed out to the ship with our faces toward the shore. Clutching the oar's shaft in hands blistered from digging, I could not wave good-bye.

And now, as I stand here at the ship's rail watching End Harbor slip out of sight, I can let myself remember the feel of the pillow in my hands pressing down on the old man's face, and the way he had jerked and shuddered as his body fought to breathe. The sea air is sharp with spray, and the voices of my new shipmates are loud with fear and hope, for, sailing before the wind, we do not know what world's ocean we will see by the light of tomorrow's sun.

8: SUMMER ICE

Today Manon arrives at a different time, and sits at a different table. Her sketchbook stays in her bag: a student had lingered after class to show her his portfolio of drawings and her mind is full of his images. Thick charcoal lines smudged and blended without much room for light. She has not found solace in her own work since she moved to the city and began to teach. Her life has become a stranger to her, she and it must become reacquainted. She has always been tentative with strangers. Art has become tentative with her.

The table she sits at today is tucked against the wall opposite the glass counter that shields long tubs of ice cream. Summer sunlight is held back from the window by a blue awning, but it glazes the trolley tracks in the street. Heat shimmers above chipped red bricks. Inside, the walls are the colors of sherbet, patched paint rippled over plaster, and the checkerboard floor is sticky. Children come and go, keeping the counterman busy. He is dark in his damp white shirt and apron, his hands drip with flavors as he wields his scoop. An electric fan blows air past his shaved head. Through a doorway behind him Manon sees someone walk toward the back of the store, a man as dark but older, slighter, with tight gray hair and a focused look.

Manon scoops vanilla from her glass bowl and wonders at the fan, the hard cold of the ice cream. This small store must be rich to afford so much electricity in a power hungry town. She imagines the latest in roof solars, she imagines a freezer crowded with dessert and mysterious frozen riches. The dark man in white clothes behind curved glass is an image, a movement, that defies framing. A challenge. Her sketchbook stays in her bag. The last of her ice cream hurts the back of her skull. She does not want to go back to the apartment that has not yet and may never become home.

The stream of customers pauses and the counterman drops his scoop in a glass of water and turns his back on the tables to wash his hands. Through the doorway Manon sees the older man open the freezer door. She catches a glimpse of a dark, half empty space: part of a room through a door through a door behind glass. Depth and cold, layers of distance. The fan draws into the storefront a chill breeze that dies a moment after the freezer door slams shut. Manon rises and takes her bowl to the counter. The young man thanks her, and as she turns to the door he says, "See you."

"See you," she says. She steps into the gritty heat and carries with her the image of dimness, depth, cold. The memory of winter, except they don't have winters like that here.

*

In the winter Manon and her sister tobogganed down the hill behind their mother's house. Snow would sometimes fall so thickly it bowed the limbs of pine trees to the ground, muffling charcoal-green needles in cozy coats of white. Air blended with cloud, snowy ground with air, until there was nothing but white, shapes and layers and emptinesses of white, and the plummet down the hill was a cold dive on swan wings and nothing. Manon and her sister tumbled off at the bottom, exalted, still flying despite the snowmelt inside cuffs and boots. Perhaps to ground themselves they burrowed down until they found the pebbled ice of the stream that would sing with frogs come spring. Black lumpy glass melted slick and mirroring beneath their breath and tongues. Then they would climb the hill, dragging the rebellious toboggan behind them, and begin the flight again.

*

The city is still greening itself, a slow and noisy process. Pneumatic drills chatter the cement of Manon's street, tools in the hands of men and women who seem to revel in the work, the noise, the destruction of what others once labored to build. The art school is already surrounded by a knot-work of grassy rides and bicycle paths and trolley ways, buildings are crowned with gardens, the lush summer air is bright with birds and goat bells, but Manon's neighborhood is rough with dust that smells of dead automobiles, the dead past. She skirts piles of broken pavement, walks on oily dirt that will have to be cleaned and layered with compost before being seeded, and eases herself under the plastic sheet the landlord has hung over the front door to keep out the grime. A vain attempt, all the tenants have their windows open, hopeful of a cooling breeze.

Manon opens the bathtub tap and lets a few liters burble into the blue enamel bowl she keeps over the brown-stained drain. The darkness of the clear water returns the image of the frozen stream to her mind. She takes off her dusty clothes and steps into the tub, strokes the wet sponge down her skin. The first touch is a shock, but after that not nearly cool enough. The bathroom is painted Mediterranean blue, the window hidden by a paper screen pressed with flowers. It smells of dampness, soap, old tiles, some previous tenant's perfume. Manon squeezes the sponge to send a trickle down her spine. Black pebbled ice. Layers of distance. The counterman's eyes.

She turns her attention to her dirty feet, giving the structures of imagery peace to build themselves in the back of her mind, in a place that has been empty for too long.

*

Ira, the landlord of Manon's building, has been inspired by the work racketing in the street below. Even though the parking lot that once serviced the four-story building has already been converted to a garden (raised beds of the same dimensions of the parking spaces, each one assigned to the appropriate apartment) Ira has decided that the roof must be greened as well.

"Native plants," he says at the tenant meeting, "that won't need too much soil or water." That way he can perform the conversion without reinforcing the roof.

Lupe, Manon's right-hand neighbor, says as they climb the stairs, "The old faker. Like we don't know he only wants the tax rebate."

"It will mean a reduction in rent, though, won't it?" Manon says.

Lupe shrugs skeptically, but there are laws about these things. And anyway, Manon likes Ira's enthusiasm, whatever its source. His round pink face reminds her of a ripening melon. She also likes the idea of a meadow of wild grass and junipers growing on the other side of her ceiling. Lupe invites her over for a beer and they talk for a while about work schedules ("We'll have to make sure the men do their share, we always do, they're a bunch of bums in this building," Lupe says) and splitting the cost and care of a rabbit hutch ("'Cause I don't know about you," Lupe says, "but I'd rather eat a bunny than eat *like* a bunny."). Then Lupe's son comes home from soccer practice and Manon goes back to her place. The evening has gone velvety blue. In the quiet she can hear a trolley sizzle a few blocks away, three different kinds of music, people talking by open windows. She lies naked on her bed and thinks about Ira's plans and Lupe's earthy laughter so she doesn't have to wonder when she'll sleep.

*

The art school can't afford to pay her much. The people who run the place are her hosts as much as her employers, the work space they give her counts as half her salary. She has no complaints about the room, tall, plaster-walled, oak-floored, with three double-hung windows looking north and east up a crooked street, but her tools look meager in all this space. She feels meager herself, unable to supply the quantity of life the room demands. Create! the bare walls command. Perform! She carries the delicate lattice of yesterday's images like a hollow egg into the studio, hopeful, but cannot decide where to put it down. Paper, canvas, clay, all inert, doors that deny her entry. She paces, she roams the halls. Other people teach to the sound of industry and laughter. She teaches her students as if she were teaching herself how to draw, making every mistake before stumbling on the correct method. Unsure whether she is doing something necessary or cowardly, or even dangerous to her discipline, she leaves the building early and walks on grass and yellow poppies ten blocks to her other job.

During the years of awkward transition from continental wealth to continental poverty, the city's parks were abandoned to flourish or die. Now, paradoxically, as the citizens sow green across the cityscape these pockets of wilderness are being reclaimed. Lush lawns have been shoved aside by boisterous crowds of wild oats and junipers and laurels and manzanita and poison oak and madrone and odorous eucalyptus trees shedding strips of bark and long ribbon leaves that crumble into fragrant dirt. No one expects the lawns to return. The city does not have the water to spare. But there are paths to carve, playgrounds and skateboard parks and benches to uncover, throughways and resting places for a citizenry traveling by bike and foot. It's useful work, and Manon mostly enjoys it, although in this heat it is a masochistic pleasure. The crew she is assigned to has been working together for more than a year, and though they are friendly people she finds it difficult to enter into their unity. The fact that she only works with them part-time does not make it easier.

Today they are cleaving a route through the wiry tangle of brush that fills the southwest corner of the park. Bare muscular branches weave themselves into a latticework like an unsprung basket, an organic form that contains space yet has no room for storage. Electric saws powered by the portable solar generator buzz like wasps against dead and living wood. Thick yellow sunlight filters through and is caught and stirred by dust. Birds and small creatures flurry away from the falling trees. A jay chooses Manon to harangue as she wrestles with a pair of long-handled shears. Blisters start up on her hands, sweat sheets her skin without washing away debris, and her eye is captured again and again by the woven depths of the thicket, the repeated woven depths hot with sun and busy with life, the antithesis of the cold layered ice of yesterday. She drifts into the working space that eluded her in the studio, and has to be called repeatedly before she stops to join the others on their break.

Edgar says, "Do you ever get the feeling like they're just growing in again behind your back? Like you're going to turn around and there's going to be no trail, no nothing, and you could go on cutting forever without getting out?"

"We have been cutting forever," Anita says.

"Like the prince who has to cut through the rose thorns before he can get to the sleeping princess," Gary says.

"That's our problem," Anita says. "We'll never get through if we have no prince."

"You're right," Gary says. "All the other guys that tried got stuck and left their bones hanging on the thorns."

"Man, that's going to be me, I know it." Edgar tips his canteen, all the way up, empty. "Well, come on, the truck's going to be here in an hour, we might as well make sure it drives away full."

The cut branches the crew has hauled to the curbside lace together like the growing chaos squared, all their leaves still a living green. As the other three drag themselves to their feet, Manon says, "Do you think anyone would mind if I took a few branches home?"

Her crewmates glance at each other and shrug.

"They're just going to city compost," Edgar says.

Manon thanks him. They go back to work in the heavy heat of late afternoon.

*

She kneels to wash spiders and crumbs of bark out of her hair, the enamel basin precarious on the rim of the tub. Lupe and her son have guests for dinner. Manon can hear talk and laughter and the clatter of pans, and the smell of frying and hot chilies slips redolent under her door. She should be hungry, but she is too tired to cook, and is full with loneliness besides. Her sister's partner introduced the family to spicy food. He cooked Manon a celebratory dinner when she got this job at the art school, and everyone who was crowded around the small table talked a lot and laughed at jokes that no one outside the family would understand. They were pleased for her, excited at the thought of having someone in the southern city, a preliminary explorer who could set up a base camp for the rest. Her sister had promised she would visit this summer before she got too big to travel, but the last Manon had heard they were in the middle of suddenly necessary roof repairs and might not be able to afford the fare. Manon puts on a favorite dress and goes with wet hair into the dusk that still hovers between sunset and blue. It is hard to look at the rubbled street and not think of armies invading.

The ice cream shop is dim behind glass, but the open sign is still in the window so she goes in. Bad to spend her money on treats, bad to eat dessert without dinner, bad to keep coming back to this one place as if she has nowhere else in the whole city to go. There is no one behind the counter, no one at the tables—well, it is dinner time—or perhaps the sign is meant to say closed. But then the older man with tight gray curls comes through the inner doorway and smiles and asks her what he can get for her. Vanilla, she says, but with a glance for permission he adds a scoop of pale orange.

"Lemon-peach sorbet," he says. "It's new, tell me what you think."

She tastes it standing there at the counter. "It's good."

He nods as if he'd been waiting for her confirmation. "We make everything fresh. My cousin has trees outside the city."

"It's really good."

He busies himself with cleaning tasks and she sits at the table by the wall. Despite the unfolding night, he does not turn on any lights. When the counter's glass is spotless he steps outside a moment, then comes in shaking his head. "Still hotter out there than it is in here." He lets the door close.

While Manon eats her ice cream, the vanilla exotic and rich after the sorbet, he scrapes round chocolate scoops from the bottom of a tub and presses them into a bowl. He takes the empty tub to the back, and she sees the shift of white door and darkness as he opens the freezer. The fan snares the cold and casts it across the room, so the hairs on her arms rise. The freezer has its own light and she can see the ice cream man shifting tubs, looking for more chocolate. There is a lot of room, expensive to keep cold, and what looks like a door to the outside insulated by a silver quilt. When he comes back with the fresh tub and drops it into its place behind the counter, she gets up and carries over her empty bowl. "Thanks. The peach was really good."

"Good while it lasts. You can only make it with fresh fruit." He rubs his hands together as he escorts her to the door. "Time for the after-dinner rush," he says, and he flips on the lights as she steps outside.

It is still hotter out than in.

*

The house at the top of the tobogganing hill grew long icicles outside the kitchen window. Magical things, they were tusks spears wands to Manon and her sister. The side yard was trampled by the playful feet of white boars that could tell your fortune, and warriors that clad themselves in armor so pure they were invisible against the snow, and witches who could turn your heart to ice and your body to stone, or conjure you a cloak of swan's down and a hat of perfect frost. Two angels, one a little bigger than the other, lay side by side and spread their wings, giggling at the snow that slipped down their collars, and struggled to rise without marring the imprints of their bodies, their pinions heavy with snow. Thirsty with cold and the hard work of building the warriors' fortress, they would snap off the sharp ends of their tusks/spears/wands and with their tongues melt them by layers as they had grown, water slipping over a frozen core, almost but not quite clear, every sheath catching a bit of dirt from the roof, or a fleck of bark, a needle-tip of pine. Half a winter down their throats, too cold, leaving them thirstier than before.

*

Manon does her share for the roof garden on the evenings of her teaching days. Her other job has made her strong, and the physical work helps drive out the difficulties of the day. Too many of her students are older than she is, she hasn't figured out how to make them believe her judgments and advice. Or perhaps they are right not to believe her, perhaps she is too young, or too inept. Lupe's son shovels dirt from the pile left in the alley by the municipal truck, loading a wheelbarrow that he pushes through the garden beds to the bucket which he fills so Manon can haul it up on the pulley and dump the contents in the corner where Lupe leans with her rake. The layers of drainage sheets, pebbles, sand have already been put down by the tenants on other floors. Dirt is the fourth floor's responsibility.

"I've got the easy job," Lupe says again as Manon dumps the heavy bucket. "Let's switch."

Manon grins. Lupe is in her forties, graying and soft. Manon has muscles that spring along her bones, visible under her tanned skin in the last slant of sun. It feels good to drop the bucket down to Marcos, warm slide of rope through her hand, and then heave it up again, competent, strong. Lupe rakes with elegant precision, a Zen nun with a haywire braid crown and a T-shirt with a beer slogan stretched across her breasts. The third floor tenants have spread the sand too unevenly for her liking and she rakes it, too, in between bucket loads of soil. Marcos and Manon, communicating by the zizz of the dropping bucket and the thump of shoveled dirt, decide to force Lupe to abandon her smooth contours. She catches on and grins fiercely, wielding her rake with a virtuosic flourish. They work until Marcos, four stories down, is only a shadow among the lighter patches of garden green. Then they go to Lupe's apartment for beer and spicy bean tacos.

"Don't worry about the dirt," Lupe says. "Living with a teenage boy is like living in a cave anyway."

Marcos scowls at her and slopes off to his room.

Lupe rolls her eyes. "Have another beer. And try the salsa, it's my mother's recipe. She always makes this one with the first tomatoes from the garden."

*

Manon had taken the branches from the park to her studio, and this morning she carries a canvas knapsack full of left-over roof pebbles to join them. The strap is heavy on her aching shoulder. She isn't strong enough yet not to feel the pain of work. Spilled on the wood floor the stones, some as small as two knuckles, some as big as her fist, look dull and uninteresting, although she chose them with care.

Next to the twisted saw-cut branches of manzanita and red madrone, they look like what they are: garden trash. She kicks them into a roughly square beach and tries binding the branches with wire, an unsturdy contraption that more or less stands on its own, footed in pebbles. She steps back. Weak, clumsy, meager. The word keeps recurring in this room. Meager.

She has to teach a class.

Life drawing is about volume and line. She tells her students to be hasty. "Throw down the lines, capture some space, and move on. Be quick," she says. "Quick!" And then watches them frown earnestly over painstaking pencils while the model sits, naked and patient, and reads her book.

"Look," Manon tells them. She takes her pad and a pencil and sweeps her hand, throwing down the lines. "Here, here, here. Fast! A hint, a boundary, a shape. Fast!" Her hand sweeps and the figure appears. It's so easy! See the line and throw it down.

They don't get it. They look at her sketch with admiration and dismay, and are more discouraged than before.

"Start again," she says.

They start again, painstaking and frowning.

After class she goes back to her studio and takes apart the pathetic bundle of wired twigs. Meager! She doesn't get it either.

*

Lupe has a meeting, Marcos has soccer. Manon spends some time in her garden bed, weeding herbs and carrots and beans. She uncovers an astonishing earthworm, a ruddy monster as thick as her thumb that lengthens absurdly in its slow escape. Mr. Huang from the second floor comes out and gives her a dignified nod as he kneels to weed his mysterious greens. Manon's mother always planted carrots and beans, but Manon's carrots don't look right, the delicate fronds have been seared by the sun. Mr. Huang's greens, like Lupe's tomatoes, burgeon amongst vivid marigolds. The blossoms are as orange as the eyes of the pigeons Lupe strings netting against, thieves worse than raccoons and wandering goats. Manon's tidy plot is barren in comparison. She has planted the wrong things, planted them too late, something. When she goes in she finds a message from her sister on her telephone.

Sorry I missed you. It looks like I might not be coming after all . . .

*

One of the other art teachers has a show opening in a gallery across town. Manon finds a note about it in her box in the staff room, a copied invitation, everyone has one. She carries it up to her studio where she is confronted by the mess of branches and stones. The madrone cuttings have begun to lose their leaves, but the red bark splits open in long envelope mouths to reveal pistachio green. She picks up a branch, carries it around the room, pacing, thinking. Nothing comes but the reminder of someone else's show. The teacher is one she likes, an older man with a beard and a natural tonsure. She has thought about asking him for advice on her classes, but has not, yet. He was on her hiring committee. She knows he did not invite her especially, but it would be rude not to go. She puts the branch down and digs into her bag to consult her trolley timetable.

She cuts brush in the park again this afternoon, and is relieved to find that her vision of layered space and interstitial depth repeats itself. Branches crook and bend to accommodate each other, red tawny gray arms linked in a slow maneuver, a jostle for sky. She thinks back to her studio and realizes she has missed something crucial. Something. She works her shears, then wrestles whole shrubs out of the tangle without stopping to cut them smaller, determined on frustration. When, on their break, Edgar asks if she is going to join the rest of the crew for a beer after work, she tells them she has a friend's opening to attend. Then berates herself, partly for the "friend," partly because now she will have to go.

*

She wears her favorite dress again, the long blue one patterned with yellow stars, the one her sister gave her. The trolley is crowded, the windows all wide open. She stands and has to cling to a strap too high for her, her arms and shoulders hurting, the hot breeze flickering through the armholes of the dress. A young man admires her from a seat by the door, but she would rather be invisible. The trolley car sways past lighted windows, strolling pedestrians, a startled dog that has escaped its leash. She has never been to the gallery before. She only realizes she has missed her stop when one of the bright windows blinks an image at her, a colorful canvas with the hint of bodies beyond. She eases past the admiring boy, steps down, and has to walk back four blocks. She remembers how tired she is, remembers she won't really know anyone there. The sunwarmed bricks breathe up her bare legs in the darkness.

Karl, the artist whose show this is, is surrounded by well-wishers. Manon gives him a small wave, but cannot tell if he sees her. The gallery is a remodeled house with many small rooms, and there are many people in each one. Every corner sports an electric fan so the air rushes around, bearing odors of bodies, perfume, wine the way the waiters bear trays of food and drink. They are casual in T-shirts and jeans, while most of the guests have dressed up, to be polite, to have fun. The people stir around, looking at the canvases on the walls, looking for friends, talking, laughing, heating up the rumpled air, and they impart a notion of animal movement to the paintings. Karl works in pillows of color traced over by intricate lines. Nets, Manon decides, to keep the swelling colors contained. She likes the brightness, the warmth, the detail of brushwork and shading, but recognizes with a tickle of chagrin that she still is more fond of representative than abstract art. Immature, immature. She takes a glass of wine and then wishes she hadn't. She is thirsty for water or green tea, for air that has not been breathed a hundred times. She decides she will pay her respects to Karl and go.

"Hi!" one of the waiters says.

"Hi?" Manon says, and then realizes the young man with the dark face glossy with heat is the counterman from the ice cream store. "Oh, hello."

"I wasn't sure you'd remember me," he says. He rearranges glasses to balance his tray.

"Of course I do," she says, then wonders why of course.

"Big crowd," he says.

"Yes, it's good."

"Good for business. We do the catering, my family I mean."

Someone takes one of the full glasses on his tray and he rebalances the rest.

Manon looks for something to say. "I teach with Karl. At the art school."

"Who's Karl?"

"The artist?"

"Oh." They both laugh. He says, "I'm Luther, by the way."

"Manon."

"It's nice to meet you."

She smiles.

"Well, I'd better get back to work. I'll see you around, huh?"

"Yes."

Luther raises his tray and turns sideways to slip between two groups of talkers, then glances back at her. "Manon?"

"Right."

He grins and eases himself into his round. Manon smiles. A lot of people don't get her name the first time around.

She works her way into Karl's circle and he introduces her around as "the brilliant new artist we managed to snare before some place with real money snapped her up."

*

Lupe decides to make a pond for the roof garden with left over plastic sheeting and stones. She and Manon dig out a hollow in the dirt, line it with plastic, fill the bottom with pebbles from the left-over pile. Ira the landlord, who is impatient to sow some seeds, points out that it will have to be filled by hand in the dry season. Lupe smiles with implausible sweetness and says she knows. When he bustles off on other business, Lupe goes downstairs to fill the bucket at the garden tap, leaving Manon to haul it up on the pulley. The first time, Lupe fills the bucket too full and gets a muddy shower when Manon starts to pull (her swearing sounds more fiery than her salsa) so after that she only fills it halfway, which means Manon is raising and carrying and pouring and lowering until dark. She doesn't mind. The sky is a deep arch of blue busy with evening birds, and there is something good about working with water, which has voice and character but no form. The wet pebbles glow with color and the water swirls, the pond growing layer by layer, dark mirror and clear window all at the same time. She goes to bed with that image in her mind.

*

At the end of winter Manon and her sister dug out the stream at the bottom of the tobogganing hill, as if by their excavations they could hasten spring. The packed toboggan run stood above the softer subli-mating snow, a ski-jump track grubby with sled-marks. They walked down this steep ramp, stomping it into steps with their boot soles, and at the bottom frayed their wool mittens by terrier digging. The ice revealed was a mottled shield over mud and sand. Suspended brown leaves made stilled layers of time out of the fall's spilling water. Although Manon and her sister would never drink from the summer stream, they broke wafers of ice free from the edges of stones and reeds and melted them on their tongues. There was always a muddy, gritty taste. The flavor of frogs, Manon's sister insisted, which made Manon giggle and squeal, but did not prevent her from drinking more ice. She always looked, too, for the frogs buried under ice and mud, waiting, but never saw them. The first she ever knew of them was their tentative peeping after dark in the start of spring.

*

Luther is behind the counter when she returns to the ice cream store a day or two after Karl's opening. He has a cheerful smile for the succession of customers (the store is busy today) but lights up espe-cially when he sees Manon standing in line.

"Hi!" he says. "Vanilla, right? It'll be just a second."

"I'm in no hurry," she says. He has lovely eyes, dark and thickly lashed.

"So, Manon," he says when he hands her the dish, "can you stick around for a little while? My dad's out on a delivery, but he wanted to talk to you, and he should be back soon."

"Talk to me?"

Luther grins. "We have a proposition to make." Then, as if worried he has been too familiar, "I mean, about work, about maybe doing some work for us. As an artist."

There is a boisterous family behind her deciding on flavors. She smiles and shrugs. "I'll be around."

"Great," he says. "Great!" And then the family is giving him their requests.

Engaged by curiosity, she doesn't mind sitting at the narrow counter shelf at the back of the room. She feels as if last night's work, last night's idea, has turned a switch, shunted a trolley from a siding to the street, set her running back on the tracks of her life. A happy feeling, but precarious: it is, after all, only an idea. Even good ideas sometimes die. But this idea inside her head has met its reflection (perhaps) in the ideas of the ice cream family, and this, she feels, is a hopeful thing. Hope, like inspiration, is fragile, and she tries to think of other things while she eats her ice cream and waits for Luther's dad.

He arrives not long after she has finished her bowl. The store has emptied a little, and after a brief word with his son he comes around the counter and suggests she join him at a table. He says his name is Edward Grant. "Call me Ed."

"Manon."

"That's French, isn't it?"

She nods.

"I've got a cousin in New Orleans." He shrugs that aside. "Anyway, about this proposition. We've been working to expand our catering business, but we haven't had much to spare for advertising. Word of mouth is pretty good for the kind of business we do, but lately I've thought even just pamphlets we could hand around would be good. I know Luther said you're a real artist, so I hope I'm not insulting you by asking. I just thought how everyone can use whatever work they can get these days."

"I could use the work. I mean, I'd be happy to, only I don't know much about graphic design," Manon says regretfully. "That's computer stuff, and I'm pretty ignorant."

Ed shrugs that off too. "We've got a computer program. What I was thinking was maybe you could come up with a picture for us, not a logo exactly, but an image that would catch peoples' imaginations, and then," he takes in a breath, as if this is the part that makes him uncertain, and he is suddenly very much like his son, "maybe you could paint it for us, too, here in the store. So what do you think?"

Manon eyes the melting-sherbet walls. Luther takes advantage of a lull and comes out from behind the counter to wipe down the tables. He leans over his father's shoulder and says, "So what do you think?"

"We can pay a flat fee of five hundred dollars," Ed says. "And materials, of course."

"Well actually," Manon says, "I was thinking maybe we could barter a trade?"

Ed looks doubtful. "What kind of trade?"

Manon smiles. "How about some space in your freezer?"

*

After that, everything becomes folded into one.

The savor of Ed's cinnamon rolls mingled with the watery smell of acrylic paint and the electric tang of the first trolley of the cool and limpid morning.

The busy hum of her classes, that she feels she has stolen from Karl's, except he gave his advice freely, as a gift.

The gritty sweat of work in the park, sunshine rich with sawdust, and after, the cool of conversation and bitter beer.

The green sprout of tough roof seeds, careless of season, and the plash of birds bathing in the pool that has to be filled by hand, and the recipe for Lupe's mother's salsa that calls for cilantro fresh from Manon's garden bed.

The cold enfolding fog of the freezer and the chirp and crackle of ice as another layer of water gets poured into the wood and plastic form.

Vanilla, dusk, and Luther's smile.

And somehow even time. The southwest corner of the park has been cleared to reveal a terrace floored in rumpled bricks and roses.

The tree of winged fruits and ripening birds burgeons on Ed's and Luther's wall. The form in the freezer is full. And there is a message on Manon's telephone. *I can come, I can come after all! The train arrives at dawn, call and tell me how to find you—*

*

Manon's sister arrives on the first trolley from the station. The early sky is a blue too sweet to become the furnace glare of noon, a promise that delights though it does not deceive. The demolition crews have taken their jackhammers to another street, leaving quiet and a strange soft carpet of turquoise where the pavement used to be, the detoxifiers that will leach spent oil from the earth. Manon walks to the trolley stop, happy to be early, and then stands amazed when her sister climbs down, balancing a belly and a bulging yellow pack.

"Elise!" cries Manon. "You're so big!"

Elise laughs and maneuvers into an embrace. "You're so slender! Look how beautiful you are, so fit and tanned!"

"Look how beautiful you are!" Manon says, laughing back. The sister's known face is new, round and gently shining, warm with the summer within. Manon takes the pack and says, "You must be so tired. Are you hungry? Or do you just want to sleep? It's only a couple of blocks."

"What I really need," Elise says, "is a pee. But we can wait if it's only a couple of blocks."

"Two and a half," Manon says. And then, "We!"

They link arms and laugh.

While Elise sleeps, Manon walks to the ice cream shop where Ed and Luther are waiting. Margot, Luther's mother and Ed's wife, is also there. She and Ed have collaborated on a feast of a breakfast, eggs scrambled with tomatoes and peppers, fresh bread and rolls, peaches like soft globes of sunrise, cherries like garnet jewels. There is so much food they can feed Edgar when he comes with the park crew's truck, and Lupe and Marcos when they finally show up, almost an hour late. Edgar can't get over Manon's tree on the sherbet-colored wall, he keeps getting up to stand with his back to the counter and stare at it all over again. "There's something new every time I look," he says. When Lupe arrives she stands next to him to admire Manon's work, while Marcos slumps sleepy-eyed over the last of the eggs.

It takes all of them to lift the form full of frozen water. They crowd into the freezer, breath smoking extravagantly, and fit poles through the pallet that makes up the bottom of the form. Edgar opens the freezer's alley door and the back of the truck, and in a confusion of warmth and cold the seven of them jockey the heavy thing outside and up onto the truck bed. Margot and Lupe massage their wrists. Edgar, in the back of the truck, leans against the crate-like form and says, "Wow!" Manon grins in secret relief: she had wondered if they'd be able to shift it at all. But now everyone except Margot and Ed pile into the truck that farts and grumbles its anachronistic way through the green streets to the park.

*

Elise declares herself to be amazed at the city. "I thought it would be all falling down and ugly. But look!" She points out the trolley window. A grape vine weaves its way up a trellis bonded to tempered glass and steel, drinking in the reflected heat of noon. "It's like that game we used to play when we were little, do you remember? Where we'd pretend that everyone had vanished from the earth except for us and everything was growing back wild. Remember? In the summer we used to say the old barn was the town all grown over in blackberry canes."

Manon remembers. "Like a fairy story. Sleeping Beauty, or something."

"Right! And I'd make you crawl inside and wait for me to rescue you." Elise laughs. "And we'd get in so much trouble for ruining our clothes! Good thing no one ever knew where we were playing, we'd never have been allowed."

The trolley drops them at the northeast corner of the park. Manon leads her sister through the half-wild tangle of chaparral and jungle gyms.

"I can't believe you made this whole park!" Elise says.

"There's still a lot of poison oak," Manon says absently.

Elise breathes in dry spicy air. "It smells so good. Ooh, what is that, it's like cough drops only delicious?"

Manon laughs. "Eucalyptus trees."

Elise's belly slows her down and her nap is still mellow in her, or maybe that's pregnancy too. She is happy to stroll, to stop and sniff the air, to peer after the jay she hears chattering in the bush. Manon keeps starting ahead, she can hear people talking and laughing on the rose terrace, but then she has to wait, to pause, to stroll, until she is ready to burst like a seed pod with anticipation. But finally the path takes one final curve and it is Elise who looks ahead and says, "Oh look, I wonder what's happening."

Manon takes her sister's hand to urge her on.

Amongst the determined roses a crowd of people mills. There are people from the park crews, people from the art school, people from the ice cream store, people from the city who have come to see the new/old park, people who were passing by. At the heart of the crowd, on the center space of the rose garden where a fountain once had played, surrounded by a lively ring of children, stands Manon's sculpture. Free from its wood and plastic form, it gleams in the late morning sun, an arc of ice, a winter stream's limb, an unbound book written on sheets of time. The sunlight fingers through the pages, illuminating the suspended branches of red and green madrone, the butterfly bouquets of poppies, the stirred-up stream-pebble floor: layers and depths all captured by the water poured and frozen one day after another and already melting.

"Did you make this?" Elise says, her eyes unaccountably bright with tears.

"Yes," says Manon, suddenly shy.

"Oh," says Elise. "Oh." And carrying her belly she pushes gently among the children to drink.

9: VARIATIONS ON A THEME

1916:

The main stairway of Masters Hall was a funnel for sound. Music from the practice rooms on the third floor, voices and odd, semi-musical sounds from the lecture rooms on the second floor, conversations from the ground floor foyer: they all spun through, mixing and clashing like water in a narrow channel at the change of tide. But that was the wrong metaphor, Berenice thought. She paused on the second floor landing, her music folder hugged against her breast, and looked out the tall leaded window. Green lawn, red maples, the roofs of the town just visible through the thinning leaves. Low blue hills were visible farther yet, but no ocean, no naked cluster of masts, no seagulls hanging on the wind. Homesickness swelled in Berenice's throat, tasting of brine. She stared fixedly at the blurring scene and prayed no one would come by to witness her tears.

A class was working on sight reading, the sol-fa syllables out of tune against the precise notes of a flute running scales on the floor above. Silver arpeggios and ragged chanting drifted like flotsam on the ground swell of muddled chords and voices, footsteps and closing doors. Out of the mix rose a voice of sudden, shocking clarity: Dr. Kingsley, with whom Berenice had just had a lesson, crossing the foyer below.

"—almost wonder why the school remains open. It is quite clear this war will *not* be over by Christmas, and by the time the young men are looking to be educated rather than killed in France, we shall have garnered the happy reputation of being an excellent ladies' finishing school. Where will all the real students be going then?"

"I think you'll find—" Dr. Kingsley's interlocutor did not share the Doctor's ringing tones: Mr. Martin, Berenice thought, who only raised his voice at orchestra rehearsals. "—that scholarship girl? The pretty red-haired—"

Dr. Kingsley said, his voice half-lost against the groaning of the front door's hinges, "Yes, there's talent of a kind, if you like. But what's the point in training it when the girl will only ever play at church fundraisers and—"

The big door banged shut. A moment later, a cool wash of air drifted up the stairs, carrying the scent of burning leaves. The view of lawn and trees and town had come clear in Berenice's sight again. She wiped tears off her face, and found her hand moving of its own accord to brush the piled mass of her hair, red as the maple leaves burned by frost. *Talent of a kind.* Perhaps, from a great man like Dr. Kingsley, that was something to be proud of?

The sol-fa class came in triumphant unity to the end of the sight-reading piece. The flute rippled to the end of its scale. For one strange moment, the whole musical beehive hum of the building fell away, and in that breath of silence, the air in the stairway seemed to change, to become something pellucid, crystalline, like pure water frozen in a well. In that moment, the only sound was of the breeze sifting leaves from the trees outside, and in that sigh was echoed the sough of waves. Of a single wave, green and cold with sunlight, curling onto a white sand shore. One moment, a single wave. Then a door crisply closed, the flute began a tedious whole-note scale, and the beehive was humming again.

Berenice sniffed, and remembered how glad she had been to win her scholarship and leave her father's cold, cramped, grieving house, the white-washed church, the smell of fish. She turned to climb the last flight of stairs, and was nearly knocked off the bottom step by the youth who came hurtling down the banister.

"Hold fast, dearling!" he cried, gripping her shoulders. Since he was still recovering his own balance, this only served to throw her further off of hers.

"*Mister* Green!"

He clasped her to his breast and began to dance her in tight circles across the landing. "*Master* Green, if you will, for I am indeed a master of all things, including of Masters Hall. *Masters of this ha-all*," he burst into song.

She pushed him away. "It's a little early in the year for Christmas carols, Master Green."

"It is always too early in the year. Unless it's too late." He smiled a ravishing smile, a beautiful boy who knew his own beauty all too well. He took Berenice's hand, bowed over it so his white blond hair hid his face and brushed her wrist, and kissed her fingers. "Until our next meeting, Mistress Red, fare thee well." He backed away, trailing his fingers against her palm, until his foot found a step, and then he was gone, taking the stairs three at a time.

Berenice stood, biting her lip, until she heard the great front door groan open and thud close. Then she laughed and gathered her skirt to climb the stairs.

*

2003:

It was an old school with new buildings. The brochure did not seem to know which fact to emphasize more, and as a consequence was a mess of mixed metaphors and much poesy about the illustrious past and the brilliant future of musical instruction. There was also a lot of bumpf about the generosity of the donor who had mostly paid for the new buildings, and about the prize-winning architecture, but there was nothing to prepare Brona for just how odd the school really was.

The construction had barely been completed in time for the autumn term, so the school grounds were still weed-choked and scarred by the tracks of heavy machines. The fence by the highway was sagging steel mesh, the main drive was rutted gravel, and there were still two portable annexes remaining from the interim between old and new facilities; and all of that only served to emphasize the weirdness of the new buildings. Huge cubes of white, unpolished stone, each one of different dimensions, were joined at seeming random, tumbled together, Brona thought, like salt crystals spilled from a cosmic spoon. Dropped down in the midst of the scarred, half-finished landscape, the school looked like an alien fortress transported complete from another world.

The cab pulled up in front of the wide unsheltered steps at the main entrance, and the driver pressed buttons on the meter before turning around to say, "Twelve even. You need a hand with your bags?"

Brona, unsettled, took a moment to reply. "No, thank you." She gave the man a ten and a five and told him to keep the change. Used to students, he was surprised enough to get out anyway and pull her bags from the trunk. There were only two, and neither was very heavy. He dropped them on the bottom step and looked up at the egg-shell-white façade.

"Used to be a real nice place," he said, shaking his head. "What some people think is progress. Have a nice day."

"Thank you," Brona said. "You, too."

The cab drove off, leaving her on the front steps alone.

The interior wasn't quite so odd. The walls were livened up by building plans Xeroxed on colored paper and scribbled with Day-Glo markers to show You Are Here; the stone floors had been laid with anti-slip rubber matting. The broad window above the receptionist's counter at Administration showed the usual clutter of desks, computers, filing cabinets, ringing phones, and busy, harassed, cheerful people. One young woman gave Brona some forms to sign and some other forms to take to the residence office to prove she was who she said she was and thus entitled to the room that was part of the Fayant Scholarship. Room, board, and tuition, all paid for by the same man who had paid for the new buildings. Nice man. Nice, and rich. Nice and rich. Brona tucked the forms into the back pocket of her jeans and, smiling, hefted her bags.

"I won't try and give you directions," the administration woman said. "Just wander around and you'll get there eventually. I'll call Residence, and if they haven't seen you in an hour we'll send out a search party."

Brona laughed.

By the building plans, the basic design was in fact quite simple. Within each cube, a single interior corridor traced a square; rooms on the outside edge had windows; rooms on the inside edge had skylights, as did the corridors. What made it confusing was how the cubes were joined together. As she wandered, Brona found the uneasiness settling around her again like a flock of invisible birds. Cool light, white stone, silence.

A demanding place, she thought. A place it would be hard to live up to.

She circled in on the residence office, was given a key and painstaking, though not hopeful, directions to her room, the laundry room, the dining hall. The residence cube was one of the largest, with two floors and a glass-roofed atrium of the sort Brona had come to associate with banks and high-end shopping malls. There was furniture on the atrium floor, blocky sofas the colors of granite and sand; and a circling gallery off of which opened dormitory rooms; and two double doors onto the dining hall. There was also, on a sunken section of floor in the middle of the room, a grand piano.

Really nice, Brona thought, and really, really rich. The temptation was impossible to resist. She dropped her bags on a sofa, and sat down at the keyboard. A Steinway, and, she was relieved to see, not a new one. She played a chord. The sound thrummed and soared, fluttered against the glassy ceiling and trailed away down the stony corridors. She smiled. In tune. She shifted the bench, found the peddles with her foot, and began to play Satie's *Gymnopedes*.

Deceptive simplicity was made rich by the echoing space that wove and rewove the steadily pacing chords and wandering melody. For one of those timeless moments that only seemed to happen when she played, the door of her memory cracked open and gave her a glimpse—a half-glimpse—the barest hint of movement at the corner of her eye. A flash of wings, the flutter of an embroidered sleeve. She played the last chord, the last note, and, sitting desperately still, cast her mind after the retreating sound, following it as if it were the thread that would lead her out of the labyrinth—or lead her further in—

"Wow."

"Totally wow."

Voices snapped the thread, slammed the door, startled her eyes open. A dozen or more people sat on the atrium's sofas, watching her. Someone started to clap, and others took it up. Someone else stood and dropped the single step down to the sunken floor where the piano sat in solitary splendor. He was of less than average height, slight, with a fine-boned poet's face that was marred just now by a salesman's grin.

"You," he said, holding out his hand, "must be the Fayant Scholarship."

Brona gave the hand a cool look before taking it in hers. "Brona Roswell."

"Valentine." The grin twisted into something bitter, yet also more attractive, more real. "The Fayant son."

*

1916:

There was a storm raging in Mrs. Potter's boarding house, an oppressive womanly storm of sobs buried in pillows, shouts locked behind doors, tiptoes and whispers in the hall. Berenice sat in Mrs. Potter's parlor studying her theory book in the dreary November light from the window—or rather, pretending to study—while the storm within was matched by a cold, sleet-laden wind without. There were term-end exams in two weeks, and a recital at which Dr. Kingsley had forbidden her to play the Chopin she had been learning all fall, but try as she would, she could not make herself deaf to the uproar. Miss Salter had been seen walking arm in arm with Miss Teale's young man, and when confronted, Miss Salter had pointed out that no promises had been made to Miss Teale and so she, Miss Salter, had every right to step out with the young man in question. It was probably the truth of this last that had provoked Miss Teale to attack Miss Salter on every front, from her morals to her figure to her breeding . . .

The parlor door opened and Mrs. Potter put her head through. "Thank goodness one of you has some sense. Light the lamps if it gets too dark, dear, you don't want to strain your eyes."

Berenice smiled and Mrs. Potter withdrew. Soon, the stairs creaked under the landlady's ascending weight; not long after, there was a fresh outbreak of weeping from above. Clearly, Mrs. Potter's brand of housewifely diplomacy did not meet the demands of high romantic drama. Berenice closed her book and rose to draw the curtains and light the lamps, but when she was standing at the window, with the cold gray street before her and the stuffy parlor behind, she changed her mind. Leaving the book on the parlor table, she went into the hall, donned boots, coat, and hat, and left the house.

She walked the two blocks to the train station, crossed the tracks and the road, and started up the muddy path into the woods that lay between town and school. It was only a narrow band of woodland, for the school had sold off most of the old manor grounds, but the trees were tall and thick-boled, their roots buried in drifts of leaves, their bare branches so interwoven they blocked much of the wind. Berenice lifted her chin from her scarf in relief from the cold, but kept her eyes on the path. It was mucky, and her boots were thin.

Masters Hall surprised her by being unlocked. She had only come this way out of habit, and because there was nowhere else to go on a Sunday. But the front door groaned open when she leaned her weight against it, and she slipped inside to a dim, beeswax-scented warmth. There was even music being played somewhere in the depths of the building. A flute shone out, lilting and clear, and beneath it lay a murmur that might have been strings, or singers, or both. Music on a Sunday, and not devotional music either: Berenice, her father's daughter, was mildly, automatically shocked, but it was a very cheerful tune.

Tentatively, she followed it to the door of the smaller recital hall, really just a room with rows of wooden chairs and a low dais for the piano. Standing outside the door, she was sure she could make out a viola's strings besides the flute, and voices that sang and laughed, such a merry sound that she smiled as she opened the door. The music played on, somewhere in the building, somewhere, but not here. The room was empty but for the piano and the chairs, and a light gray as dust, and the sound, just as gray, of rain beating on the windows. The flute ended its tune with a flourish. The voices laughed and chattered on. Somewhere.

Berenice slipped into the recital room, took off her coat and hat, and sat down at the piano. She played scales to loosen up her fingers, and the sheer tedium set her dreaming. She imagined the drab room made brilliant by candles, mirrors, gilt. She imagined the chairs crowded with men in tuxedos and women in gowns bright as butterfly wings, their jewels shining like captive stars. She imagined herself in green—no, black—no, brown, rich raisin-colored velvet with gold embroidered on the tight cuffs, so that it glittered with the dancing of her hands. Smiling, she closed her eyes and played.

The empty room swallowed sound, the growing dusk drank it down. After the final note, the piano murmured to itself a moment, then fell silent when she took her foot from the peddles. She let her hands rest in her lap, her eyes still closed. For one giddy moment, she heard applause, but it was only the patter of sleet against the window glass. She opened her eyes and was startled by the darkness.

And was startled again when a voice said, "Mistress Red, you should play before kings."

She jumped. Her hand pressed down on the keys. Discord. She could only see a dark shape with pale hair amongst the empty chairs. She saw for a moment a thin old man, but of course she knew who it was. Miss Salter's beau, and Miss Teale's. She took her hand from the keys.

"Mister Green," she said, breathless.

"Did I startle you?"

"Yes."

"I thought I might." He stood and began to work his way to the end of the row.

Berenice stood as well, and quickly moved to retrieve her coat and hat from the chair at the back of the stage. As quick as she was, he was nevertheless beside her in time to take her coat and hold it while she slid her arms into the sleeves. She stepped away and put on her hat.

"Ah," he said, "the fire's out. Now there is only the dark."

She couldn't help but smile. "You should put a hat on yourself, Mister Green, if you want that to be true."

He raised a hand to his hair, which seemed paler than ever against the background of night. "Moonlight rather than fire," he said ruefully. "Perhaps you will lend me a little warmth?"

"Perhaps I will not!" she said sharply, and a little nervously. She maneuvered past him and stepped off the stage. He jumped down and ran, coltish and loud on the bare floor, to the door which he opened with a bow.

"I shall lend you a little moonlight, then," he said, "and walk you home."

"Really," she said, more nervous than sharp now, "that isn't at all necessary, Mister Green."

He laughed and tucked his arm through hers. "You're very prim, Miss Ross, for red-haired girl who plays Chopin with her eyes closed in the dark."

Stung, she pulled free. "And you, sir, are very forward for a man so careful of his own skin!"

Too careful, she meant, to serve his country in a time of war.

"But it is not my country," he said softly, reading her thought with discomfiting ease, "and it is not my war. And, my dear Miss Ross, the woods are very dark tonight."

Something in his voice, absent its usual gaiety— Something in the echoes in the dark foyer, the ghosts of music and daytime voices— Berenice shivered, and when he opened the heavy door, she stepped through and let him take her arm.

*

2003:

Brona's piano teacher said early on, half in despair, "I don't have anything to teach you. I think you should be teaching me."

Brona shrugged. There was little point in pretending otherwise. "Let's talk about interpretation," she said, and they did that during most of their lesson times.

Leona, her teacher, had a soft gray mob of curls and a round, light brown face that was webbed with lines, like fine tissue paper that had been folded and unfolded too many times. The creases changed patterns whenever she spoke, smiled, frowned. She was an inarticulate philosopher, a thinker who spoke in dreams, who wrestled with the keyboard to make it communicate more clearly than she could. Brona liked her immensely, and when Leona recommended a book that Brona had already read, she decided to look it up and read it again, for Leona's sake.

The library, like the main residence and the recital hall, was a two story cube with an atrium in the middle and a gallery running around all four walls. Music and listening stations below, books and archives above. Even with students cluttering all the tables, even with a gray sky pressing down on the glass, it was a strange room, severe, elegant, and bright. Brona had heard a lot of complaints about the new school, how cold it was, how confusing, how noisy the classrooms and hallways were, but she was developing a personal fondness for the generous Mr. Fayant and his imaginative architect. It *was* a building to live up to, and she thought it would probably do most of these students good to try.

She found Leona's book and sat on a low, deep window ledge, the book unopened on her knee. The window overlooked glassy roofs hemmed in by weedy ground, the highway, the town. The library fluttered like a dovecote with whispers, turned pages, music that seeped from earphones. It was a lovely, breathy sound, like leaves in a breeze, water at the slack of tide. Brona closed her eyes and drifted, half asleep and not quite dreaming.

A nearby voice came clear. "You pretend very well, my dear, but why should you? Why should you hide what you are?"

Brona opened her eyes. The speaker was out of sight somewhere in amongst the bookshelves, but she was shocked by the conviction, the absolute conviction, that the woman had been speaking to her.

She had not been. Someone else responded, a masculine murmur too low to admit to words.

The first voice said, "I will not argue. Every light shines, every fire burns. You can't hide a fire, you know. If you try you'll only put it out." She laughed. "That has to be an exit line. I shall see you soon, though, Valentine."

In the wake of the voices, the library's murmur swelled back into the fore, a gentle foaming wave of sound that washed over Brona, making her skin prickle with cold. Not really sure why, she set the unopened book aside and got up from the window ledge. Two rows away, Valentine Fayant stood with his hands braced against a half-empty bookshelf, his arms stiff and his head bowed. Beside him was a cart loaded with grubby folios.

"Who were you speaking to?" Brona asked him.

He jerked upright, staring. It took him a moment to muster a response. "What's it to you, Scholarship?"

"I don't know. What fire are you trying to hide?"

"I don't know, I—" His look of angry bafflement intensified. "Is eavesdropping a lifestyle choice, or just something you do in your spare time?"

Brona laughed and leaned against the bookshelves. "I was sitting just over there." She pointed a thumb, shrugged. "I was curious who you were talking to. She sounded—" What? Brona waited to hear. "—familiar." She was chilled, realizing this was true.

Valentine ducked his head. Seeming to notice the cart for the first time, he picked up a folio and put it on the shelf. "Jade. She's in strings. Second year. I doubt you know her, she doesn't live in res." He listlessly put another folio on the shelf.

Jade, Brona thought. *Jade.* Did it ring a bell, or did she only wish it would?

"She's a little bit crazy," Valentine went on. "I don't know what she's talking about half the time."

Brona studied him. He looked sulky, and very young. "Perhaps she's talking about how you pretend to be less talented than you are. Or perhaps she's talking about the way you work so hard to deserve the scorn people lay out for the rich donor's son."

Valentine flushed, and looked at her sidelong. "You're another weird one, aren't you, Scholarship?"

"Probably." She took a folio off the cart, untied the faded red ribbon and looked inside. A handwritten score for a flute quartet, an illegible name scrawled across the upper corner, and a date. 1936. "What is this?"

He took the folio from her hands, tied it closed, put it on the shelf.

"Part of the archives." He continued shelving, a twist to his mouth. "I get a cut in my tuition for helping do the catalogue. Everything got mixed up in the move. Not that it's any of your business."

"No, it isn't. Was the job your father's idea, or yours?"

Shelving, he pointedly did not answer.

She laughed, took her weight off the bookshelf, turned to go.

He said, "You want to go into town for a beer sometime?"

Without looking back, she said, "I don't have any ID."

She was several rows away when she heard him say, "How about a coffee, then?"

She smiled to herself. But as she descended the gallery stairs the smile faded. Jade. Jade. She didn't think she knew the name, but the voice—

*

1917:

Berenice played Mozart at the recital, and afterwards went home for a cold, prayerful Christmas in her father's house, her father's church. She did not think much about school while she was home. The usual round of housework and churchly visits closed over her head without a ripple to prove that she had been away, and the changes to the village were so minor they could scarcely be seen. The Fabers had repainted their boat white with green trim. The board-walk outside the general store had three new slats, bright yellow amidst the gray. The grief her father bore for his only son, dead in France, had become a clean, rigid structure on which he hung his life. In the new year, as she boarded the train that would take her back to school, she felt that she was drawing breath for the first time in two weeks. Like a seal, she thought. Seals could stay under for a very long time, but even they could drown.

In town the snow was everywhere stained with coal smoke and mud, but it was white around the school. A white blanket on the ground, white lace upon the trees. On the first day of classes, Berenice walked with the other girls, foregoing the path through the woods in favor of the cleared drive. Almost with the other girls, not quite. Miss Salter walked ahead with her group of three, Miss Teale behind with her two seconds, and Berenice, neutral party, walked alone. She was too glad to be back, and too glad not to be drawn into the continuing feud, to regret it much. The red brick of Masters Hall loomed warm and cheering at the end of the drive.

Just as cheerful were the voices of the young men lobbing snow-balls at one another across the drive. They were using the shoveled drifts of snow as fortifications, and all Berenice could see of them were the tops of their heads and the scything motions of their arms as they threw. Miss Salter's group, clucking in dismay, came to a disor-dered stop in the drive.

A boy with pink cheeks and brown hair popped up from behind the right-hand drift. "Hullo! Non-combatants. I say—" was as far as he got before a snowball caught him in the face. He yelped and sat down out of sight.

"Cease fire!" cried the forces on the right, while those on the left shouted, "Surrender or die!"

Snowballs were thrown, from both sides.

"For pity's sake," shouted the brash Miss Salter. "You might stop long enough to let us by!"

Several figures stood up at that, faces red and clothes mottled white. There was some startled and sheepish laughter. "I *said* there were non-combatants on the field," the brown-haired boy said, and a young man from the other side, whose hair was nearly as pale as the snow, cried, "Ladies! Forgive these cads, they know no better," and slid down the drift onto the drive. He bowed, shedding snow, and by some deft alchemy of gesture and smile he parted the clutch of girls to single out Berenice.

"Mistress Red, the very sight of you reminds me of summer's warmth. Will you allow me to escort you from the field of battle?"

"Certainly not," she said, and brushed past his outstretched hand.

He smiled. The girls, both Miss Salter's and Miss Teale's camps, glared.

She had a lesson with Dr. Kingsley first thing. Rather than worry about Mr. Green or her fellow boarders, she worried about how cold her hands were, and how stiff her fingers would be on the keys. He was very critical of her technique, Dr. Kingsley was. She was sweating and red-faced by the end of the lesson, her fingers finally loose, her throat tight with throttled tears.

"Very well," Dr. Kingsley said, but by his tone of voice he meant, Very ill.

"It's hard to practice at home, sir. I do better here."

"You will have to," he said, unrelenting. He got up from the stool he had placed intimidatingly close to her elbow and rummaged through the music on the shelf beneath the window. Even bent over, he blocked much of the light. He was very large, barrel-shaped in his dusty black suit, with a mane of hair and side-whiskers that should have dated him, but only made him more imposing. He pulled out a score and handed it to her. Satie, some of his pieces for students. She took them without being able to hide her dismay.

"But I wanted to go on working on the Nocturnes."

"Miss Ross, ambition may not be a cardinal sin, not even in the female, but it is a foolish one when the female in question does not have the necessary foundation upon which to build such edifying structures as those of which she dreams. Chopin requires strength, technique, and a certain vigor of soul, none of which you, at this moment, can muster. It will take a great deal of work to convince me that you ever will. I am not wholly optimistic. However, if you still wish to try, I suggest, in my humble role as teacher and guide, that you begin with these."

"Yes, sir," she whispered.

He opened the door and ushered her into the hall.

The second floor landing was the usual eddy of noise, music and voices washing through each other like the hot air from the radiators and the cold draft from the foyer below. Berenice got no further before the tears came. She leaned her forehead against the window frame, and when her breath misted the pane, she wiped it away to make the snowy ground, the black-trunked snowy trees come clear.

A hand touched her cheek, a voice said, "What is this?"

She turned, shocked, in time to see Mr. Green touch his fingertip to his tongue.

"A tear!" He gave her a strange look, solemn and bright. "But what marvel has wrung ocean spray from fiery maid?"

"You're so odd!" she blurted.

"But then, this is such a very odd world." He brushed his hand over her cheeks, touched his knuckle to the end of her nose, and smiled at her blush. "There. Fire again. Why did you weep?"

Berenice looked from his pale, beautiful face to the snowy world, but it made no difference. The one was a cold and as mystifying as the other. "Doctor Kingsley says I may not play Chopin. He says I cannot. He says—"

"Fools say much. The wise listen rather less."

She glared at him. "Doctor Kingsley is one of the most famous, the most reputable—"

"Fools. And cowards, who crop pretty birds' wings because they cannot, themselves, fly." Mr. Green gripped her chin. "Listen, my chick, didn't I say you should play before kings?"

She was mesmerized by his touch, by the cold-water brightness of his eyes. For a moment, shocked and undefended, she thought the whole building fell silent, the very air washed through by the winter ocean that lay behind his regard. Then he released her chin with a last caress across her cheek.

"Called away, alas." He stepped back. "Play Chopin, Miss Ross. Play Chopin in the dark with your eyes closed."

She sniffed. "And will you find me a king to play before?"

Delighted, he laughed. "I will, my chick, and so I will."

He bowed, and scampered down the stairs.

*

2003:

Brona played at night when the practice room with the concert grand was free. She no longer thought of it as practice—could not, in truth, recollect a time when she had, though she supposed she must have done. Perhaps when she was a child? But now she simply played, and the acoustical curtains that clothed the walls folded the sound away. No echoes to chase, no reverberations rung from memory's shrouded bell. Nothing but the music.

She came to the end, and stopped. The soundproofed silence was perfect. She opened her eyes. And although she saw nothing but the practice room, the creamy curtains pleated by blackness with only half the track lights burning, and though of course she saw no one, she was surprised, and did not know why. Somewhere in her mind, as elusive as a remembered perfume, there was an expectation of a different room (but what room?) and of an audience (but what audience?). She frowned at the black and white keys, but as always, the hunt after memory only chased it deeper into the recesses of her hidden past. It was late. She closed her eyes and rubbed at the lids, then got up from the piano bench.

Like a mockery, the faint hiss of distant applause broke through the room. Absurdly, she wondered if there was a concert in the recital hall, then remembered the soundproofing. The applause sank, swelled again, soft as a low-tide surf—and as cold, by the prickling of her skin. It wasn't sense but instinct that tipped her head back and showed her how the wind washed the first snow of the year against the skylight. She saw the snow drift and swirl like foam at the dying end of a wave. She saw herself, foreshortened in the night-backed mirror of glass, face pale, hair and clothes bereft of color, equally dark. She lifted her hands towards her reflection, and her reflection looked liked a woman in mid-dive, arcing towards the depths. She shook her head and left the room, flipping the lights off and changing the In Use sign as she closed the door.

The practice rooms were on an upper level, and a half-flight of stairs led to the hallway of the next cube. The upper landing was wide enough to accommodate a table and a couple of sofas; a stone balustrade guarded the drop to the hall below. Against the balustrade sat Valentine Fayant, his head tipped back and his face still with the stillness of a troubled man too tired to worry about his troubles. His eyes were open and he watched Brona approach without changing expression or lifting a hand.

She hunkered down beside him and saw the flute case he cradled in the curve of his arm. "So you do practice." She slipped the case out of his grasp and opened it.

"How do you know I haven't been sitting here *refusing* to practice?" His eyes were on her hands.

"With such a fine instrument? It would be a crime."

"Do you know, that's almost exactly what Jade said just now."

The flute shone with the deep, polished wealth of old silver. "Jade was just here?"

"Not two minutes gone. She was giving me another one of her pep talks from the eighth dimension, so if you were planning to cheer me up or inspire me or kick me in my lazy butt, feel free to give it a miss."

Brona took the flute from the case, fitted the pieces together, adjusted the head. A subtle warmth clung to the metal, the memory of his breath and hands. "Eighth dimension?"

"Or somewhere," Valentine said on a sigh. "She's almost as weird as you, Scholarship."

Brona smiled so she would not frown, thinking, *The elusive Jade.* She lifted the flute, blew a note, and then another, and then a melody came rippling out of somewhere, dancing in her fingers, singing in her breath. The song tripped through the school's stony labyrinth as if Jason had not come back weary and wounded from the Minotaur, but happy, laughing, drunk on forbidden wine and with life rather than death behind him.

The melody ended. Brona knelt with the flute still held to her lips, head cocked, listening to the echoes. Valentine reached out and took back his flute, his hands sliding warmly around hers, then gone.

"Are you trying to seduce me?" he said. "Or are you merely trying to destroy what's left of my ego?"

She smiled at him. "That's a very good flute."

He looked down at the shining instrument. "Better in your hands than in mine." He pulled off the head section and reached for the swab in his case. "Is there anything you can't do, Scholarship? Please tell me there is, because it's very difficult going to school with a genius."

"I can't remember where I learned that tune."

Valentine gave his flute the familiar bitter smile, and took off the foot. "Thank you. Really."

"I can't remember when I learned to play—"

"Brona." He fitted the cleaned flute into the velvet compartments of the case and closed the lid. "I don't need more proof of your brilliance. I need more proof of your humanity."

"God! So do I!"

He stared at her. She stared back, as startled as he was. After a moment, she grimaced and shook her head.

"It's late, isn't it?"

"Yes," Valentine said slowly. "Yes, it's pretty late."

*

1917:

Berenice was descending the stairs to the foyer of Masters Hall, juggling her music folder as she wound her scarf about her neck, when she saw Miss Salter with another girl standing by the door. She hesitated. Miss Salter's friend glanced up and said something to Miss Salter. Miss Salter said loudly, "Why should we wait? I have no doubt she'll find someone to walk her home," and opened the door. The two girls went out into the snowy day. Three young men loitering by the radiator watched them go, then looked up at Berenice, murmuring quietly amongst themselves. Berenice turned to climb back up the stairs. She reminded herself, salve to her pride, that Dr. Kingsley *had* told her to practice more. But that was more an abrasive than a salve.

In the practice room, with the door safely closed and the hated Satie still in her folder, she played one mind-numbing exercise after another. Played? She pounded through them, stretching her hands, dredging power from her arms, shoulders, spine, banging out machine-gun arpeggios and artillery chords, until the blood throbbed in her temples and the tears dried on her reddened face—

A cool hand covered her eyes. Her fingers stumbled in mid-flight. A cool voice said, "What happened to the Chopin?"

"Nothing!" she cried into the dark of his touch. She caught her breath. "What *could* happen to the Chopin? I am forbidden— Forbidden!"

"Shh." Without taking his hand from her eyes, he settled on the bench beside her. "Who is powerful enough to forbid you music? All you have to do is play."

She caught her breath again, lifted a hand from the keys to touch his wrist. "If Doctor Kingsley gives me too low a grade, I lose my scholarship. My father cannot afford to pay the school's fees. I would have to leave."

He leaned his forehead against her hair and whispered, "There are other places to play."

She gave a shaky laugh. "Have you found me a king, then?"

"I have found a king for you," he said, "and I have found a musician for a king. Am I not a clever wight?"

"Oh, Mister Green, I only wish it were true." She let her hand drift back to the keys, pressed them too softly to make a sound. Her voice was almost as quiet. "I do not think I can go home again. I do not know how to live there anymore."

"There are other places to play. Yes, and live."

Finally, she pulled his hand from her eyes. His countenance was so lively she felt laughter scud like sea spray across the surface of her misery. She said, "Where, Mister Green? In the hollow of a tree?"

"In a moonlit palace where you shall play for the king and all his starry court. But we might be able to find you a tree if it would please you." He stood, pulling her up with him, and sang,

"Come, follow, follow, follow, follow, follow, follow me.
Wither shall I follow, follow, follow,
Wither shall I follow, follow thee?
To the greenwood, to the greenwood, to the greenwood, green-
wood tree!"

She laughed and put on her coat. When he began the round again as he opened the practice room door she joined in on the *Wither shall I follow*, and they sang their way down the stairs and out of Masters Hall.

Out of the hall, across the snowy lawn, into the snowy trees. New snow was falling, downy as a swan's breast, burying the path to town. Berenice might have gone by way of the drive instead, but Mr. Green pulled her on. He quit his song as they came under the eave of the wood and they went in silence save for the crunch of their boots and the hush of snowflakes touching on snow. She held fast to his hand, unaccountably nervous. The narrow band of woods seemed to widen, or deepen, or keep abreast of them as they walked. The trees went on and on, and they were very large and dark against the snow. But then, at last, she could see the end of them, a brightness that grew even brighter as a wind from nowhere plowed the snow clouds away. The sun scattered jewels across the ground, dazzling Berenice's eyes so that she could not make out the familiar soot-smudged roofs of town.

And then from somewhere, impossibly, she heard the sound of the sea.

*

2003:

Leona offered to buy Brona a coffee after her lesson. They went to the "café" by the recital hall where refreshments were sold on concert nights, and sat by a tiny round table that bore a constellation of sticky rings.

Leona said, "I've never said this to a first year student before, but I want you to seriously consider entering one of the national competitions in the spring."

Brona shook her head as she blew across the top of her cup.

"Why not?"

"I'm not ready."

"Are you indulging in a fit of humor? Fishing for compliments? You're as good or better than anyone in this place, including the faculty, and you know it." The wrinkles around Leona's mouth deepened. "You aren't concert-shy."

"No." Brona sipped, set the cardboard cup down, matching the bottom carefully to one of the older stains. "But I'm not ready for a career."

"Oh, lord," Leona groaned. "If I had a dollar for every student that said she wasn't ready. You'll never be ready. Ready doesn't work like that."

"I'm too young."

"How old are you?"

Brona shrugged. "I don't know what kind of career I want. Suppose I decide I want to go into jazz?"

"So what if you do?" Leona leaned across the tiny table. "Give me a real reason, girl. I'm seriously starting to wonder. What've you got to hide?"

"What?" Brona sat back, hot and cold moving across her skin.

"I said, what have you got to lose?"

Brona shook her head, more at herself than at Leona, and was still trying to formulate an answer when someone leaned over her shoulder. She looked up. It was Valentine, an envelope in his hand and his flute case under his arm.

He said, "I was looking for you."

She smiled at him, grateful for the interruption, though he did not look well. "Why is that?"

"I don't want to interrupt, I—"

"It doesn't matter. Sit down. Do you know Leona? She teaches piano."

"No. I can't stay. I only wanted to give you this." He laid the big manila envelope on the edge of the table, what little clear space was left beside their cups. Brona had to catch it before it fell onto the floor.

"What is it?"

"It's—Jade told me—I thought—" He took a breath, turned his head to look off over the heads of the seated crowd. When he looked back down at her, his eyes were hot and strange. "It's something we found in the archives. Something I want you to see. So you'll understand."

"Understand?" He shook his head and Brona raised her brows at him, troubled. "But what is it?"

"You'll see. Listen. I have to go." He stepped back.

"All right. I'll—"

"It was nice to meet you," Valentine said to Leona, then, to Brona: "Good-bye." He turned and threaded his way through the tables and out of sight.

"Odd young man," Leona said. "Isn't that the Fayant son?"

"Excuse me," Brona murmured, already tearing open the envelope's gummed flap. There were only a few sheets of paper inside. Photocopies, it seemed, of black and white photographs.

A wide brick building, with three stories and a steep roof, on a flat lawn against a background of trees. Brona saw within the shades of gray the red of the brick, the green of the lawn, the first flush of orange across the leaves—

—and a driftwood, moonbeam, seafoam palace spiraling up from the edge of an ocean shore.

A tall frame house with eight girls posing on the porch and on the steps, their hair swept into buns, their skirts decorously long. Brona saw them smoothing their collars, tucking in hairpins, jostling to get into the picture's frame—

—and a moon-haired figure in green-leaf motley and bells of gold dancing along the spine of a dune.

A young woman in a blouse with full sleeves and tight cuffs standing beside a piano, one hand stretched to touch the piano's lid, the other hidden in a fold of her skirt. Brona saw the deep red of the piled hair—her hair. She saw the wide, solemn mouth—her mouth. She saw the straight brows, the long, tapered eyes, the classical nose—her brows, her eyes, her face—

She closed her eyes, and felt a cool, slender hand brush her cheek, and heard a voice as richly timbred as a wooden flute. *But what marvel has wrung ocean spray from fiery maid?*

And then she heard another voice, the same voice, only an alto, not a tenor, flute. *You can't hide a fire, you know. If you try you'll only put it out.*

Jade, she thought. Mr. Green. Valentine. *Berenice.*

"Are you all right?"

She opened her eyes. Saw Leona's worried face. Saw the pages crumpled between her hands. Thought, Berenice and Mr. Green. Valentine and Jade.

"Brona?"

She groped for a reply, and in that moment the clatter and growl of the busy café was drowned beneath the heavy booming surge of surf—of her blood, but they were one and the same. Berenice and Valentine. Jade and Mr. Green.

And Valentine had been carrying his flute case.

She stuffed the photographs into the envelope, crumpled as they were. "I have to go," she said, and she went.

There was no path through the wood. There was no wood, just the rutted, snow-swept grounds, the sagging fence, the highway rushing with traffic beyond. As Brona ran down the front stairs of the school, winter's cold biting through her sweater, she saw two figures walking across next-year's lawn towards the highway. Brona, running after them, stumbled over frozen lumps of dirt, caught her feet in snow-buried hollows. She lost her grip on the envelope and let it go. Jade and Valentine were nearly at the fence. The traffic roar softened to a sobbing sigh. The bright flash of cars blurred into the gleam of a sunlit ocean, their speed into the ageless curling collapse of a foam-capped wave.

"Wait!" Brona cried. "Valentine, wait! *You don't know what they are!*"

Valentine stopped, turned back. The small, dark-haired figure beside him only glanced over her shoulder, but she also stopped. The wave hung on the verge of dissolution. The town was still visible beyond.

Brona came up to Valentine, panting. "You don't know," she said.

"I know you're Berenice Ross," he said, almost angrily. "You were a scholarship student in 1916. You disappeared halfway through your second term, and now you've come back again with more skill, more talent than, than—" He groped for a word.

"Than seems humanly possible," Jade said in her sweet voice. She smiled across her shoulder at Brona, her eyes pale as seafoam under her black, arching brows.

"Than I could ever dream of," Valentine bitterly said.

"Is that how she told the story?" Brona asked him, ignoring Jade. "There and back, with a small gift to show I'd been?"

"A small gift." Valentine's eyes were fixed on hers. "A *small* gift?"

"Valentine, listen. Perhaps they've told you more this time than they ever told me. I could not have guessed—I could not have dreamt—where it was they were taking me. And I can't tell you it is any less wondrous than they've made it seem. I *can't*, because they took every memory of it from me when they let me go."

Jade finally turned to face her. "My dear, is that what you—"

"You've had your turn," Brona said harshly without taking her eyes from Valentine. "Yes, I have skill. But do you think it was something they gave me? I walked back into this world with nothing, no family, no home, no *name*, because they had taken away my past. And it's been *years*, Valentine. If Berenice— If I left here in 1917, that means they only kept me for a year. One year. And ever since then I've had to invent myself and my life with nothing but a bit of talent to do it with. Can you imagine what that would be like? Adrift in time, unable even to *guess* why I go on, and on, never aging, never knowing who I am, or what I am, or where I am from?" She snatched at a breath. "I'm good because I've had ninety years to practice in!"

Valentine listened, his face stark as bone. "Then why, for God's sake, are you going to school?"

She laughed. Humorless as it was, it eased the tension. She looked away, scrubbed her face with her palms. "Because I got tired of playing in hotel lounges."

"What?" Valentine laughed, too, in surprise.

"You think I should be making the grand tour, recording with the great symphonies, living in Europe maybe?" She gave him a twisted smile. "Try being rich and famous when you can't get a social security number, or pay your taxes, or apply for a passport. This school, all the schools, they're like holidays. They're havens, really. I didn't even know—would you believe it?—that I'd ever been to this one before."

Silence fell. In the worlds beyond where the three of them stood, traffic growled, surf sighed and boomed. And finally, finally, Jade spoke.

"But Lady Red," she said, "sweet berry, fiery child. We took nothing from you."

Brona groped for her voice. "Only my life. Only my name!"

"But those were only what you left behind." Jade cocked her head like a puzzled bird. "My dear, we did not send you away. It was you who chose to go."

Brona fumbled after memory, and caught only rags. A gown of kelp leaves. A red bird with a trailing white tail. "But *why?*"

"You did not believe us when we told you how much you had changed."

Brona did not know what to say, what to believe. After another long moment, it was Valentine who spoke.

"I would not want to leave," he said.

Jade laughed and clapped her hands. "You are coming, then?"

He drew himself up and braced his shoulders. "Yes."

"Hurrah!" Jade laughed again. "And you, little fire bear? Are you ready to come home?"

Home, Brona thought—Berenice thought. Home. She did not know what or where that was, but she thought, she was almost certain, that she would never know until she learned where it once had been.

And the wave, cold and green in the winter sun, rolled foaming across the sand.

Printed in the United States
27864LVS00001B/76-234

9 781894 815581

MAY   2005

$ 29.95